Aidan IN A KILT

The Ballachulish Trilogy, Book Two

ANNA DURAND

JACOBSVILLE BOOKS · MARIETTA, OHIO

AIDAN IN A KILT

ISBN: 978-1-949406-74-0 (paperback)
ISBN: 978-1-949406-75-7 (ebook)
ISBN: 978-1-949406-76-4 (audiobook)

Manufactured in the United States.

Jacobsville Books
www.JacobsvilleBooks.com

Publisher's Cataloging-in-Publication Data
provided by Five Rainbows Cataloging Services

Names: Durand, Anna, author.
Title: Aidan in a kilt / Anna Durand.
Description: Marietta, OH : Jacobsville Books, 2021. | Series: Ballachulish Trilogy, bk. 2.
Identifiers: ISBN 978-1-949406-74-0 (paperback) | ISBN 978-1-949406-75-7 (ebook) | ISBN 978-1-949406-76-4 (audiobook)
Subjects: LCSH: Man-woman relationships--Fiction. | Scots--Fiction. | Americans--Fiction. | Michigan--Fiction. | Virgins--Fiction. | Romance fiction. | BISAC: FICTION / Romance / Contemporary. | FICTION / Romance / Romantic Comedy. | GSAFD: Love stories.
Classification: LCC PS3604.U724 A33 2021 (print) | LCC PS3604.U724 (ebook) | DDC 813/.6—dc23.

Praise for Anna Durand's Books

"Durand's Hot Scots series has been loads of fun to read, and [*Irresistible in a Kilt*] is no exception. [...] The author's action-packed and suspenseful plot keeps the reader on their toes, and the grown-up sizzle never disappoints."
Jack Magnus, Readers' Favorite

"[*Lethal in a Kilt* is] full of hot sex, adventure, and so much laughter. I found myself laughing-out-loud at the antics of the Witches of Ballachulish (Logan's sisters) and the hilarious flirting and sexy banter between Serena and Logan. [...] Recommend highly!"
Sharon Clayton, The Eclectic Review

"[*Insatiable in a Kilt*] smokes from the very first pages... Durand's characters are a delight and seeing how they mix business with their increasing attraction for each other is entertaining indeed. [...] Durand's Hot Scots family saga just keeps on getting better."
Jack Magnus, Readers' Favorite

"I loved the Scottish in Ian and the strength of Rae, but the love of one little girl makes [*Notorious in a Kilt*] something to behold."
Coffee Time Romance

"*Gift-Wrapped in a Kilt* is a marvelous continuation of the author's MacTaggart family saga. Durand's story has an entertaining plot, and her steamy interludes are well-written...a celebration of healthy relationships between loving adults written in a tasteful and compelling manner."
Jack Magnus, Readers' Favorite

"I have enjoyed this whole series, but Emery and Rory [from *Scandalous in a Kilt*] have stolen my heart and are now my favorites!"
The Romance Reviews

"An enthralling story. [...] I highly recommend the writing of Ms. Durand and *Wicked in a Kilt*, but be warned you will find yourself addicted and want your own Hot Scot."
Coffee Time Romance & More

"There's a huge hero's and heroine's journey [in *Dangerous in a Kilt*] that I quite enjoyed, not to mention the hot sex, and again, not to mention the sweet seduction of the Scotsman who pulls out all the stops to get Erica to love him."
Manic Readers

Other Books by Anna Durand

Lachlan in a Kilt (The Ballachulish Trilogy, Book One)
Rory in a Kilt (The Ballachulish Trilogy, Book Three)
The American Wives Club (A Hot Brits/Hot Scots/Au Naturel Crossover Book)
Brit vs. Scot (A Hot Brits/Hot Scots/Au Naturel Crossover Book)
Dangerous in a Kilt (Hot Scots, Book One)
Wicked in a Kilt (Hot Scots, Book Two)
Scandalous in a Kilt (Hot Scots, Book Three)
The MacTaggart Brothers Trilogy (Hot Scots, Books 1-3)
Gift-Wrapped in a Kilt (Hot Scots, Book Four)
Notorious in a Kilt (Hot Scots, Book Five)
Insatiable in a Kilt (Hot Scots, Book Six)
Lethal in a Kilt (Hot Scots, Book Seven)
Irresistible in a Kilt (Hot Scots, Book Eight)
Devastating in a Kilt (Hot Scots, Book Nine)
Spellbound in a Kilt (Hot Scots, Book Ten)
Relentless in a Kilt (Hot Scots, Book Eleven)
One Hot Chance (Hot Brits, Book One)
One Hot Roomie (Hot Brits, Book Two)
One Hot Crush (Hot Brits, Book Three)
The Dixon Brothers Trilogy (Hot Brits, Books 1-3)
One Hot Escape (Hot Brits, Book Four)
One Hot Rumor (Hot Brits, Book Five)
One Hot Christmas (Hot Brits, Book Six)
Natural Passion (Au Naturel Trilogy, Book One)
Natural Impulse (Au Naturel Trilogy, Book Two)
Natural Satisfaction (Au Naturel Trilogy, Book Three)
Fired Up (a standalone romance)
Echo Power (Echo Power Trilogy, Book One)
The Mortal Falls (Undercover Elementals, Book One)
The Mortal Fires (Undercover Elementals, Book Two)
The Mortal Tempest (Undercover Elementals, Book Three)
The Janusite Trilogy (Undercover Elementals, Books 1-3)
Obsidian Hunger (Undercover Elementals, Book Four)
Unbidden Hunger (Undercover Elementals, Book Five)
Willpower (Psychic Crossroads, Book One)
Intuition (Psychic Crossroads, Book Two)
Kinetic (Psychic Crossroads, Book Three)
Passion Never Dies: The Complete Reborn Series

Chapter One

I, Aidan MacTaggart, have a plan. Find a wife, but not just any wife—an American one. If Lachlan, my bossy oldest brother, could accidentally meet a woman who became his bride and his soul mate, then the actions that led him to happiness ought to work for me. I am "Don Juan" MacTaggart, after all. I have more skills in attracting lasses than my workaholic brothers. So that's how I wind up inside Dance Ardor, a dimly lit club in Chicago far from my home in the Scottish Highlands, determined to get myself an American girl.

My plan might have a few…flaws.

Aye, Lachlan met Erica here. And they are blissfully happy. But I wonder if my brother may have pulled a joke on me when he said every night was kilt night at Dance Ardor because I seem to be the only human in this place who wears the plaid. *Bloody Lachlan.* I know he wants revenge ever since I almost tricked his new bride into saying a slightly naughty Gaelic phrase. If he thought this would humiliate me, my brother doesn't know me as well as he thinks.

The lasses in the club watch me. Smiling. Batting their lashes.

Although I've been here for only a few minutes, already I've learned an important lesson. American women love a man in a kilt. Must be my legs they find intriguing.

I wander around the edge of the dance floor, past tables occupied by couples and groups. Ladies cast their appreciative gazes in my direction, but none of them interest me. I want a woman with substance and heart and—

My thoughts and my feet stumble to a halt. I've seen her. The woman of my dreams.

A redheaded girl has just exited a set of double doors that access some deeper region of the club. Her emerald-green dress matches her eyes, and its hem stops well above her charming knees. The daringly low neckline draws my focus to the slopes of her generous breasts. As I watch, she halts to glance around, as if she's looking for someone.

Please, don't let her have a man waiting for her.

Every sweep of the multicolored strobe lights ignites stunning high-lights in her fiery red hair and green eyes. *Bod an Donais*, those eyes are hypnotizing. Even from this distance, their color reminds me of jewels, and her lips... I want to catch them between my teeth and taste their flavor, then plunge deep into her mouth.

I rush toward her.

Aye, Lachlan and Rory would never do this. My brothers think things through, but I act on impulse. If they saw this woman... I would shove them out of the way to get to her. She is the most enticing lass I've ever laid eyes on, and I have to know her.

The beauty's gaze travels the club, everywhere but in my direction.

Just as I reach her, she turns and bumps into me.

The wee lass yelps and throws her hands up. They land on my chest, the delicate weight of them begging me to clasp her hands in mine. I can't stop my gaze from flying to her cleavage, to the half-exposed mounds of her breasts. Since she's much shorter than I am, I have a perfect view down the neckline of her dress. I shouldn't gawp at her cleavage—it's rude, I know that—but I can't help it.

The lovely curve of her throat snares my attention. And those perfect earlobes. I fight the urge to lunge down and take one in my mouth.

She stares at my chest, the bit of it visible where the top buttons of my shirt are undone.

I can't resist the urge any longer. I settle my hands over hers on my chest. Her skin is soft as silk and warm too, and my hands almost completely cover hers.

"Well now," I say, "I've been looking for a bonnie lass, but I didn't expect to literally run into one."

She stumbles backward a step, blinking rapidly, like she's dazed. Her gaze sweeps over me, from my leather boots up my legs and over my hips to my arms, and finally to my face. She angles her head back and blinks again, slowly this time, as our eyes meet.

Desire simmers inside me, heating up more every second. I want her—in my bed, in my life, and maybe as my wife. Only one way to know if she is the woman I've been looking for.

A lock of her flame-red hair has fallen over her eyes.

I brush the lock away from her face. "Your dress brings out the green of your eyes. But this lighting can't do justice to your beautiful red hair."

She sweeps her appreciative gaze over me again, and her tongue darts out to moisten her lower lip. With a tiny shake of her head, she seems to rouse herself from a fantasy—of me, I hope—and a faint blush dapples her cheeks.

Bonnie, adorable lass.

I tilt my head to study her face. "You're the one I've been looking for, I think."

My future wife smooths out her dress, clears her throat, and lifts her chin. Whether it's defiance or a simple need to look up to meet my gaze, I don't care. She's so luscious and cute that I want to drag her into my arms just to feel her soft, warm body against me.

"Are you looking for the party?" she asks.

Party? No, I hadn't been looking for one. If this lass wants to take me to a party, though, I'll go along. Anything to spend more time in her presence. I let my lips slide into my best wicked smirk, the one the ladies always appreciate. "Aye."

One word is all I can speak. Her eyes, aimed straight at mine, glimmer with an emerald fire that transfixes me.

"You're not a firefighter," she says.

Is she barmy or just fixated on firemen? Makes no difference to me, because this lass entrances me like no other woman I've ever seen. "I didn't realize American women are so specific about what they want."

"As long as you look good without your clothes, you'll do."

No clothes? What sort of party has she come from? I'd prefer a private session involving nudity, but I can be flexible.

"You're direct, aren't you?" I say. "Yes, I've been told I look quite good naked."

"Naked?" Her brows lift, and she glances down at my kilt. "Please tell me you're wearing a G-string under that thing. That's the protocol, isn't it?"

"A G-string protocol?" I can't keep from laughing as I shake my head, confused and enchanted at the same time. "You're adorable, but I'm beginning to think you're off your head."

"Are you calling me crazy?" Before I can respond, she raises a hand to silence me. "Never mind. Come with me."

The bonnie wee bampot turns away, crooking a finger to beckon me to follow.

How can I refuse her? This girl is a mystery, a sexy one, and I plan on examining every clue she offers me. All night. Naked. In a back room of this club if necessary. I need to have her, one way or another.

"Ah, lass," I purr, "I'll follow ye anywhere, even if ye are a bampot."

"Whatever, just hurry up."

She leads me toward the double doors. I drink in the view of her round little erse shimmying with every swing of her full hips. Dear God, but she has curves in all the right places. The sort of curves that make a man want to explore every one of them with his hands, his mouth, and aye, his cock sunk into her sweet flesh.

The woman I intend to marry glances over her shoulder at me.

I hit her with my signature smile, a slow and sensual expression that leaves no doubts about my desire for her. "After the party, may I buy you a drink?"

"I don't drink. Not morally opposed or anything, but I've never tasted an alcoholic beverage I liked."

"Water is a drink, you know." I would offer her a glass of mud-puddle water if it keeps her close by, but instead, I peer down the hallway past her. "Where are we headed?"

"The party, of course." She scrunches her eyebrows in the sweetest way, then waves for me to pick up speed as she does the same. "Come on, they're waiting."

"They?" Although she had mentioned a party, I still have no bloody idea what I'm walking into, but I'd meant it when I said I'll follow her anywhere. Especially if I get to admire that beautiful erse along the way.

"It's a party," she says, sounding a bit peeved. "Just come along, will you?"

"Aye." As we push through the swinging doors, I move up alongside her. Gazing down at her smooth shoulder, I can't resist gliding a hand up her arm. The silken feel of her skin makes the desire flickering inside me flare into a bonfire. "I'm yours to command."

"Um…" She stumbles to a halt, sweeping her gaze over me. Her breathing has grown heavier, and she loosely bites her lower lip. Clearing her throat, she shakes my hand off. "Where were you, anyway? I've been looking everywhere."

She'd been looking for me? Well, I've been searching for a woman like her all my adult life. Does she feel the same attraction I do?

Please, merciful heaven, make it true.

"Have ye, then?" I ask.

"Yes." She seizes my arm, hesitating for the briefest moment. Her eyes flare wide like she's surprised, or maybe aroused, by my biceps. Then she tugs my arm. "Get a move on."

"Lead on, lass. Lead on."

She hauls me straight to a room inside which women's voices laugh and shout. My future wife releases my arm and hesitates with her hand on the knob. "I hope they're not too disappointed you aren't a firefighter."

"Is it really that important to every American woman?" Lachlan hadn't mentioned this trait of American lasses. Had Erica been so specific? Do women in this country make lists of the exact qualities they want in a man, including desirable professions?

Bloody hell, I hope not. That sort of behavior reminds me of Rory, my older brother who makes rules for every ruddy thing.

"Never mind," she says, and flings the door open, gesturing for me to go inside.

Women's voices erupt in wild whoops.

Something about their shouts makes me freeze. They sound…ravenous.

Mhac na galla. What sort of orgy is this lassie dragging me into?

"He's here!" someone hollers, and louder whoops erupt.

I stagger backward half a step.

The siren who'd lured me here lays a hand on my back and pushes. I stumble across the threshold.

Women scream and whoop and whistle.

Holy heaven. My eyes fly so wide I feel a breeze drying them out. Across the room, a blindfolded woman holds a paper shaped like a penis—and painted like one too—while she flounders around, moving in the direction of a board that holds a cartoon-like image of a man without a dick. The woman stabs her paper cock onto the image, pinning the appendage to the man's groin.

I wince. The lad might be made of paper, but I sympathize with what this mob of lunatic women has done to him.

The woman whips off her blindfold, pumps her fists in the air, and shouts, "Woo! Time to get the party started!"

A mob of screaming women barrels toward me.

"Take it off, baby," one says. "Show us what you got."

I flail backward, smacking into the redhead behind me.

"Shit!" she yells, as she tumbles to the floor.

Faced with a throng of crazed women, I shed all my masculine pride and hurry backward out of the room. Hercules himself would've fled from this onslaught. I trip over the redhead's legs and hop sideways to avoid falling onto her. My weight would crush the little siren. I fling out a hand to halt my own fall, my palm slapping on the wall.

Inside the room, someone shrieks. A tiny woman rushes to the doorway, eyes wide, face blanched, her attention on the redhead. "Calli, are you okay? What happened?"

The woman of my dreams pushes up onto her elbows and blows hair out of her face. "The exotic dancer trampled me."

Exotic dancer? I feel my brows pinch together, tightening my forehead.

The tiny lass offers a hand to the redhead—Calli, the other one had called her—and helps lever her off the floor. When my dream girl's foot contacts the linoleum, she winces and hisses, grabbing the doorjamb for support.

She frowns at me. "What's wrong with you? A stripper ought to be used to being pawed by salivating women."

The other girl aims a chastising look at me and slips an arm around Calli's waist. "Yeah. What's your damage, Kilt Boy?"

With my palm still flat on the wall, I gawp at these women. I might be horribly confused, but I know one thing for certain. I hurt Calli, and though it had been an accident, I worry I've ruined my chances with her.

"I'm getting a refund," the tiny one says. "I don't want a nutso stripper, even if he is wicked hot."

"Refund for what?" I ask, glancing from one bampot to the other. "Did you call me—You women are cracked. Ahmno a stripper."

Chapter Two

The tiny lass huffs. "Of course you're a stripper. We paid for you."

"Paid?" I move away from the wall, straightening to my full height. "I donnae take my clothes off for money."

"Who else but a stripper would wear a kilt?"

I clench my jaw. "A man from Scotland would."

Calli hobbles between the angry elf and me, holding up a hand to each of us. "Let's all calm down. This was obviously a huge misunderstanding, and that's my fault."

The elf points at Calli's ankle. "He broke your leg."

"Don't be so melodramatic. I twisted my ankle, that's all."

I glance down at her ankle and grimace. How could I have hurt a woman? Even if it was an accident, I feel awful about it. So I rub the back of my neck, rolling my eyes up to look at Calli. "I'm sorry. Didnae mean to hurt you."

"She needs medical attention," the elf pronounces. "I'm calling nine-one-one."

"No," Calli says. "A twisted ankle is not an emergency. I need to sit down, that's all."

The tiny lass eyes Calli warily. "You sure?"

"It was an accident, and I will be fine." Calli raises a hand, palm out. "I swear it."

The doors to the club proper swing open, and a man in a firefighter outfit saunters down the hallway toward us. He holds a boom box on one shoulder. Pouting like a male model, he nods at Calli. "Hey babe, where's the bachelorette party?"

She hooks a thumb over her shoulder. "In there."

The real stripper pushes past her. She tries to sidle out of the way, but her ankle gives out, and she staggers into me. I catch her by the shoulders, steadying her against my body with both hands. She turns her gaze up to mine.

"Thanks," she whispers.

She has the most beautiful green eyes I've ever seen.

Whoops and catcalls erupt inside the party room once again. Music starts up too, full of pounding bass and electric guitars.

I lean closer to Calli to be heard above the din. "You need to rest your ankle. Let me help you find a place to sit."

The angry elf lingers nearby, but her focus is on the festivities inside the room. She bites her lip, casting Calli a sideways glance.

Calli waves me away. "Go on, I'll be fine. I appreciate your concern, but you must want to be out there. Don't let me disrupt your plans." To the elf, she says, "You go on too, get to your party. I'll be right there."

The other lass squints at me, probably because I still have my hands on Calli's upper arms. "I can't leave you alone with a stranger."

"I'm not a stranger," I say. Then I offer my hand to Calli. "Aidan MacTaggart. There, now you know me."

The woman I want to marry settles her hand in my palm. I love the feel of her delicate, warm hand in mine.

My future wife coughs and says, "I'm Calli. Nice to meet you."

"Enchanted to meet you." I lift her hand to kiss it. "But I feel responsible for your injury. Please let me take care of you."

"No need. I can get my own butt into a chair."

The corners of my mouth twitch, almost forming a smile, because she is the most wonderful woman I've ever met. "I'm sure you can, but a gentleman offers aid to a lady in distress."

"That's sweet, but—"

"I'll see you to a chair and leave you be." I place a hand on her back and spread the other arm wide, indicating the doorway to the party room. "After you."

Kicking off her shoes, Calli starts to reach down for them, but I snatch them up and offer her my arm. She hooks her arm around mine, curling her hand around my forearm as she lets me guide her toward the doorway. Thankfully, her limping improves with each step.

At the threshold, she pulls away from me. "Thank you, but my ankle is feeling much better. You can go back out there and find a hot chick in a slinky dress to occupy your time."

My gaze travels the length of her succulent body, down to her toes, and back up to her face. "Donnae need to go anywhere to find that. You are exceptionally hot, and your dress is slinky enough to capture any man's interest."

Is she blushing? I like that. The dusting of pink on her cheeks is becoming.

"Let me have a look at your ankle," I say, because I'm desperate to keep her near me, "to make sure I haven't wounded you grievously."

"I'm fine, really," she says. Calli studies me for a moment, then seems to realize the futility of trying to make me go away. She shuffles across the threshold. "See? I can walk all by my itty-bitty self."

"You aren't itty-bitty." I can't resist raking my gaze over her from head to toe one more time, paying special attention to her breasts and lips before I look into her eyes again. "You're a full-grown woman with soft, inviting curves in all the right places."

"Thank you for helping me. And I'm really sorry I thought you were a stripper."

I shrug. "I suppose it's a compliment. My offer to buy you a drink after the party is still open, even if you want to sip apple juice."

"I'll probably be too tired later, but I appreciate the offer."

"Come find me if you change your mind." I take her hand and kiss it one last time. "Till we meet again, Calli."

Though I don't want to leave her, I realize I have no choice. She has a party to attend, one that involves paper penises and a stripper. What else can I do? I stride down the hallway and out the swinging doors.

Somehow, I need to convince that lass to date me.

I stand at the bar, sipping a glass of whisky, though it's the American variety instead of the Scottish sort. For the past fifteen minutes, I've waited here, hoping Calli will find me. Maybe I had come to this club to find a wife, or at least a girlfriend, but I don't want to do that anymore. Not unless the woman I marry or date is Calli. I don't even know her surname, but I want her like I've never wanted any other lass.

Several women have approached me, and although they were bonnie, I couldn't muster any desire for them.

My mobile chimes, telling me I have a new text. When I check, I see it's Lachlan the lying ersehole.

How goes it? he wants to know.

Bloody brilliant. I have a fiancée already.

Lying cacan.

He's calling me a wee shit? And a liar? I type, *Lachie "Every Night is Kilt Night" MacTaggart shouldn't criticize.*

Don't get in too much trouble.

Why do my brothers insist on treating me like a bairn? They've both got cabers up their erses. So I tell Lachlan, *Go shag your wife.* He replies with an emoji of a devil face, though I have no ruddy idea what that means. Stuffing the mobile in my pocket, I scan the crowd inside this club and frown at my rubbish luck. The only woman I want just walked away from me. None of the scantily dressed lasses here make me want to do anything other than go home.

Aye, running home with my tail between my legs would make Lachie and Rory smile with smug satisfaction. Aidan screws up again.

Still frowning, I survey the club's patrons again—and I see Calli.

When our gazes intersect, I can't stop my mouth from curving into a grin. She smiles at me too, so brightly that I swear I light up from the inside out. Why does she affect me this way? I don't know, and I don't care. Examining every minute detail of everything I do is not my style. So I saunter toward Calli, wondering how long it might take for me to convince her to marry me. I should probably start with getting to know her, but I've never liked waiting for anything.

Slow down, ye eejit. Donnae scare her away.

Am I an idiot? Possibly. Then again, maybe I'm just very focused on my goal.

I stop inches away from Calli and slant my head down toward hers. "This is a lovely surprise. Thought I wouldn't see you again."

"Here I am."

"Aye." Settling my hands on her upper arms, I slide them down to her elbows. "I'd love to spend more time with you."

"I'd like that too."

"What about a private booth?" I point down the short hallway that leads to curtained booths. "I promise to take no liberties without your express consent. Will you come with me?"

She gazes up at me with an almost dreamy expression, her lips parted slightly. Then she nods.

I take her hand, guiding her down the hallway toward a booth that has its curtains open, revealing no one inside. I'd noticed this hallway while I was waiting and hoping Calli would find me again, and I'd asked the bartender about the booths. Now, I usher the bonnie American into the empty space, pulling the purple curtains shut behind us.

Calli stares at the semicircular table and the plum-colored velvet that upholsters the curved sofa behind it. The tabletop has a plum surface too, with a thick, flickering candle at its center. Wax gathers within the candle's concave top, forming a lava-like pool at its center and dribbling down the sides.

I place a hand on the small of her back. "Have a seat."

Calli is staring at the ledge that backs the sofa, where I notice a small bowl, deep purple in color and filled with condom packets. This is a true hedonist's heaven, isn't it? I love women, but I am not that sort.

My future wife seems shocked by that bowl and its contents.

I wince. "Didn't know about those. I swear, I didn't."

"I believe you. First time at Dance Ardor?"

"Yes. Have you been before?"

"No. Came for my cousin's bachelorette party."

Lowering onto the sofa, Calli shimmies sideways until she's behind the table with the bowl of condoms behind her.

Maybe we could make use of that bowl…

No, that would be pushing her. I need to take it slow.

I slide in beside her, draping an arm across the sofa's back behind her shoulders. She smells wonderful, like all sorts of womanly things I can't describe. Sitting beside her like this, I have a perfect view of her bonnie tits, thanks to the plunging neckline of her frock.

Smoothing out her dress, she clears her throat. "Sorry I shoved you into that room with all those ravening bridesmaids. They're actually nice ladies, but they've had a little too much champagne tonight."

"Have you been drinking?"

"No. Told you I don't drink."

"Thought maybe you were desperate enough to try it after being in a room with those bampots. Are you the one chosen to drive everyone home?"

"I'm not the designated driver." She squirms a little. "We came in a van with a professional driver."

"Hope he's not in this club getting jaked." When I realize she seems confused, I explain, "Getting drunk."

"No, *she* is waiting in the van watching TV on her phone."

"Ah." I glance down at her feet. "How's the ankle?"

"Okay. Hurts a little when I walk, especially in these heels."

"May I have a look? I'm no doctor, but I've had my share of injuries." And been the cause of someone else's pain. But I'm in America to forget all that rubbish.

Calli gnaws on her lip. "It's not necessary. Really."

"Humor me?" I say. "I won't bite. Unless you want me to."

Can't help it. I give her my wickedest grin. Since her lips tick upward a wee bit, I think she likes my devilish side.

The lass leans back against the plush cushioning and raises her foot.

I clasp it in both hands, bringing her leg up and onto my lap with everything from her knee down in contact with my body. I slip her shoe off and set it on the table, then skate my hand over the sole of her foot and down to her delicate toes that have curled slightly as if she loves my touch. The sensation of her skin on mine arouses me even more, and a brilliant idea occurs to me. Though I'd offered to examine her injured ankle, I don't want to give up the feel of her skin just yet, and maybe I can use my examination as an excuse to keep touching her. I rub the ball of her foot with leisurely strokes, letting my fingers roam over her skin while I knead her flesh and revel in the pleasure of touching her and seeing the desire on her face.

"It's my ankle," she says, "not my toes."

Does she think I've forgotten? No chance I'd ever forget even one tiny thing about her. I smirk. "Aye, but I thought to check your whole foot to be sure. All right?"

"Okay."

Keeping my hand on her sole, rubbing with measured strokes, I place my other palm on her heel and glide it up to her ankle, shamelessly fondling her flesh, which I mean to do until she tells me to stop. Doesnae seem likely she will. Her cheeks have acquired a faint blush, and she rubs her lips together over and over as her breath hitches and her body tenses.

"Oh…" she says, then seems to lose her train of thought while I explore every contour of her ankle and foot.

Suddenly, it occurs to me that her expression might not signal mounting desire, but instead, indicate pain. I freeze with my hands on her skin. "Is this uncomfortable?"

"No."

Ah, so it is desire after all. Calli wouldn't lie. Maybe I've known her for less than an hour, but I can tell she's an honest lass.

"I've been looking for a woman like you," I say, not even trying to keep my lust from coloring my voice. "A woman with substance and heart and sensuality."

"You don't know me. Maybe I'm obsessed with my looks and never pick up a book, except to prop open my bedroom door for the long line of men waiting for their turn."

I chuckle while I return to massaging the sole of her foot. "You aren't like that. I can tell."

"Exactly how can you identify my character traits after a few minutes in my presence?"

"The way you talk is one clue." I slide my hand from her sole to the top of her foot, gliding my fingers up her skin from her toes to her ankle and down again while, with my other hand, I keep massaging her ankle with lazy strokes. "The way you carry yourself is another clue. You're a real woman, not a silly girl."

And with every minute that ticks by while I'm in her presence, I become even more convinced that she's the one for me.

I release her foot, moving it off my lap, and notice out of the corner of my eye that she's slipping her foot back into her high-heeled shoe. I edge closer until my bare knees brush against hers. *Bod an Donais*, I love to feel her skin against mine. Her foot has fallen back to the floor, and my kilt grazes her thigh. I brace one hand on the sofa behind her head, then settle the other on her thigh. Our faces hover inches apart, and I swear I can taste her breaths as they tease my skin.

Leaning in close, I whisper into her ear. "I want to kiss you."

She stops blinking. Stops breathing too, I think. Our gazes are bound by an invisible thread, a connection I've felt since the moment I first saw her. She might think I'm off my head if I tell her that, so I'll keep it to myself for now. The last thing I want to do is scare her away. I drag my tongue across my lower lip while I imagine it's her skin I'm tasting, and my eyes drift half-closed. What will she taste like? I burn to know the answer—right now.

I slant my head closer, my gaze locked on her mouth.

Though I desperately need to kiss her, I pause with my lips millimeters from hers and let myself enjoy the sensation of her breaths whispering over my skin. I roll my gaze up to meet hers, certain mine is rife with a hunger only she can satisfy. Maybe I love to flirt with the lasses, and kiss the lasses, but I've never needed to taste a woman as much as I need to taste Calli.

I cradle her nape with my palm and tilt her head back a touch, enough to bring her mouth within kissing distance of mine and expose the tender flesh of her throat. I press my lips to hers, keeping the touch soft and sweet, brushing my mouth back and forth.

Calli's lips part on a delicate gasp.

I withdraw a few inches. "May I kiss you?"

"Yes," she whispers.

That's all I need to hear. I claim her mouth in a ravenous crush of lips against lips, loving the way she dissolves into me with a soft wee whimper. I clasp her nape more firmly as I flick my tongue out to explore the seam of her lips. She tastes even better than I'd imagined, though I could never describe her flavor. Donnae need to. Experiencing her is enough for me, and words are unnecessary.

She grasps my shirt, her fingers crooking into the fabric, and opens her mouth to me like she's begging for a deeper kiss.

Well, I never turn down an invitation from a sexy lass.

At the instant I thrust my tongue into her mouth, I lash my free arm around her waist to bind her supple, sensual body to mine. She swings one leg over me to straddle my lap and clings to my shirt, her breasts mounded against me while she surrenders to the demands of my tongue and lips, her body plastered to my chest. She coils her tongue around mine. Christ, I love her passion. And I love this kiss. I want it to go on forever, and longer even, until after the universe collapses in on itself and a new one explodes into existence.

When did I become a poet? It's barmy rubbish.

Calli moans as I slide my hand down from her nape and trace a path along the bare skin of her back, following the curvature of her spine until I feel the edge of her dress, just above her erse. She arches into me while we ravage each other's mouths with increasingly frantic lashes of our tongues.

I groan low in my throat.

She rips her mouth away from mine and scrambles off my lap, banging her hip on the table as she flounders to get out of the booth. Tripping over her own feet, she grabs for the purple curtain to stay her fall.

I thrust an arm out, intending to catch her.

She steadies herself before I get the chance and shrugs away from my outstretched hand. I feel air rushing into my mouth, though I hadn't realized I'd opened my mouth. Well, I am gawping at her slack-jawed, baffled by her abrupt exit.

"I'm sorry," she says, shaking her head. "I can't do this."

Before I can speak a single syllable, she bolts out of the booth.

Chapter Three

I try to leap off the bench, but my kilt gets caught up on the velvety fabric, slowing me down. By the time I race out of the booth, I can't see Calli anywhere. A redhead wearing a backless green dress ought to be easy to spot. I scan the crowd—all right, I might be frantically searching for her—while I barge through groups and brush past individuals, desperate to catch the lass before she vanishes from my life forever.

What had I done? She legged it like she was fleeing from a ravenous beast.

Though I sprint out the doors and into the car park, I don't see her. Where did she go? In those high heels, I doubt she could run faster than I did. I jog down every row of cars, hunting for a sign of the lass who captivated me, but she's not in any of the vehicles parked here.

I've lost my dream girl.

Shuffling back toward the club's main doors, I let my head drop forward and my shoulders slump. It figures. I find the woman I want to marry, and she runs away from me. I pushed too far. I must've done. But I didn't feel like I had. How does asking her permission for a kiss lead to a panicked escape? I thought I was being a gentleman, or at least the closest I can ever really get to behaving like a gentleman.

Somehow, I cocked it up.

I've just rounded a corner, halfway to the club's entrance, when a flash of red hair snags my attention. It's her. She's getting into a taxi.

Though I run faster than I ever have in my life, I arrive three seconds too late. The taxi has just pulled out of the car park and is rushing down the street. I didn't even get a glimpse of the name of the taxi company, so I have no way to track the lass down.

Or do I? Calli came to the club for a bachelorette party. Her cousin's party.

I head back inside the club. Some people, the ones I'd almost run over in my desperation to catch up to Calli, glare at me or give me baffled looks. I am not sprinting this time. I walk at a normal pace. Well, slightly faster than normal, but still just walking. I ignore all the gawpers and push through the swinging doors into the hidden hallway and straight to the door Calli had shoved me through earlier. The door is closed, and I have no desire to burst in on those wild lasses stabbing more paper cocks onto paper laddies. That sight had been rather disturbing.

So, I knock on the door.

Nothing.

I hear music, but it doesn't sound like the stripper's pounding boom box. Assuming they didn't hear me the first time, I knock again.

The door swings inward, and the lass who had urged me to take it all off stares at me. Her eyes go wide. "Oh. It's you."

"Aye. May I come in? I need to speak to the bride."

"Sure, come on in." The lass moves aside to let me pass her while she shouts, "Tara! Kilt Boy is back. Do you think he'll show us what he's got this time?"

The lass wags her eyebrows at me while grinning.

"I only need to speak to the bride," I say, feeling a wee bit uncomfortable. What if these tipsy women abduct me and make me their sex slave? I stifle a groan. Aye, I'm so bloody irresistible that women can't stand to let me go. Calli had no problem doing that.

The wee elf who had called me Kilt Boy earlier, and who treated me like a sexual predator, rises halfway off her chair and flaps her hand at me. "Over here, Aidan."

At least she's not glaring at me anymore.

I wend my way through the crowd to where Tara sits on a plastic chair, set apart from her mates. I sit on the chair beside her. "Thank you for speaking to me. I'm sorry to interrupt your celebration."

"Don't worry about it. The party's winding down, anyway."

Relaxing a little, I dive in. "The reason I'm here is that I'm worried about Calli. She took off so fast I couldn't catch up to her, and I have no idea what I did wrong."

"She's okay, I think. Calli mentioned you guys kissed, and I'm sure that's what has her freaked." Tara sighs. "She's not big on dating. Don't know why. But based on what little she told me, I'm guessing you two had an instant connection, and it scared the bejesus out of her."

"Oh. Are you sure she's all right?"

"Yeah, Calli will be fine. She's stronger than she thinks."

I shouldn't ask, but I can't stop myself from doing just that. "Did she say anything about me? Whether she, ah, likes me."

Tara laughs softly and pats my knee. "She does, trust me. Calli must like you a whole bunch to panic like that."

Not sure if that's a compliment, or if I should apologize for scaring Calli.

Her elfin cousin studies me for a moment, then gives me a sly smile. "I have a great idea."

"You do?"

"Mm-hm." She leans toward me and whispers, "You should come to the wedding reception."

"But ye cannae want a stranger there."

"You aren't a stranger. I know you're Aidan MacTaggart." She offers me her hand. "I'm Tara Douglas, soon to be Tara Adams."

I shake her hand. "It's a pleasure to meet you, Tara, officially. But are you sure you want me at your wedding reception?"

"Positive." She slaps her palms on her thighs. "Calli will be so happy to see you again. Now, let me give you directions to the reception venue. It's at the Morton Arboretum in the Ginkgo Room."

She rattles off the directions, but I must look confused, because she nabs my mobile and types the address into the maps program.

"Thank you, Tara," I say, getting up from my chair. "I'll let you lasses finish your party. And I will see you tomorrow."

"Good night, Aidan. See you then."

I leave the party and catch a taxi back to the house where my sister-in-law, Erica, used to live. Her parents own the house, but they retired to Florida a few years ago, so Erica lived there until she married my brother Lachlan. Now, the place is empty—except for me. Lachlan wanted to pay for a luxury hotel suite for me, but I put my foot down. A normal house is fine for me. Not sure what I'd do with a gigantic suite, anyway. Since Lachlan doesn't like that kind of hotel either, I can't see why he tried to talk me into staying there. I won that battle, but I surrendered to the next one, agreeing to fly to America on Lachlan's new private jet, which he shares with Rory.

Lachlan might not have come to America to find a wife, but he got one anyway. None of us know exactly what Lachlan's ex-wife did to him, but he was terrified of falling in love again. So naturally, he broke Erica's heart and spent two months trying to win her back. It only worked because Erica is a very sweet and forgiving woman.

No, I will never be as daft as my brother. If I broke a woman's heart, I'd get her back right away. That's what I'm doing with Calli, though I didn't abandon her. She left me. And tomorrow, I'll find out why.

Though I sleep that night, it's not the most restful experience. Dreams of Calli torment me. Her smile, her body, her kiss…

I wake up in the morning not as refreshed as I'd like, but I don't mind. I'll give up sleep entirely if I can have Calli. Dreams of her couldn't satisfy this need that urges me to find her and win her and marry her. Maybe I'm moving a bit fast, but it's only in my thoughts. I'll take it slower when I see her.

Probably.

Since the wedding reception won't start for several hours, I decide to give my oldest brother a piece of my mind. I ring Lachlan while I start getting dressed. I sleep naked, of course. No respectable wicked seducer would have it any other way.

"What trouble have you gotten into now?" Lachlan asks instead of saying hello.

"Any trouble I had last night is your fault."

"Now I'm all-powerful and can affect your actions from thousands of miles away?"

"You did that before I left Scotland." I wander over to the dresser and pick up the kilt I'd left there in a lump. "Every Friday is kilt night, that's what you told me. Good one, Lachie."

"Maybe I needed to get my revenge for your behavior at the wedding."

"What did I do? Your wife wanted to learn Gaelic."

"Aye." Lachlan lowers his voice to a growl. "But ye tried to trick her, Aidan. My sweet, innocent wife."

I chuckle. "Innocent? The way I hear it, you debauched that poor lass like a demon."

"Who told you that?" He huffs. "It was Rory, wasn't it?"

"No, it was Iain."

Lachlan clucks his tongue. "Now I know you're feeding me a porky. Iain doesn't gossip."

"No, he's even older than you, which means he's even more boring."

My brother huffs.

"Got to go, Lachie," I say. "I have a date with an enchanting lass, and I willnae be throwing her over because I'm too uptight to know how to treat a woman."

"*Thalla's cagainn bruis*, Aidan."

Away and chew a brush? I guess he's not as clever as I thought if he can't come up with a better insult than that. "I love you too, Lachie."

He snarls a few more Gaelic curses, finding less polite ways of telling me to bugger off. I disconnect the call while chuckling. Aye, my brothers are both uptight and no fun. That's why I will have no trouble winning over Calli.

Unless she runs away again.

Maybe I should plant a GPS chip on her, so I can track her down anywhere.

Discarding that idea, I consider my clothing options. Calli loved the kilt, but I think it might be too showy for a wedding reception. After all, I wouldn't want the women in attendance to be distracted by seeing my legs.

Aye, I'm joking. Even I am not that much of an erse.

But the kilt is too much for the occasion. I choose my dark-blue suit and a white shirt, the outfit lasses always love. I don't wear it often, though, since I don't attend many formal events. Will Calli like my clothes?

I'll find out soon.

After showering and dressing, I march out the door with my mission clear in my mind: Get the girl.

Chapter Four

When I arrive at the wedding reception, I'm not sure what I'm meant to do. Tara didn't give me explicit instructions. How will I find Calli? I'm standing in a crowd of wedding guests, having a nice conversation with an elderly couple who say they're the groom's grandparents, but I haven't seen the bride or her sexy cousin. I don't think the groom's grandparents know anything about Tara inviting me or why she did that.

Maybe I'm starting to feel a wee bit odd about crashing a wedding reception. But Tara did invite me.

The groom's grandparents excuse themselves to go talk to their grandson, and I watch couples shuffling around the dance floor.

Suddenly, the crowd thins a bit and I see her. Calli. She's sitting at a table near the windows with her cousin. Tara says something that makes Calli's eyes go wide and her mouth drop open. Then she wriggles in her chair and fusses with her dress. Even from this distance, I can tell she's wearing a bonnie mint-green frock, a color that looks good on her and compliments all that fiery red hair.

Tara glances my way, smiling and waving to me.

She wants me to go over there, right? I stride through the crowd headed for the woman of my dreams, and excitement rushes through me as I draw closer to the bonnie redhead. Does she want to see me? Or did her cousin trick her into this?

Calli sees me, and I can't help grinning.

Tara says something to Calli, then rises and walks away.

I'm close enough now that I can see Calli is poking at the food on her plate while trying not to look at me. I halt beside the chair Tara had vacated. "May I sit with you?"

"Um… sure."

I sit down, settling one arm on the tabletop. Our shoes almost touch, our knees too, but I don't mind.

She crosses her right leg over the left one.

My gaze snaps to her right thigh and the high slit in her dress that exposes nearly all of her shapely leg. I can't stop myself from licking my lips. Her green frock drapes over one shoulder, leaving the other bare. She looks incredible, sexier than at the club, and I want to pick up where we left off last night.

But I won't do that. Not yet.

Calli glances down at her dress and freezes for a moment as if she's only just realized the slit has fallen open to reveal her leg. She drops her right foot to the floor, yanking the dress to cover her thigh, and crosses her left leg over the right one.

No slit on the left side. She's embarrassed, I think, by her accidental exposure. It was only her leg, though. Cannae see why she'd feel uncomfortable, but women can be odd that way.

I gaze into her emerald eyes while she gazes right back at me. "Calli Douglas, I was hoping to get you alone again."

She folds her hands on her lap. "We're not alone. We're in the middle of a packed wedding reception."

"Everyone else is over there." I wave a hand toward the other side of the room where the rest of the party loiters. "And we are over here."

"How do you know my last name?"

"Your cousin told me."

Calli points at my trousers. "No kilt?"

"Don't wear one every day."

"Only at nightclubs?"

"Ah…" For some reason, I'm feeling embarrassed now, which is barmy. I scratch the back of my neck, grimace, and mumble, "Bloody Lachlan."

"Is that some kind of Scottish cocktail?"

"No." I sigh. "My brother, Lachlan. He told me every Friday is kilt night at the club. Now I'm thinking he said that so he could get his revenge on me."

"Revenge?" she says, slanting toward me. "What did you do to him?"

I clear my throat, shifting in my seat, and wonder why I feel anxious about telling her the truth. She might think I'm an erse, or maybe she'll think it's entertaining. Might as well confess.

A smirk tightens my lips. "At Lachlan's wedding last fall, I tried to trick his bride into repeating a Gaelic phrase. She's American and didn't know the language."

"What did you get her to say?"

"*An toir thu dhomh pòg.*" My smirk widens into a grin. "It means will you give me a kiss. Lachlan, the uptight man he is, warned her before she said it. Erica's a bonnie lass, and I really don't see how he can blame me for trying."

Calli sighs, almost smiling, and shakes her head. "You are a wicked one, aren't you?"

"Noticed, have you?"

Leaning back in her chair, she studies me with a touch of suspicion. "What exactly are you hoping to accomplish here?"

"Have a good time. Drink mediocre whisky." I gaze into her eyes. "Dance with a beautiful woman."

She watches me again, but this time, her cheeks turn faintly pink. Is she remembering our kiss last night? I am, for sure. Calli kisses with passion, with all her heart and soul, and I've never enjoyed a kiss that much in my life.

Coughing, she gestures toward the throng of people in attendance. "Plenty of pretty girls to choose from."

"Only interested in one." I stroke the tabletop with my fingertips. "Dance with me, Calli. Please."

"I think you've gotten the wrong impression of me."

"You're a bonnie, sexy lass who's well-spoken and charming. Am I mistaken?"

"Well-spoken?"

I sit forward, hands linked between my knees. "I heard your speech at dinner this evening. You're eloquent, entertaining, and clearly love your cousin very much."

"Oh." She bites her lip. "I still think you might have the wrong idea about me. Despite my behavior last night, I'm not the kind of girl who makes out with strangers in nightclubs."

"I never thought that." I glance down at the floor, wondering how to convince her I'm not the way I might've seemed to be last night. Well, all right, I am that way sometimes. But I've never been as forward with any other lass as I was with Calli. Honesty seems like the best option, so I look up at her with a sheepish expression. "I don't normally take so many liberties with a woman."

She stares at me. "You don't?"

"No."

Bagpipe music emanates from my trousers.

Calli points at my pocket. "I hope that's your phone."

"It is."

Mouth tight, growling a sigh, I extricate the mobile from my pocket, upside down, and try to flip it over. I lose my hold on it, and the device flies through the air to crash-land on her lap.

Calli picks it up, though I'm sure it was a reflex and not nosiness. She seems to glance at the screen, then her mouth crimps and she tosses the mobile at me.

I catch it in both hands, turning it so I can see what's on the screen. It's a text message from my sister Jamie. *Have you found your quarry, Don Juan? Expect details about American fling.*

I let out a long groan. *Mhac na galla.* No wonder Calli seems annoyed. She doesn't know my baby sister is as sarcastic as my brothers and loves to torment me—affectionately. I love my siblings, but they often inspire me to curse in my thoughts. "Son of a bitch" is what I most often think when they harass me, but I usually go for the Gaelic version, *mhac na galla.*

Planting both feet on the floor, Calli tugs her dress as if she's making sure it covers all of her. "So, Don Juan, am I right in assuming I'm your quarry? The hapless American you tried to lure into a fling?"

"It's not like that." I sink back in my chair, shoving the mobile into my pocket. "My brothers and sisters have a strange sense of humor. They call me Don Juan because I like women, but I don't use them, and I'm not out shagging a different woman every night."

"Shagging? What a funny word for sex."

I struggle to keep from smirking and succeed, though just barely. "I could've said 'fucking.' Would that be more acceptable?"

"Normal people call it having sex."

Smiling, I chuckle softly. "I've never been accused of being normal. But why does the word fuck fash you?"

"Why does it what me?"

"Fash." My lips tighten, and I bluster out a sigh. Lachlan had warned me about this problem, but I assumed he was having me on. But no, it's true that Americans are confused by Scottish words. "Sorry. Fash means bother. Why does 'fuck' upset you?"

"I—The word doesn't offend me, but could you please stop saying it?"

"Dance with me and I will." I offer her my hand, palm up. "Otherwise, I'll have to remind you about our time in the club."

"Blackmail, hm?"

"Anything to get you in my arms again." I stand, still offering my hand. "Please, Calli. One dance. I promise to behave. Mostly."

She considers my hand, which is callused and rough from the construction work I do for a living. I'm not ashamed of having a job that involves hard labor, but some women have complained about my rough hands. Calli doesn't seem bothered by that, though she does seem curious.

"One dance," she says, slipping her delicate palm into mine.

I close my fingers around her hand, loving how warm and soft hers is.

"Aye, one dance," I say while I lead her toward the dance floor. Cannae resist flashing her a mischievous smile over my shoulder. "But I will make the most of the single dance I have with you."

Hand in hand, we wend our way through the couples twirling across the floor in time with a sedate instrumental played by a small string ensemble. Calli bumps into Tara, shoulder to shoulder, as the wee elf dances with her new husband. The newlyweds both grin at me and Calli, and Tara winks at her cousin. Calli gives Tara a sarcastic scowl, probably because her elfin cousin had orchestrated my reunion with her.

None of that matters now. Once we find an open spot, I raise our joined hands, snake my other arm around her side to spread my palm over the small of her back, and tug her close. Despite her high heels that make her a few inches taller than she would be in her bare feet, I still tower over the lass.

Finally, I have Calli Douglas in my arms.

While we sway our hips and shuffle our feet, I marvel at how lucky I am. On my first night in America, I met the perfect woman, a lass who's beautiful and well-spoken, sexy and sweet. All right, maybe she ran away from me last night, and I know virtually nothing about her. But I'm dead certain, in a way I can't explain, that Calli is the right woman for me.

Her breasts brush against my chest while I hold her close and we glide around the dance floor. Everyone else in the room seems to fade away, leaving only the soft strains of the music and the feel of this woman cradled in my arms.

I bend my head to whisper in her ear. "Couldnae stop thinking about ye. All night, all morning, every second till I found ye here."

Spinning us round and round the floor, I maneuver between other couples while keeping my mouth near her ear. All I see is her. All I want is her.

"Did you think about me?" I purr into her ear.

"Yes."

"Good." I pull her even closer, our bodies pressed together, her breasts mashed into my chest. "I went too far last night. I'm sorry."

"I gave you permission to kiss me. Which makes it my fault, not yours."

"You're not angry?"

"No."

"The party's almost over," I say. "Spend the evening with me."

"What?" She pulls her head back to stare at me. "I don't know you."

"Get to know me, then." I skate my hand up her back, then down again, my fingers teasing the upper curve of her erse through her dress. "I want to know you. Give me the rest of tonight, please."

"I'm flying home to Michigan in the morning. Have to pack and get some sleep."

"Can't you stay an extra day?"

"Why are you so determined? We're essentially strangers."

"Been told I'm impulsive, and you are the most captivating woman I've ever met." I lift our hands to my lips, feathering kisses across her knuckles. "When I see what I want, I donnae give up easily."

Calli glances at something past my shoulder.

She disentangles her hand from mine. "The bride and groom are heading out. I have to see them off, so please excuse me. It was nice meeting you."

My mouth opens and then shuts again as I track her journey across the dance floor away from me. She's leaving? Just like that?

Calli glances back at me once, then she's gone.

Chapter Five

After Calli disappears, I stand frozen on the dance floor, wondering why the lass seems determined to get away from me. She likes me. Why else would she have kissed me last night and danced with me today? *It was nice meeting you*, she said. Nice? Meeting her is the best thing that's ever happened to me, but I can't seem to convince Calli to stay in the same room with me for more than ten minutes.

Most of the guests have wandered away to enjoy the buffet or to chat to each other while seated at the tables that surround the dance floor. Calli had said she was going to see the bride and groom off. Does that mean she'll come back?

I have never been the sort of man who waits for a lass to summon me.

When I check the hallway, I don't find her there. I head outside where Tara had told me the wedding took place, though I hadn't attended that event. I understand why Tara didn't invite me to the wedding. I'm a stranger, after all, and it was kind of her to let me come to the reception.

A glassy pond catches my eye, and I amble over there in search of the lass who keeps fleeing from me. I don't expect to find her there, but I do. Calli stands beneath a large tree with its canopy of branches spread out above her while she gazes at the pond with a bleak expression. What fashes her? I want to know because I need to learn everything about her—if she'll let me.

She lays a hand on the tree trunk and shuts her eyes. Her expression softens as if she's enjoying a happy memory.

I walk over to her. "There you are."

With a yelp and a jump, Calli whirls toward me.

"Did I scare you?" I say with a smile. "Sorry. I've been looking every-where for you and finally spotted a red-haired woman in a green dress out here, looking melancholy."

She stares at me, not blinking.

I stride closer, narrowing the distance between us to an arm's length. "I was hoping for a real goodbye."

"I said goodbye."

"No, you excused yourself and told me it was nice meeting me."

She offers me her hand. "It was nice meeting you. Goodbye, Aidan."

As if that will satisfy me. The more she tries to get rid of me, the more I want to know why. I've been told, often, that I'm charming. And lots of fun. She likes me, but she won't let herself enjoy spending time with me. Somehow, I will unravel the mystery of Calli Douglas.

I slide my hand into hers, letting my fingers graze the underside of her wrist. "I'd like to kiss you goodbye."

She holds perfectly still for a moment, her gaze locked onto mine. Then she clears her throat. "On the cheek."

"On the lips." I draw her closer until I can hold our joined hands to my chest. "Please. One last taste of you before you go."

Peripherally, I notice the last of the wedding guests are loitering inside the Gingko Room, maybe thirty feet away, with nothing but floor-to-ceiling glass between us and them. Though I don't care who sees us, I have a feeling Calli does. But I also feel fair certain she won't care about the guests anymore once we're kissing, considering the way she'd abandoned herself to our kiss last night.

She bites her lip. "Okay."

Okay? That means a kiss on the lips. I get to taste her again.

Moving forward, I ease her backward until the tree shields us from the windows of the Gingko Room. My pulse accelerates, and I feel more excited by the prospect of kissing this lass than I've ever felt with any other woman. I back her up all the way to the tree, our bodies inches apart, and clasp her hand to my chest. With my other hand, I cup her cheek and rub my thumb across her lips. She parts them for me, and I push the tip of my thumb inside, though only for a second. Her eyes drift half shut as she exhales a long breath and her shoulders sag, her body going limp against the tree.

Christ, she is the most sensual woman on earth.

I sweep my hand up her cheek and dive my fingers into her hair, cradling her nape. We gaze into each other's eyes without glancing away, not even for half a second.

"Thank you," I say, my voice rougher.

"For what?"

"This."

I brush my lips across hers, and the first touch makes my cock twitch and my pulse pound even faster and harder. I catch her upper lip between my teeth, pulling it into my mouth and licking at it with swift, light strokes. Releasing her lip little by little, I shift my hand to her nape to angle her head back for the deep kiss I crave. Calli's eyes flutter closed. I nip at her bottom lip and sweep my tongue over the seam of her mouth.

Calli rocks her hips forward, nudging my growing erection.

I groan, long and low, the feral sound resonating in my chest. This woman turns me into a beast, but I like it.

She thrusts her free hand into my hair, clawing at my scalp like she's desperate to drag me in for a passionate kiss.

Cannae wait any longer. I seize both her hands, pinning them to the tree above her head while I press my body against hers, firmly enough to hold her in place, but not so forcefully that she might want to run away again. Her body feels so bloody good. For a moment, all I can do is gaze into her eyes, certain my raw hunger for her shows, though she doesn't seem to mind. I'm breathing harder, and suddenly, I need to do this right now. I adjust my hold on her, clasping both her wrists in one of my hands while I skim my other palm down her bare arm and across her exposed shoulder to her collarbone. I dance my fingertips up her throat to her chin. With light pressure from my thumb, I encourage her to open her mouth wider.

And she surrenders to me.

I drop my hand to her hip, curling my fingers around it, and claim her lips in an open-mouth kiss, diving my tongue deep to ravish her with possessive strokes. She writhes against me, rubbing her breasts on my chest and rolling her hips into my hard cock. I can't stop myself from scraping my erection over her belly while I groan into her mouth. She keeps writhing, like she's desperate for me to shag her, and *bod an Donais*, I need to fuck this woman right now. A frustrated noise bursts out of her while the kiss grows wilder, our tongues tangling and our lips crushed to each other.

A frantic, lustful noise erupts out of her.

I peel my mouth from hers, fighting to catch my breath, and let my head fall forward until our foreheads touch. "Let me see you again. Please."

"I live in another state."

"And I live in another country." I free her hands, step back half a step, and hold her face in my palms. "May I visit you sometime?"

She hesitates, but only for a heartbeat. "I guess so."

I touch my lips to hers. "Meant to give you a simple kiss, but I lose my mind when I touch you."

"I liked it. Both times."

Reaching into my trouser pocket, I pull out my mobile. "May I have your number?"

Calli bites her lip like she's considering how to answer. Then she gestures for me to give her my mobile. "Sure."

I hand the device over to her.

She finds the address book and types in her number and name, then hands my mobile back to me. "There you go."

A smile stretches my lips. I'm probably more thrilled than I should be, but I don't care. Calli has agreed to let me ring her sometime. She might be leaving Chicago, but she wants to talk to me again.

Calli pushes away from the tree and smooths her dress. "Well, it's time for me to head out. Goodbye, Aidan."

I lift her hand to my mouth and brush my lips over her knuckles. "Till we meet again, Calli Douglas."

She mutters something I can't understand, her cheeks turning pink, and starts to walk away. But she stumbles over a tree root and winds up half staggering back toward the building. I consider offering to help her, but I don't want to push my luck. I have Calli's number. I can talk to her again, which means that she just might agree to let me see her again too.

Oh aye, last night I found my dream girl.

Tomorrow, I'll come up with a plan to win her over.

Chapter Six

Am I slightly insane? Even I'm starting to wonder about that after another restless night of trying to sleep but not having much success. I keep thinking about Calli and how I can convince her to give me a chance. I've never had trouble getting dates, which means I could go to another club or a bar or even the beach and meet eligible women who won't run away from me like I'm a crazed pervert who has leprosy.

But I don't want just any woman. I want Calli Douglas.

Maybe I'm just being stubborn, but I don't think so. There's something about Calli, something more than her sexy body and her passion. She's a mystery. Maybe that's why I can't stop thinking about her and can't talk myself out of tracking her down.

In the morning, I decide I should get a second opinion about my sanity—though not from my brothers. I know what Lachlan and Rory will say, and it's not what I want to hear. So, I ring my sister Jamie, the baby of the family, because she might understand what I'm doing here in America and give me unbiased advice. Aye, my sister will be impartial. The lass who frequently says she wants to fall in love as often as possible is going to give me sound guidance concerning my love life.

"Have you been arrested yet?" Jamie says when she answers her mobile.

"Arrested? I've never done anything illegal, and you know it."

"Just thought I'd ask. You have run away to another country to find a wife, so I thought you might've been arrested for wearing a kilt with no shorts underneath."

"Would I do that?"

She laughs. "You brag about 'swinging free' under your kilt. Honestly, I didn't need to have that image in my head, Aidan."

"Then let's never discuss that subject again." I really didn't need to hear my sister talking about whether I wear shorts under my kilt. Maybe ringing Jamie hadn't been such a brilliant idea after all, but I might as well try. "I rang you for advice, Jamie. About a girl I met."

"You're wanting advice from me? I thought 'Don Juan' MacTaggart knew everything about women and didn't need pointers from anyone." She lowers her voice to a sarcastic whisper. "If you're asking me for help, you must be desperate."

"Never mind. I'll talk to Evan."

"Evan?" Jamie says with a laugh. "Unless you're wanting a security system, he won't be any help. Evan doesn't date."

Of course he doesn't. Everyone knows that. My cousin might be a genius, but he doesn't socialize much. I really have lost my mind, haven't I?

"Sorry, Jamie. I shouldn't have bothered you. This is a problem I need to solve on my own."

"Well, you can always ring Lachlan or Rory."

"Ah...thank you for the suggestion."

She snorts. "Which means 'hell will freeze over before I take your advice, you daft bairn.' Aye?"

"I'll talk to you later, Jamie. And please don't tell Lachlan or Rory about this call."

"Maybe I should go to America. Lachlan met Erica there, and now you've found a girl there too. Does America have magic air or water or something?"

"Bugger off, ye cheeky bairn. And no, do not come anywhere near the United States of America."

She makes a snarky huffing sound. "If it's good enough for you and Lachlan—"

"No, Jamie."

Have I convinced my sister to stay away from America? Probably not, but Rory and Lachlan will straighten her out if she mentions her daft idea to them. At least Jamie agrees not to tell our brothers that I rang her, and we say goodbye. Honestly, I thought Jamie would be more understanding. I'm on my own.

All right. What should I do now?

While I mull over my plan, which consists of nothing so far, I make myself breakfast in Erica's kitchen. Or her parents' kitchen. Does it really matter who claims ownership? I'm using it now. After eating, I take a shower. Then I decide I really should go to a gift shop and buy presents for my family. Lachlan always does that when he's away, and I wouldn't want anyone to think I'm too skint to afford to treat my brothers and sisters. I am skint, but I have a credit card. Lachlan would probably buy gifts at a shop so expensive I couldn't afford to buy a toothbrush without overtaxing my credit card.

I take a taxi to the area the driver tells me is a popular district for shopping, especially for tourists. Am I a tourist? I guess I must be. I wander down the street for three blocks, but don't see any shops I like. So much for that plan. By the time I get back to the house, it's lunchtime, so I make myself a sandwich and eat it before considering my next move. I wash the dishes too. And take the rubbish out to the bin behind the house. Then I get online and hire a car without leaving the sofa. Aye, I might be procrastinating. Maybe I'm afraid Calli will tell me to sod off, or however Americans tell someone to go away.

Afraid? Me? Bloody hell. That won't do at all.

I grab my mobile, find Calli's number, and dial it.

After two rings, she answers. "Hello?"

"You sound sleepy. Did I wake you?"

Silence.

"Are you there?" I ask.

"Yes."

I clear my throat. "Is it too soon to ring you?"

"No, I guess not. You don't waste any time, do you?"

I sigh and chuckle. "Impulsive, remember?"

More silence.

"What are you doing?" I ask, hoping to sound casually interested and not desperate to hear the answer. Aye, that means I'm lying with my tone of voice.

"Not sleeping," she says, sounding a touch snippy. "Sorry. I get grumpy when I'm tired. Exhausted from the trip."

"Tell me one thing before we say goodbye."

"What do you want to know?"

"Are you with anyone? A husband, a boyfriend, a lover?"

She hesitates. "I'm not interested in starting anything."

"Hmm." I hesitate now, because I'm not sure how to proceed. "You seemed interested at the club and again after the wedding."

"I'm not having sex with you."

"Sex? Didnae mention that. I meant seeing each other as in dating." Since I have my opening, I can't resist lowering my voice to a husky murmur. "But if you'd rather skip straight to the good part…"

"No. I wouldn't rather." She groans. "I have to go. To sleep. Not with you, just to—Oh forget it. I'm exhausted, and I have no idea what I'm saying."

"I'm sorry for disturbing you, but I'd love to see you again. I'm tired of the city, hired a car for a drive…anywhere." Maybe I hadn't hired a car specifically to visit her, but I came up with my plan two seconds ago. I clear my throat, dismayed by how hesitant I sound when I ask, "May I come to see you?"

She says nothing for a few seconds. "Well, we could meet in a public place. When will you get here?"

"I could be there tomorrow. Mid-morning."

"Okay. Meet me at the beach." She rattles off directions to a beach in Michigan, punctuating her words with a yawn.

I grab a pen off the table beside the sofa and scrawl those directions on my palm. "Better let you go. Get some rest."

"See you tomorrow."

We hang up. And I hunt down a notepad so I can transcribe Calli's directions onto paper and wash the ink off my hand. Tomorrow, I'll get to see her again. At a beach. That means neither of us will wear much clothing, right? People wear swimsuits at the beach. Maybe she'll choose a bikini. She did wear a slinky frock on the night we met, and another one yesterday at the wedding reception. What are the odds she'll treat me to that body in a skimpy swimsuit?

Honestly, though, I won't care if she shows up in a clown costume. I'll want to shag her no matter what.

But I will take it slow. Not my strong suit, but Calli is worth the extra effort. I know she is.

A quick check on my mobile tells me I have a long drive ahead of me. Sure, I could probably get Lachlan to buy me an airline ticket, but I don't want to tell him why I need to go to Michigan. Not yet. He won't understand. Besides, I'd like to drive there and see more of this country. It's my big adventure, isn't it? Might as well make the most of it. After packing my bags, I head out to my hired car that was just delivered to me and use the map software on my mobile to type in the destination Calli gave me.

And I'm away.

By the time I reach Milwaukee, Wisconsin, I'm already knackered. It's evening now, anyway, so I find a small motel where I can spend the night. Lachlan would not approve. My room didn't cost a small fortune. But it's comfortable, and I sleep better tonight because I know what will happen tomorrow.

Calli Douglas will be waiting for me.

Chapter Seven

Thin white clouds glide across the blue sky as gentle waves lap at the golden sand on the beach, the water shimmering a pale aqua blue. The four-foot cliff behind us juts out to our right, sequestering us from the beachgoers who occupy the long, straight stretch beyond. Calli chose this spot for us, and I can't help wondering what she wants to do with me that requires this much privacy.

Oh, I have ideas. I always do when I'm with a beautiful woman.

I've never seen a beach like this one. The lochs in Scotland are deep and dark, and though Calli told me Lake Superior is very deep too, this inlet seems more like the Caribbean bays I've seen in movies. I had no idea Michigan looked like this.

Calli sits cross-legged on a beach towel, gazing out at the view of the lake, though she keeps glancing at me too.

I'm relaxing on the beach towel adjacent to hers, but I don't even try to stop looking at her. Lying on my side, propped up on one elbow, I admire the view of Calli—though she's not wearing a bikini, like I'd hoped she might. Still, her outfit is sexy enough to satisfy me until the day I can convince her to try a string bikini. Or nudity. Do they have nude beaches in Michigan?

I skim my gaze over her for the tenth time, drinking in the sight of her legs, mostly exposed by tan shorts that cover only one-third of her thighs. A bright-pink tank top covers her torso, with glitter-coated red flowers over her chest, and the neckline plunges low enough to make my mouth water. I'd love to fondle and taste those tits. The semitransparent, loose-fitting white shirt she wears only makes her more enticing. Even her white socks and walking shoes appeal to me—because *she's* wearing them.

I arrived in jeans and a T-shirt, both tight enough to show off my body without being overt about it. Why shouldn't I show it off? Women like to look at me, and I like watching them do that.

Especially when it's Calli admiring me.

I gaze at her face until she finally notices. "You like me."

"You have no idea what I think about you. And vice versa."

Maybe I've started to smirk a wee bit. She can't convincingly deny the fact, so she claims I can't know the truth. "If ye donnae like me, why would you bring me to a private place?"

I'd arrived before Calli, so I waited in the car park for her. A nice elderly couple took pity on me and kept me company, and the three of us wound up laughing like we'd known each other for years. They live in Michigan, though not here in the Upper Peninsula, which they explained is not physically connected to "The Mitten" aka the Lower Peninsula. It's all very confusing. That part of the state is vaguely shaped like a mitten, though.

Once Calli arrived, I said goodbye to my new mates.

"I'm starting to think," I say, "you have lascivious intentions."

She tries to pull off a nonchalant attitude, but it's not convincing. "I like the shade. Too much sun makes me feel sweaty and icky."

"I like a sweaty lass. Watching the drops of perspiration run down between a woman's breasts makes me want to lick it away."

She glances down at her tits like she's afraid there might be sweat there and I might actually lick it away. Then she fiddles with the lid of the plastic cooler full of provisions for our picnic. "Do you want to eat yet?"

"In a bit." I settle a palm on the sand between us, moving my fingers in a petting motion since I can't pet her, not yet. "First, I'd like us to get to know each other better."

"Okay, but we need to be perfectly clear on a few things before we share our life stories or whatever."

"Such as?"

Calli wriggles her bonnie erse on her towel, adjusting her position to turn partway toward me and look straight into my eyes. "You need to understand the rules I live by."

Oh, bloody hell. Rules? She's as uptight as Rory, isn't she?

Donnae care. I can loosen her up.

I push up into a half-sitting position, still on my side, held up by one hand flat on my towel. "Tell me your rules, then."

She bites her upper lip, then inhales a deep breath and blows it out. "These are my rules. No sex, no love, no marriage."

This has to be a joke. A sensual, vibrant lass like her wouldn't take a celibacy vow, not after the way she kissed me. "I don't understand. Not wanting marriage, that's not too unusual. But no love? Giving up sex is one thing but—"

"I haven't given up sex."

My brows lift, and I open my mouth two seconds before I manage to speak. "You just said—"

She silences me by holding up one finger. "I said exactly what I meant. Don't make assumptions about what you think it means, take it at face value."

Take what at face value? I have no ruddy idea. Maybe she is a bampot after all, but I still want her like mad. I like insane women? Ah well, I learn something new about myself every day. I probably look confused—because I am.

Calli seems to realize that. She sighs, and her shoulders crumple. "I've never had sex, therefore I can't give it up. I am a twenty-five-year-old virgin."

I shrug. "Are you thinking I'll be shocked? I'm not."

She folds her arms atop her knees. "No one in this day and age believes a person over the age of eighteen could be a virgin unless there's something terribly wrong with them."

Ah, so that's the problem. I lean forward to touch her arm. "I've been with virgins older than you."

"They must've been nuns, right?"

"No. Each had her reasons for staying innocent, and I'm sure you have yours."

"I'm not innocent."

She might not be insane, but she seems determined to drive me off my head. I stare at her for several seconds while I try to puzzle out the meaning of what she said, but I fail. "You are a confusing woman. How are you not innocent if you're a virgin?"

"You're making assumptions again." She shivers faintly when I start to caress her skin with my fingertips. Sidling away from me, beyond my reach, she faces the lake again and stretches out her shapely legs, leaning back to brace her hands on the towel behind her. "I've never had sexual intercourse with anyone, but that doesn't mean I'm ignorant of all sexual knowledge."

I scan my gaze up and down her body one more time, from her shoe-covered feet, up her bare legs, past those mouthwatering breasts, and finally to her lovely face. "You're very comfortable with your body, aren't you? Not embarrassed to show it off."

"I don't usually dress this way. Sweats and baggy T-shirts are my MO. What does my clothing have to do with the topic at hand?"

"You say you're not innocent, and I'm noticing how you're at ease with your sensuality. But I could use a wee bit of help connecting the dots here."

She avoids my gaze even when I sit up to look at her. "Tell me, what do you think being a virgin means? In terms of sexual experience?"

"Means no experience, of course."

"Not for me." Calli squeezes her eyes shut like she needs to force herself to speak the words. "Just because I've never been touched by a man doesn't mean I have no idea what pleasure feels like. There are other ways to, um...have orgasms."

She winces, eyes still firmly shut.

Naturally, she expects me to be horrified or...something. The bonnie, barmy lass really doesn't understand me yet, does she? I chuckle. "You masturbate."

Opening one eye only, she peeks at me.

I can't help grinning while my body quivers with contained laughter. I'm not laughing at her. I'm laughing because she's so bloody adorable that I want to pull her into my arms and kiss her.

With both eyes open now, she makes a peeved face. "You think it's funny?"

"No." I brush the backs of my fingertips down her cheek, no longer laughing, and smile softly. "I think it's charming."

Her brows snap together. "Charming? I intend to stay a virgin for the foreseeable future, but meanwhile I—do naughty things to myself in the privacy of my bedroom. How can you not think I'm demented?"

I shrug one shoulder. "I knew you were a passionate woman the night we met. And I was right."

"It's not passion when you're alone."

"Of course it is." I lean in close to murmur in her ear. "I plan to take full advantage of your secret passion."

"Remember the rules, Aidan. No sex, no love, no marriage."

My breaths fan over her ear and cheek, reflecting onto my face, while I murmur, "Ye cannae stop from falling in love."

"Yes I can." She sits forward, clasping her hands on her lap. "I can control my feelings, the same way I control my behavior."

I shake my head. "Emotions are uncontrollable. You can't keep from feeling."

"I disagree."

"Maybe you are daft," I say with a teasing smile. "But since you can't control your behavior, that doesn't bode well for your no-love plans."

"What do you mean I can't control my behavior?"

"The other night. At the club." One corner of my mouth lifts. "You molested me."

"I did not—Well, maybe I did. But you started it, begging to kiss me like that."

"Guilty. I wasn't begging, though." I move back just enough to see her face. "You've been honest with me about your rules. I should be honest with you about what I want."

"Okay," she says slowly, like she's unsure if she wants to hear it.

"I came to America to find a wife."

"Don't they have women in Scotland?"

"Been dating in Scotland since I was fifteen, but I've never met the right kind of girl."

She draws her knees up, wrapping her arms around them. "Doesn't explain why you came all the way to America."

"Ah…" I bow my head briefly, then give her a tight-lipped smile. "My brother Lachlan found an American wife. Met her at Dance Ardor. If it worked for him, why not for me?"

"Let me get this straight." She taps her fingers on her crossed arms. "Your brother, the one who told you every Friday is kilt night at the club, met his wife in that very same club."

"Aye."

"Was he, by any chance, wearing a kilt at the time?"

Clearing my throat, head down, I peek up at her. "Yes. It was kilt night then, which is why I believed him when he said every Friday was for kilts."

"I see. And what will you do with this American wife once you find her? Do you plan on kidnapping her back to Scotland?"

"Not kidnapping anyone." I twist my mouth up, then groan. "And I don't know. Haven't thought that far ahead. Find a wife first, talk about living arrangements later."

"Uh-huh. A good, specific plan."

"Everything can be worked out when I find the right woman." I slant toward her again, our mouths almost touching. "I knew the moment I saw you, Calli, you could be the right one for me. Give me four weeks to convince you, and if I can't, I'll go away and never pester you again."

She gets a suspicious expression on her face. "Why four weeks? That's an awfully specific timeframe. Most people would say a month."

Bugger. She would have to notice that.

I scratch behind my ear, my face pinched. "Lachlan spent four weeks with Erica."

Calli throws her head back, groaning at the heavens before she returns her attention to me. "I don't want to participate in a reenactment of the epic love affair between the Amazing Lachlan and Erica the American Wonder-Wife."

"Ahmno trying to—" I contort one side of my mouth, then exhale a long breath, relaxing my face. "Forget about Lachlan and Erica. Please, Calli, give me four weeks."

"To do what, precisely? You'll never convince me we belong together."

A sly smile steals across my face. "I mean to seduce you. If I can tempt you to break your first rule, the rest will follow."

"The rest meaning love and marriage. You can't make me fall in love with you."

"I can, and I will." I don't say that with sarcasm. I mean it. Winning Calli is my mission, and I'm too stubborn to give up on her because she's afraid of love.

She snorts, and the sound seems to imply she doesn't believe I can make her love me.

I slide a fingertip along her jaw, down her throat, over her collarbone. When my finger teases the upper curve of one breast, she sucks in a breath. The sound makes my cock twitch. My God, she's beautiful. I want her to love me because I know I can love her—if she'll let me. Maybe my determination to win her is an aftereffect of the rubbish I've been through this year, but no, it can't be. Calli is the woman for me, full stop.

"You like me," I say. "Otherwise you wouldn't have invited me to visit you or brought me to a secluded beach. You want me, otherwise you wouldn't have kissed me twice—with breathtaking passion and sensuality." I coast my fingertip down the valley between her breasts until it collides with the neckline of her T-shirt. "Those facts give me hope that you will fall for me. Ye willnae be able to stop it."

"Because you're so irresistible."

"That's not the main reason." I withdraw my hand but keep my mouth near hers while our gazes connect. "It's because I'm lovable."

Laughter bubbles out of her, the light, feminine sort that's as melodic and sweet as music.

"You are bonnie all the time," I say, "but when you laugh, you're the bonniest of the bonnie."

"Thanks."

I study her for a moment, entranced by Calli in every way imaginable. Can I win her over? It might be the most difficult task I've ever undertaken, but I'm as stubborn as she is. I won't give up easily, and I absolutely will not leg it back to Scotland if she says she loves me, like Lachlan did when Erica told him how she felt.

Glancing at the waters of Lake Superior, I squint at the sunlight glancing off the surface. "What is Calli short for?"

"Nothing. It's my name. Calli Bethany Douglas."

"A good Scottish name, Douglas."

"I'm American." She stretches her legs out again, wiggling her feet. "Is Aidan short for something?"

Ah, she really ought to know better by now. Asking me a question like that… Of course I have to take advantage of the moment to show her more of my wicked side. I shoot her a grin infused with all the lust she inspires in me. "Aidan the Magnificent. It's my full, Viking name."

"Thought you were Scottish."

"Vikings came to Scotland, you know. I've probably got at least a wee bit of Norse blood in me."

"What part of Scotland are you from?"

"Ballachulish. A village in the Highlands, on the shores of Loch Leven." I gaze out across the blue waters of Lake Superior, and an impulse hits me. "Maybe I'll have a swim. The water's making me sentimental."

"Did you bring swim trunks?"

"I don't need them." Springing to my feet, I lift my shirt, intending to shed it.

"What have you got on under those jeans?" Calli asks.

I pause with my shirt partly lifted. "Skin."

She stares at my abdomen like she wants to nibble on my abs, which I'd love for her to do, but she holds back.

I pull my shirt up a little higher.

Calli raises a hand. "Hold up, Flipper. That water is frigid. Why do you think we didn't see a single person swimming or wading? It comes straight from the depths of Lake Superior, which is very deep and cold. They don't call it an inland sea for nothing."

I flatten my lips. She can't think I care about that. "I'm Scottish. Chilly water doesnae scare me."

"Maybe you should dip your toes in first to test how cold it is." When I scoff and roll my eyes, she says, "Trust me. You don't want to swim this early in the year unless it's an inland lake, or a protected bay. Even then… Well, trust me. Okay?"

Grumbling, I let my shirt fall back down and nod. If the lass insists, I will test the water. Stripping off my shoes and socks, I roll my jeans up to my knees. While I amble toward the water, Calli leans back, braced on her arms, to watch me. I can tell by the look on her face that she's admiring my body again. I love that.

Her head lolls to the left as she moistens her lips, all her attention riveted to my erse.

I wade out into the gently lapping waves without stopping until the water reaches my knees. This doesn't feel so bad. What was she on about? This water isn't as cold as she—

Mhac na galla. The frigid water has suddenly hit me, and my entire body freezes. My shoulders bunch up. I can't seem to pull in a full breath, and I curl my fingers then snap them straight and stiff. I clench my teeth, a breath exploding out between them. I've swum in cold lochs, but this… I suck in a shuddering breath, sure my feet are about to freeze solid and break off to float away on the tide.

"Ah!" I hiss, backing out of the water as fast as my half-frozen feet can move. "*Bod an Donais*!"

Calli slaps a hand over her mouth to stifle a laugh.

Whirling around, I drop onto my beach towel, rubbing my feet furiously. "You think it's funny? I've probably got frostbite."

"I warned you." Canting her head, Calli grins while I give an exaggerated shiver. "What was that you said a minute ago? Sounded like another language."

"Gaelic. I was cursing at the bloody freezing water."

"What does it mean? The phrase you said."

"*Bod an Donais*. Means the devil's penis."

Laughter erupts out of her and doesn't stop until she's clutching her belly and her eyes are watering. I observe her with a half-smile, half-frown until she wipes her eyes and catches her breath.

"You think that's funny too?" I say. "It's a legitimate Scottish curse. Though I could've said *bod a' chac*, which means shit's penis."

The lass bursts out laughing again and collapses onto her back on her towel, hands clutching her belly.

Her giggles die away when I recline beside her, my head supported on one hand and my focus squarely on her. "I can teach you plenty of dirty Gaelic phrases—starting with the ones about sex."

"Let's eat now," she says as if I didn't just offer to talk dirty to her.

"Not yet," I murmur, bending closer, my face positioned over hers. "First, I want to kiss you."

"No sex. Rule number one."

My mouth twists into a half-suppressed smirk. "You keep assuming I'm wanting sex, which makes me wonder if you're the one who can't stop thinking about it."

"No comment."

"Let me kiss you. Unless you're afraid you can't keep from fucking me, right here on the beach."

She clasps her hands more tightly over her belly.

I let my lips slide into a devilish smile. "Ready to break your first rule?"

"No." She squirms, adjusting her position though she seems like she can't quite get comfortable. "But we can kiss. Only kiss. No clothing will be removed, and no parts of you will sneak under my clothes to touch parts of me. Understand?"

"Aye. I willnae stroke your *boicionn* unless you beg me to."

"My what?"

"*Boicionn*." I sweep a hand down her body, hovering it a bare inch above her skin, and halt it over her groin. "Your sweet, pink, slippery folds. The ones I'll lick and stroke when I finally have you naked under me."

"Never going to happen."

"We'll see."

"Are you going to kiss me or what?"

I lay a hand on her cheek, drawing circles on her skin with my thumb and grazing the corner of her mouth. Slanting closer, I hover my lips millimeters from hers. "Desperate for me?"

"Patience is not my forte. When I decide to do something, I want to get it done right away."

"I like that about you."

Her lips drift apart like she's begging me to kiss her.

"I like everything I've learned about you," I say. "Even your rules."

Before she can speak, I brush my lips across hers—once, twice, three times. Even that delicate contact drives me mad with a hint of what her mouth will taste like this time. I skate my lips over hers, teasing her until she fists her hands in the towel beneath her and lets out a soft, hungry moan. When I dart my tongue out to flick it across the seam of her mouth, back and forth, she exhales another long, ravenous moan and seizes my head in her hands, pulling me in. Our lips crash together as she sinks her fingers into my hair and opens her mouth wider, urging me to take control.

How can I resist that?

A groan resonates in my chest and throat as I dive my tongue inside her mouth, lashing and coiling it around hers, starved for the flavor and sensation of this woman devouring me as completely as I'm devouring her. When we come up for air, both breathless, all we can do is gaze into each other's eyes for a long moment. My cock is halfway to a hard-on, but I don't care. Kissing Calli is worth it.

I move in for another kiss.

Calli places a hand on my chest, keeping me at bay. "Listen, you need to accept I won't ever love you. I do not fall for men called Don Juan."

I rub my eyes with my thumb and forefinger. "Bloody Jamie. Little sisters can be a trial, that's for sure. When you've got five brothers and sisters, you get used to being called all sorts of sarcastic names. Doesn't your brother annoy you that way?"

"Gavin prefers to annoy me by meddling in my life."

I nod. "Overbearing brothers. I sympathize."

"Ditto. But about this Don Juan thing…"

"I am not a Don Juan. I like women, and I like to flirt, that's all."

She still has her hand flat on my chest, the warmth of her skin penetrating my shirt. "How many women have you been with?"

"Seven."

Her eyebrows shoot up. "Seven? That's it? Doesn't sound very Don Juan-ish to me."

"Told you, I'm not like that. Jamie's exaggerating." I settle my hand over hers and slowly peel her palm away from my shirt. "I'd like another kiss now, please."

"Okay."

I set my hand on her bare thigh, my fingers grazing her silky skin, and dip my head closer to hers. And closer. And closer. Our lips come within millimeters of each other, and I'm about to kiss her when—

My mobile plays bagpipe music.

I mutter a Gaelic curse and roll away from her to dig the mobile out of my jeans pocket. When I see who the caller is, I flinch.

"Have to take this," I tell Calli. "Won't be a minute."

I spring to my feet and trot a little ways down the beach to answer my call. I face away from Calli, my shoulders tensing up while I clasp one hand to the back of my bowed head.

"What do you want, Seona?" I ask.

"You owe me, Aidan."

"Owe you? I tried to be there for you after the accident, but you told me to go away and never bother you again."

"What are you doing in America?"

I pace a short length of the beach, head down. "That's none of your concern, Seona. I'm busy, so if—"

"You owe me, Aidan," she says again with anger in her voice. "Whose fault was it? Not mine. You ruined my life, and I want you to pay."

"Ahmno sure what you're asking of me."

"Money, Aidan. For my pain and suffering, which you caused."

So she's become an extortionist, and I'm her mark. "I'm on the verge of bankruptcy, Seona. I cannae give you anything."

I suddenly realize I'm gesticulating with one hand, waving it around as if she were in front of me while issuing her demands.

"You should have paid more attention," Seona hisses. "I was hospitalized for months because of you. My pain and suffering are worth every pound in your bank account. Unless you want me to tell the world what you did to me."

The daft cow really is blackmailing me. I haven't done anything illegal or even immoral, not with her. How can she believe I'll give in to her demands?

"See a psychologist," I snarl. "That's the kind of help you need. Goodbye, Seona."

I end the call and stuff my mobile back in my pocket, then stalk back down the beach to Calli. Should I tell her about Seona? I don't want to ruin a beautiful day with a beautiful woman by bringing my problems into the mix. Seona will give up her stupid attempt to blackmail me. She has to. And I've got better things to think about—like the bonnie lass stretched out on a beach towel.

Settling onto my towel beside Calli, I reach for the cooler. "Let's eat."

"Yes," Calli says, rubbing her hands together and licking her lips. "I'm famished."

Head down, I peek up at her. "I know. You are always famished."

Aye, no more thoughts of Seona. I've got better things to think about today.

         # Chapter Eight

While I bring out plastic-wrapped sandwiches and bottles of water, I keep thinking back to my call with Seona. I don't want to keep thinking about it, but my mind has other ideas. I'd rather focus on Calli. Aye, that's what I *should* focus on. No more worries about Seona. She has worse problems than her physical injuries, that much is clear. I hope she gets the help she needs, but I can't have anything to do with her now.

I unwrap a sandwich and hand it to Calli, then unwrap one for myself.

"Listen," she says after swallowing a bite of food, "there's something else I need to tell you about me."

I bite off a chunk of my sandwich, chewing with deliberate slowness, swallowing and dragging my tongue across my lips. "I'm listening."

She picks at the crust of her sandwich while she avoids looking at me. "Even if I wanted to marry you, which I don't, I can't do it. I'm already married."

I freeze, staring at her without blinking, my sandwich hovering an inch from my mouth. "What? But you don't wear a ring. And you're a virgin."

"I am married, Aidan. Filed for divorce, but still married."

"Filed for divorce?" I set down my food. "Then you're separated. Legally."

"There's no such thing as legal separation in Michigan. But yes, I started the divorce process." She raises her sandwich as if to take a bite, then sets it down. "My husband has been trying to delay the proceedings."

"Are you still in love with him?"

"I never loved him."

"Donnae understand." I glance at my sandwich, my lip curling because I suddenly feel ill. Why did she wait until now to tell me this? She's a married virgin? I don't understand at all, so I set down my sandwich. "You don't love him, and you've never slept with him. Why did you marry the man? Why not get an annulment instead of divorce?"

"It's a long story." She holds up a hand when I open my mouth to speak. "Please don't ask any more questions. That's all I can tell you, for your own protection."

Squinting at her, I pucker my lips. "Protection? Why would I need to be protected from knowing about your relationship with your husband?"

"It's complicated."

"Has he abused you?"

"No, nothing like that."

"All right." I pick up my sandwich and devour another bite while I wonder what exactly she needs to protect me from, but I decide to give up trying to figure that out. Time to get back to enjoying my day with Calli. "Then we can kiss, and I'm free to seduce you, since you're not really another man's wife anymore."

"Maybe you should go home. I'm bad news."

"You've already been good for me. I haven't had this much fun in a long time."

She stares at me, still holding her sandwich. "Aren't you worried I'm a criminal wanted by the FBI? Or that I'll try to con you into murdering my husband for his life insurance?"

I laugh, shaking my head, and go back to eating my lunch. She really is the sweetest lass I've ever met.

"Tell me," I say, "can your husband stop the divorce?"

"No. Michigan is a no-fault state, which means the divorce will happen. He can argue about the terms and bring in his team of lawyers to slow things down, but it will go through, eventually."

"His team of lawyers? Is he wealthy?"

Calli absently draws lines in the sand, her gaze on the lake. "Yeah, he's rich. Inherited a fortune from his parents."

"Does he want to keep you from getting any of his money?"

"No." She dives her fingers into the sand. "I already told him I don't want any more of his money. I want nothing from him except a divorce."

"Any *more* of his money?" I say. "He's given you—"

"Yes and no. It's complicated, please don't ask me to explain."

"If that's what you want." I stroke the back of one finger along her upper arm. "Speaking of what you want… Since I don't want to overstay my welcome, would you rather I go back to Chicago tomorrow?"

Please say no.

"Well…" She hesitates, then says, "Stay for a week. We can reevaluate at that point."

I smile, sure my joy shows on my face and makes me glow from head to toe. Calli doesn't want me to leave. Whatever's going on with her husband, she can tell me later, after we've gotten to know each other better.

"Have dinner with me," I say.

"I'd love to."

Calli and I have just been seated in the restaurant she chose, which overlooks a waterway she calls the Portage Canal as well as a lift bridge composed of two blue towers that span the narrow waterway. Though it's seven o'clock in the evening, the sun still glows in the sky. This part of Michigan reminds me of Scotland in that respect. The sun shines late in the evening there too.

I received another call from Seona just as we walked into the restaurant, but I dismissed her with a gruff "can't talk now." That's all she gets from me. I have no time to waste on Seona's problems because they are not my problems. I feel bad for her, but I have a life of my own to worry about.

Seated across the table from Calli, I relax in my chair and focus on her bonnie face, which brings a faint smile to my lips. Calli Douglas agreed to a date. With me.

She fidgets as if my attention unnerves her. "You look pleased with yourself. Are you concocting some sort of plan to get me into bed?"

"No." I pick up my water glass and take a sip but keep my gaze on her. "Just wondering how long you'll keep pretending we're not dating."

"We aren't. Dating implies a desire to advance the relationship." She fusses with something on her lap, maybe her napkin. "There will be no advancement."

I can't help lifting my brows and letting my smile tick up a little higher. "We share meals, we talk about our lives and our plans, and we kiss. That's dating."

She growls in frustration. "We. Are. Not. Dating."

"What are we doing, then?"

"Hanging out."

Shrugging one shoulder, I swallow another mouthful of water. "Call it whatever you like, if it makes you feel better."

"Thank you. I will." She wraps a hand around her glass of fizzing soda. "You've mentioned having five siblings, brothers and sisters. How many of each?"

I lean back, eying her with curiosity and a touch of amusement. All right, if she wants to ignore the monstrously large elephant in the room, I can tiptoe around the beggar. "Are you sure you want me to answer? This sort of question might lead to accidental dating—or sex."

"Very funny." She gulps a mouthful of soda and sets her glass down a little too hard. It thunks on the tabletop, splashing the fizzy liquid inside. "I'll risk it. Hearing about your family won't make me wild with desire for you."

"In that case, I have two brothers and three sisters."

"Wow, big family. Do you get along with them?"

"Aye," I say. "Lachlan used to be the most uptight person you'd ever meet until Erica softened him up. He's annoyingly happy these days. My brother Rory has always been serious, but he hasn't found a woman to loosen him up yet. My sister Catriona is the most American of us because she went to university here and came back to take a job at a museum. Fiona's a spitfire, and Jamie doesn't know what she wants yet."

She stares down into her glass, flattening her lips, but then focuses on me again.

I sit forward to brace my elbows on the table. "As for my parents, they're embarrassingly in love after forty-five years together."

Her eyes glisten with what might be tears. She clears her throat, sucks down a third of her glass of soda, and coughs at the sudden onslaught of carbonation.

I stretch a hand across the table to clasp hers. "What's wrong? You look unwell."

"I'm fine." She takes a slower sip of her soda. "I drank too fast, that's all."

I caress her skin with my fingers, glad when she starts to relax. "I blethered on and on about my family. Should we talk about something else?"

"Actually, I'd like to know more. Like who's the oldest and where you fit into the hierarchy."

"Make us sound like a royal family." I sit back, withdrawing my hand, and rest an arm on the table. "Lachlan is the oldest. He's forty-two. Rory's next, and he acts eighty even though he's thirty-nine. Then there's Fiona who's thirty-five, followed by Catriona who's thirty-one. I'm the youngest son, but Jamie's the baby of the family at twenty-six."

"How old are you?"

"Twenty-eight." I tap one finger on the tablecloth. "Tell me about your family."

She shifts in her chair like she's got a razor blade under her erse. "I have one brother, Gavin, but I've mentioned him before. He's eight years older and very overbearing at times."

"You don't get along?"

"Oh no, we do. He's bossy because he loves me and all we've got is—" She clutches her glass in both hands, fixated on the bubbles in the liquid. "All we've got is each other. Our parents died in a car accident five years ago."

I wrap my hand around both of hers, which remain clamped around her glass. "I'm sorry. Cannae imagine how awful that must be for you."

"Not like it happened yesterday."

I peel her hands away from the glass, enveloping them in mine. "But it still hurts, I can see it in your eyes."

"Sure, it hurts once in a while. But it was a long time ago, and I'm okay with it."

"Is there more?" I ask gently.

"Yes, but I'd rather not talk about it." She pulls her hands out from between mine. "I hardly know you. Need a little more time before I share all my secrets."

I nod, because I understand the need for secrets in certain circumstances. And she's right. We don't know each other well yet. "Maybe one day you will tell me. When you feel comfortable enough with me."

She studies me for a moment, seeming like she wants to say something. "May I ask you a personal question?"

"Ask anything you like."

"Why are you really here? In America, I mean. You say you're looking for a wife, the way your brother found his, but my intuition tells me there's more to it than that."

Calli is too canny sometimes. No one else would notice the things she intuits about me. I let my gaze drift to the windows and the view beyond them, feeling a somberness creep inside me. "I need to change my life."

"Fleeing to another country seems a bit excessive. You could've changed your life in Scotland."

"Had to be somewhere else." I sink into my chair, my attention still glued to the windows. "I've been selfish, and that has to change. I have to change."

Until now, I've lived my life without worrying about the potential consequences of my actions. Flirting with lasses. Caring only about having fun. Look where that got me. Seona wouldn't be in the state she's in if I had behaved like a man and not an immature laddie. But now I know what I need to do, if it's not too late for me to change things.

I look straight at Calli. "I took a hard look at myself and realized what I really want. It's what my parents have. Love, commitment, family—children, I mean. I'm looking for the right woman, and the moment I saw you, I knew you might be the one I need."

She doesn't move or blink for several seconds, then finally, she starts blinking again. "Aidan—"

"We're virtually strangers, I know." I fiddle with my napkin, my focus trained on my lap, then raise my eyes to look straight into hers. "I trust my instincts. And they tell me you could be the one I've wanted. I'm only asking for a chance to find out if you are."

Calli straightens. "So, what do you do for a living?"

Well, I can't blame her for wanting to veer away from the serious discussion we'd been having. I've made her uncomfortable.

I pick up my fork and twirl it around my fingers. "I have a company. General contracting. I like the work, and I like being in control of my own destiny."

"What's your company called?"

"MacTaggart Construction. Afraid I'm not very imaginative."

She leans back against her chair. "Oh, I suspect you have plenty of imagination when it counts."

I smile, setting down the fork. "With you, I'll harness every bit of my creativity."

"Are you the boss in the office, or a hands-on type of guy?"

"Hands-on." I steeple my fingers. "Always. What about you? What do you do?"

"Nothing exciting. I'm a librarian, got a master's degree and everything."

"Librarian?" Is it strange that knowing she's a librarian turns me on? I bend forward, moistening my lips. "A bonnie, sexy one for sure. Where are you working? I saw a library a few streets over."

"Haven't started my next job yet."

Though I'd love to hear everything about her, my mind keeps circling back to what she hasn't said. "You haven't told me if you'll give me a chance to find out if you're the woman I've been looking for."

Elbows on the table, she drops her face into her raised hands. "Aidan, please, stop wasting your time here. I'm way too damaged to give you any of the things you want. Go back to Chicago or Scotland or wherever and find a girl who's right for you. I am not."

That's bollocks. Neither of us knows yet if we're right for each other.

I move my chair around until I'm sitting right beside her. When she lowers her hands, I settle a palm on her forearm. "Let me decide if I'm wasting my time."

"You are so pigheaded."

I smile, letting my hand linger on her bare skin. "Lachlan told me the same thing when I said I wanted to come to America. He tried to talk me out of it, but I'd set my mind to it." I slant closer. "I've decided this too. I want to spend time with you. Give me four weeks, it's all I ask."

"I agreed to one week, with the potential for extensions."

"Make it four weeks. Please. You can always boot me out after the first week."

She gazes into my eyes for a long moment. "You win, I give up. But let's not assign a time limit to this, forget one week or four. Stay as long as you like, and if I get sick of you, I'll say so."

"Thank you, Calli."

"Don't thank me. None of what you're hoping for is going to happen."

I stroke my fingers over her skin, keeping the touch light and, I hope, arousing. "At the very least, I'll have gotten to know a sweet lass and gotten to see a new place."

The waitress arrives with our food order, ending the discussion. I move my chair back to where it belongs. While we eat, we talk about normal things like tourist attractions and the weather. Even if Calli doesn't want to admit it, I'm sure she recognizes the truth as well as I do.

We are dating.

I aim my best wicked smile at Calli, the same one she'd loved when we met at Dance Ardor.

She shoves a huge chunk of broccoli into her mouth and chomps on it.

Ah, she must be imagining she's taking my *slat* into her mouth. Sooner than she wants to believe, I'll be making love to her. Is Calli the woman I've been searching for? Finding out the answer might become the best holiday I could ever have.

Chapter Nine

I expect to sleep well that night, considering that Calli finally agreed to give me a chance. I have what I've wanted since the night we met. But fate decides to throw a monkey wrench into the works. I'm sleeping soundly, dreaming of Calli and all the things I want to do with her and to her, when it starts to rain. At first, it seems like part of the dream. And it starts gradually. *Drip, drip, drip.* It's bloody annoying to hear the dripping of rain in my dream while I'm making love to a beautiful lass. Calli lies naked beneath me, her legs wrapped around me and—

The dripping of rain becomes an incessant downpour.

Bloody hell. I can't even enjoy a sexy dream in peace.

The downpour turns into a flood, roaring around me, and I start to feel like I'm lying on a waterbed that's sprung a leak. Little by little, I rouse from the dream that has become a bizarre nautical experience. The gushing of water surrounds me, and the bed squishes when I roll onto my back with my eyes still closed. I groan. What in the world is going on? Rubbing my eyes, I sit up and yawn. I'd left the bedside lamp on, so when I peel my lids open, I can see what's happening.

Water spews from the wall. It has soaked the wall, and the flimsy materials used in the structure have broken open. Water also pours out of the bathroom to pool on the floor. What sort of shoddy craftsmanship went into this motel? It had been the cheapest, least appealing place in town, but I hadn't been able to get a room at a better establishment. No rooms available, except here.

And now I'm swimming.

Luckily, I'd left my luggage on the table, so my clothes are still dry. After ringing the motel office to report the emergency, I get dressed and leave, informing the desk clerk I'm checking out early. The lad looks younger than I am, possibly a college student. When he sees my wet hair, he offers an optimistic view of things.

"At least you got in a shower," the lad says, "before the pipe burst."

Shower? Aye, but not on purpose.

I drive around in my hired car for a while, since it's too early to ring Calli. I'd hoped to spend the day with her, but now I need to find another place to stay. How long do I need to wait to knock on her door? I have no idea if she's an early riser or a late sleeper. I'm used to getting up early for my job, but she might not be. So, I stop at a local restaurant for breakfast, eating slowly to waste time. Finally, I can't take it anymore. I ring Calli's number, but there's no answer. Then I drive to Calli's house. She'd given me directions last night, and the map software on my mobile agrees with what she told me. At least I've dried out by the time I pull into her driveway, but I take a moment to run a comb through my hair. Donnae want to look bedraggled when I see my dream girl.

Now that I'm presentable, I stride up the path to the front door and knock twice. Nothing happens. I shove my hands into my trouser pockets and rock on my heels, back and forth, back and forth. When I still get no response from inside the house, I knock again—three times.

Please let her be home.

I'm about to knock again when a shadow falls over the peephole. She must be checking to see who's out here.

"Calli?" I call through the door. "Are you there?"

At last, the door swings open.

I smile. "Glad you're home. I tried to call first, but you didn't answer."

She winces and slaps her forehead. "Fudge. I forgot to recharge my phone last night. It's probably out of juice."

"Fudge?" I repeat with a laugh. "Never heard anyone say that as a curse before."

"I admit it's not as colorful as the devil's penis, but it works for me." She waves for me to enter while she trots to the kitchen bar to dig her mobile out of her purse and plug it into the wall socket there.

"That's what I love about you," I say, shutting the door. "You're not like anyone else on earth."

"Yep, that's me. A weirdo."

Two furry wee bodies erupt from the other side of the sofa, bounding over its back to crash-land on the floor. They rocket toward me. I kneel to embrace the puppies and babble rubbish to them the way anyone who loves dogs will do. They lick my face and hop up and down, panting and furiously wagging their wee tails. I've never seen puppies the color of these two, with their brown-spotted golden coats. They are almost as beautiful as their mistress.

Calli ambles over to us, smiling and shaking her head. She folds her arms over her chest. "Better watch it. They'll decide they want to go home with you."

"What are their names?"

"Misty and Mandy. They're sisters. Littermates, which means they were born at the same time from the same mother. Misty is the bigger one."

I straighten, but Misty leaps up to slam her big paws onto my stomach. I scratch behind her ears, then gently push her away. The puppies hop back and forth in front of me, panting and wagging their tails. As much as I love dogs, I came here to see their mistress, so I turn to Calli. Misty and Mandy seem to realize it's time for the adults to talk, and they bolt out through the puppy-size plastic flap set into the rear wall beside the sliding glass doors.

"Don't be jealous," I say to Calli, moving closer to curve a hand over her elbow. "The puppies are sweet, but I came for you."

"When did you do that?"

Is she flirting with me? Aye, she definitely is. The sultry tone of her teasing question confirms it.

"When did I come for you?" I say as I glide my hand up her arm, exposed by her short-sleeve T-shirt. "Last night. This morning. More often than I should probably admit to."

Her hand floats up to her throat. "Was it good for you?"

I skate my fingers higher up her arm, sneaking them beneath the sleeve of her T-shirt. "The best I've ever had."

"Guess you don't need the real me. But for the sake of total honesty, I was thinking about you right before you knocked on the door."

"Thinking?" I move my hands to her waist, tugging her closer. "Please tell me they were salacious thoughts."

"Very." She bends her head back, and our gazes collide. When I lean in, she fans her palms over my chest, swirling them in lazy circles. "If I hadn't been interrupted, I might've come for you."

Bod an Donais. Is she trying to get me hard? Whether she intends to or not, it's happening.

My breathing grows heavier with every inhalation, and I clamp my teeth together to stop myself from tearing her clothes off right now. Tugging her hips into me, I speak in a huskier voice. "*Is iomadh rud a nì dithis dheònach.*"

"What does it mean?"

"Two willing people can do many things together." I slide my hands down to her buttocks, dipping my head until our lips nearly touch. "You *fannadh* for me, I *fannadh* for you. If we're both willing, why donnae ye let me show ye all the things I can do to ye? Ye'll stay a virgin, technically. But I have to touch ye, to feel your slick little *brillean* while I make ye come for me."

She clutches fistfuls of my shirt, all but panting with need. "I only understood half of what you said, but it sounds…good."

I glide my tongue over her bottom lip, and my voice turns gravelly. Cannae stop myself from sounding like a ravenous beast, not with my *slat* rock hard and the scent of her lust inundating my senses. "*Fannadh* means masturbate and *brillean* means clitoris. The rest I think you understand. Let me show you."

Chapter Ten

I need to make her come for me. Donnae care if my cock explodes from the pressure of the need to fuck her. Giving Calli pleasure matters more to me than my own release, which is something I never imagined I would think, and certainly nothing I'd ever say out loud. But I need to do this for her.

She clings to me, her tits heaving. "Show me."

My shoulders cave in with relief, and I touch my forehead to hers. Maybe it's barmy to want this so much, but I donnae care. I move around behind her and spread my hands over her belly, drawing her snug against me so she can, I'm sure, feel the raging hard-on barely contained in my jeans. I keep one hand on her belly while the other wanders lower to slip inside the waistband of her sweatpants.

She stalls my progress with one of her hands on mine. "Are you sure I'll still be a virgin after this?"

"Positive." I nuzzle her neck, then lick at her earlobe. "Technically. It's no more than what you do to yourself."

Though I want to do so much more, I need to take it slow with her. She's very skittish.

"Should I stop?" I ask.

"No. Please don't stop."

I draw her earlobe into my mouth, suckling softly, and thrust my hand down inside her knickers to palm her mound. She sucks in a sharp breath. The hairs beneath my hand are soft, and I can feel the heat of her body plus a hint of the slickness between her thighs. I long to yank her sweatpants down so I can kneel in front of her and devour all that luscious cream. But I need to go slow. *Fuck.* Calli forces me to dig down deep to find a well of willpower I never knew I had.

But she's worth it.

I dip a finger between her folds and begin circling it around her clit.

She crumples against me, and her head falls back onto my chest, exposing her slender throat.

Bod a' chac. She will drive me mad, and I'll let her do it. I will volunteer for madness if it means I can touch her body and watch her come under my hand.

I rasp my tongue up her throat to the hollow where every woman is sensitive and the slightest touch will make her squirm and gasp. I toy with her *brillean*, first whisking my finger round and round it, then rubbing in sure, swift strokes while I feel her slickness coating my finger. Bloody hell, I need to thrust that finger into my mouth and suck on it so I can finally taste her—but I don't do it. She arches into my touch, her back bowing and her mouth falling open on a strangled moan. Christ, that sound makes my cock throb. While I torment her with my finger, I scrape my palm across her mound, loving the desperate little noises she makes. I glide my free hand up under her shirt to cup her breast through her bra, plucking her nipple with my thumb and forefinger.

"Aidan," she gasps. "Yes oh god yes."

She throws her arms above her head to lock both hands behind my neck.

While my heavy breaths gust over her ear, I rub harder and faster with that finger, up and down, then switch to sideways strokes. She whimpers, writhing against me, frantic for release. I'll *caith* any second if I don't make her come right now. So I shove my hand deep between her drenched folds, plunging one finger inside her. With the heel of my hand, I work her clit with ruthless fervor while I thrust that finger in and out, in and out, imagining I'm fucking her with my cock while I shove a second finger inside her, and then a third. I'm breathing so hard I'm starting to see black spots in my vision, but I willnae stop. I crook my fingers inside her to pet a spot I know always makes women go off like a firework.

"Oh God," she cries out. "Please, Aidan, please."

Shifting my hand, I free my thumb to flick it across her nub over and over and over while I keep petting that secret spot inside her.

Calli's body grips my fingers with spasm after spasm, milking me like I've got my *slat* inside her instead of my fingers, begging me to make her keep coming. She claws at the back of my neck, but ahmno worried about claw marks on my skin, not when she's blowing apart in my hand. Her heels lift off the floor, and her back arches wildly, rubbing that sexy erse against me. Fuck, I'm about to blow apart too. I keep rubbing until I've drawn every last bit of pleasure from her body, the muscles inside her stop contracting around my fingers, and she goes boneless in my arms.

We're both gasping for breath. I hold her against me, my arms wrapped around her, until she regains her equilibrium. I'm still reeling, so desperate to come that my heart is pounding.

She lays her hands on my forearms. "Wow. I can't think of anything more eloquent to say."

"Mm." Eloquence is out of my reach for sure. I shift my hips, hissing in a breath, and she must feel my erection pulsing against her back. Somehow, I manage to regain the power of speech. "Please excuse me for a moment. I need the bog." I clear my throat. "The bathroom."

I pull away from her and spin around, hustling toward the hallway in a slightly bowlegged fashion. Veering toward the first door on the right, I mutter a curse when I realize it's the laundry room.

"The door on the left," Calli calls out.

With a curt nod, and my entire face pinched in agony, I rush into the open doorway of the bathroom across the hall, slamming it behind me. I yank the zipper on my jeans down and pull out my cock, pumping it hard and fast while I remember the look on Calli's face when she came. I slump against the wall, grunting and gasping, working myself with so much vigor that my hand might cramp up any second, but I cannae stop. My chest heaves, my back arches, and I splutter while slapping my palm on the wall. The need to come rockets down my spine. I squeeze my eyes shut and grit my teeth while the release I desperately need barrels toward my cock.

"Aidan?" Calli says. "You okay in there?"

I mutter a strangled curse. "Aye. Fine."

Then I *caith*. Milky liquid erupts out of me while I keep pumping, letting out a sharp grunt followed by a long, low groan as the pressure in my *slat* finally eases up. I sag against the wall, breathing hard. Christ, I haven't come that hard in…ever.

Just imagine what it will be like when you take her body.

I wipe myself off and clean up the mess I've made using hand soap and a roll of paper towels I find in the cabinet under the sink. Maybe I should feel embarrassed, and maybe I do a wee bit, but this is hardly the first time I've needed to come after giving a woman pleasure.

After zipping up my jeans, I swing the bathroom door open.

I might still be breathing harder than usual.

Calli raises her brows, and her gaze flicks down to my waning erection. Arms crossed over her chest, she gestures at my groin with one finger. "Did you go in there to, uh…*fannadh*?"

Though my breathing has normalized, my cheeks feel hot from exertion. I glance down at the floor and mumble, "Yes. That's what I did."

She lays a palm on my cheek. "How can a wicked man like you be embarrassed about jerking off?"

"Ahmno embarrassed." I twist my mouth into a warped frown. Is this what they call protesting too much?

"Why did you run away? That implies you're em—"

"I am not embarrassed."

Palms out, she raises both hands. "Okay, okay. No need to get huffy with me."

I roll my eyes.

"Oh no," she says, locking her arms over her chest again, "don't give me the eye roll either. You're the one who did…what you did to me and then bolted like a kid caught stealing candy."

"I—" Shoving a hand into my hair, I grumble under my breath. After a moment of forced relaxation, inhaling deeply and exhaling slowly, I manage to compose myself. Leaning against the doorjamb, I slant my head down to gaze into her emerald eyes. "I've never had this problem before. The way you reacted when I touched you, the way you came under my hand, you were stunning. And it affected me. So much I thought I'd burst in my pants."

"Burst?" She struggles not to smile. "You can say 'fuck' in front of me, but you can't say you were about to come?"

"I can say it." Angling my body toward her, I loop my free arm around her waist. "But I never *caith* in my pants. I never lose control with a woman. This is a new experience for me."

Her arms fall away from her chest to dangle at her sides. She leans toward me just a little. "I'm sure it happens to every guy now and then."

"You don't understand." I skim my hand up and down her back. "It's because of you, because I want you more than any other woman I've known."

"Oh." Her cheeks turn faintly pink. She rubs her lips together while staring at my mouth.

An explosive whack reverberates through the living room as the puppies tear through the dog door. The magnetic plastic flap snaps back into place behind them.

Misty and Mandy barrel straight toward me.

They leap on Calli on their way to me, making her stumble into the wall. The puppies assault me with gleeful ardor. After a moment of flinging their wee bodies at me and flailing their tongues at any part of me they can reach, the puppies settle down to lie at my feet and gaze up at me with rapt adoration. I'd love for Calli to gaze at me that way.

"I have another problem," I say in a casual tone, resting one hand on the doorjamb.

"And is this one also my fault?"

"Not unless you sneaked into my motel last night and ruptured the pipes."

Feigning deep thought, she taps a finger on her chin. "No, I don't recall doing that. But I might've been sleepwalking."

"Hmm." I dance my fingertip over her lips. "Why would you want me homeless?"

"What do you mean 'homeless'?"

"My room was damaged by the burst pipe, and there are no other rooms available."

"There are lots of motels around here. I can get the phone book to look up—"

"Please don't." I grunt as Misty hops up to plant her paws on my stomach. Babbling nonsense to her, I pet the wee pup's head with one hand. "No other rooms available. There's some sort of festival happening and a conference at a nearby university."

"What will you do?"

I shrug one shoulder. "Donnae know. May have to go back to Chicago."

"Stay with me."

My eyes widen as I blink several times, sure I must've misheard. "What?"

"I have a spare bedroom. You, um, can stay here with me. As long as you understand this does not mean I'm going to sleep with you."

"Not yet."

She tries to look stern but can't quite pull it off. "Not ever."

"You want me, and we both know it." I take hold of her right hand, guiding it to my groin until her palm covers my semi-hard cock with only a single layer of denim between my skin and hers. "And you know how much I want you."

She pulls her hand away from my crotch. "You can stay here. But do try to behave yourself."

I grin. "Why? You don't behave yourself with me."

Before she can think of any reasons not to let me stay here, I trot out the front door to retrieve my bags from the hired car. I can't believe she offered to let me stay in her house, and she rushed to make that offer. I'd expected she'd need a minute or two to consider the idea. But no, she blurted out her offer the second I said I might need to go back to Chicago. Though I could go back to Erica's house, I'm glad I don't need to do that.

Calli will be my roommate.

I saunter back into the house carrying my things. "Where am I, then?"

"Follow me." Calli guides me to the far end of the hall where an open door leads into a bedroom. She points at another door, on the left, one that faces sideways to the other bedroom that must be hers. "There's the spare room. Bed's made, and extra pillows are in the closet."

I glance from the spare room to her bedroom, a mere arm's length away. "You want me close, don't you? Convenient for midnight cravings."

"You are incorrigible."

I smile brightly. "Thank you."

"I think you're the strangest man I've ever met."

"You like the way I make you feel, though." Setting my bags down, I sling an arm around her waist. "One of these nights, maybe you'll show me how you touch yourself."

Her mouth opens, but she seems unable to speak.

"Think about it," I say, then I pick up my bags.

While I lug my things into the spare room, I feel better than I have in a long time. Seona hasn't harassed me today, and if she tries to ring me again, I won't answer. Her problems don't matter to me anymore. Whatever she blames me for, I have no time to waste on thinking about it. I'm sleeping in Calli's house. She let me give her an orgasm. The lass wants me and likes me, that much I'm sure of, and she's granting me unlimited time to show her we can be good together as a couple.

How long will it take for me to seduce her?

A few days at most. She wants me that much.

Chapter Eleven

After lunch, I need to change my shirt because one of the puppies had spilled tomato sauce all over me when she tried to leap up onto my lap and give me a "doggie smooch," as Calli called it. I had offered to make lunch. The lasses always love it when I cook for them, especially since they assume I don't know what a spatula is, much less how to whip up spaghetti and meatballs. My sisters know how to cook, but every man in my family also picked up that skill because our mother insisted we learn. Sorcha MacTaggart doesn't let her sons get away with claiming manly immunity.

"You will learn how to cook," she'd told me when I was fifteen and complaining about having to help her make dinner. "No son of mine will force his wife to do all the household work. You'll learn how to dust and polish the table too."

And I had learned. I doubt Ma drilled all of that into me so the lasses would be impressed, but that has been an unexpected benefit of my mother's approach to child-rearing.

I want bairns of my own—so I can torture them with feather dusters and bread kneading. No, that's not the only reason I want bairns. Since I met Calli, I want sons and daughters of my own more than I ever have before.

After we ate, I had insisted on cleaning up. Calli seemed surprised, but in a good way. When she tried to help anyway, I chased her out of the kitchen.

When I walk into the living room after changing my shirt, Calli is gazing out the windows into the backyard, where Misty and Mandy are having a bloody good time. They leap up on their hind legs to battle like grizzly bears, without the bloodshed. The puppies slap their front paws on each other's shoulders too.

Calli notices me and smiles. Her attention shifts from my face down to my chest and the dark-blue T-shirt I'm wearing. It has a lion logo on it and the phrase "Scotland the Brave" emblazoned on the fabric.

"Cool shirt," she says. "I can almost hear the bagpipes. Or is that your phone ringing?"

"Not my phone, you cheeky lass." I veer around the sofa and plop onto the cushion beside hers. "Catriona gave me this shirt. She says American women love this sort of thing." I pluck the shirt with my thumb and fore-finger. "I think she might be pulling a Lachlan joke on me. What do you think?"

"I wouldn't say it's on a par with 'every night is kilt night,' but she might be pulling your leg. I like it, though. You look good in blue."

She likes me in blue? Calli likes me, full stop. I swivel my upper body toward her, laying an arm across the sofa behind her. "You look good in any-thing, but I loved the green dresses you wore at the club and the wedding."

"Tara picked them. She insists green is my signature color, mostly be-cause of my eyes."

"Your beautiful, luminous emerald eyes." I lean in closer, gazing into her green irises from a few inches away. "They are mesmerizing."

She swallows hard enough I can see it. "You don't talk like any other guys I've met. They said things like 'you look fine' or maybe they'd tell me I had nice eyes. Nobody's ever called me mesmerizing before."

"They were eejits."

"Can't tell if I agree or not, since I have no idea what an eejit is."

"An idiot." I slant in closer, and my mouth grazes the corner of hers as I drag my lips across her cheek to her ear. "Any man who describes your eyes as nice is blind and stupid. You are stunning, Calli."

"Thank y—" Her words die away when I nibble on her earlobe, then coil my tongue around it. "Unh."

I love every odd noise she makes.

Shoving my hands under her erse, I lift her up and onto my lap, seating her sideways across my thighs. "I like you speechless. You make the sexiest little noises."

Calli moans when I grasp her erse in one hand. "Can't think when your mouth is—mm."

I paint damp kisses along her jaw, down her throat. She turns her head to the side, granting me full access, and I take advantage of the opening to drag my tongue over her throat and nip at her flesh. She flattens her palms on my chest. When I raise my head, leveling my gaze on her, she skates her hands in circles on my chest.

"Do you know," she says, "I've never seen you shirtless. Fantasized about it, but—"

I pick her up and drop her back onto the adjacent cushion with her calves draped across my lap. In one swift motion, I whip my shirt off over my head, tossing it onto the coffee table. It slumps onto a pile of travel magazines.

Spreading my arms over the sofa's back, I give her a satisfied smile. "There. Problem solved."

Calli straightens and rakes her gaze over my torso while skimming her tongue over her bottom lip repeatedly. Her attention wanders down my abs to my waistband. She bites her lower lip, her eyes squinted like she's struggling against the impulse to unhook the metal button on my jeans, ease the zipper down, and swallow me whole.

She drops her gaze even lower, to the bulge of my *slat*. I'm not hard, not yet, but she seems impressed by the size of my cock. Honestly, no lass has ever gawped at my body this way. I love that Calli, the not-innocent virgin, is the first to admire my *slat* with such intense hunger.

I sweep a finger over her lips. "You're drooling."

"Am not." She pats her lips like she's checking for drool, then gives my chest a half-hearted slap. "You're hot, but I can control my lust."

"The way you controlled it this morning? When I had my hand inside your panties and you were screaming my name."

Is it strange that I'm proud of myself for remembering American women call them panties and not knickers?

She lays her hands flat on my chest, like she's reveling in the feel of my body. "I didn't have sex with you. That's control."

"But it was a sexual encounter." I settle a hand on her knee, gliding it between her thighs. She seems unaware that she's parting her lips for me while I skate my hand up to her groin. "I made you come for me."

"I'm aware of that."

"Only one more little step—"

"No stepping. Not even on my tippy toes."

"Hmm." I slide my hand back down to her knee, studying the lass. "Have you ever seen a man naked?"

"Not in person."

"I can remedy that."

While cradling Calli in my arms, I rise and turn around to face the sofa. Her eyes have gone wide. I set her down on the cushions and take two steps backward to stand just past the coffee table. Her gaze stays glued to me while I unhook the button on my jeans. And I cannae help it. I flash her a smug smile as I pull the zipper down slowly, loving the way her tongue pokes out between her teeth and her attention is riveted to my groin as I unveil the length of my *slat* inch by inch. She runs her tongue over her lips like I'm the most succulent treat she's ever seen and she cannae wait to taste me. The more of my body I expose, the more ravenous her expression becomes.

My jeans slump to the floor. I step out of them and roll my shoulders back. "You're drooling again."

"Am not." She roams her gaze over my body from head to toe, but her focus gravitates back to my cock once she's done with her appraisal. The lass can't seem to tear her eyes away from my hardening length, and the longer she stares at it, the more blood rushes into my *slat*. She glances at my thighs but inevitably returns her hungry gaze to my dick. She slants forward, her mouth falling open, her tongue moistening her lower lip.

Fuck, if she doesn't stop looking at my cock that way, I might *caith* right here in front of her. Is the not-innocent virgin ready for that?

I lower my erse onto the coffee table, facing her. My erection has grown stiff enough to wave in the air between us.

Calli shakes her head once, like she's struggling to cast off an erotic fantasy. I've decided that must be what she's doing, because she's been obsessed with my cock ever since I stripped off my jeans.

I tip toward her, spreading my thighs wide and letting my erection jut toward her. "One little step, that's all it takes."

She looks at me but seems unable to speak.

My cock is so amazing it leaves her speechless? I doubt that. The lass has never seen a naked man, though, so I assume that's why she can't summon any words.

"Ah well," I say, unfurling my body while my erection waves in her face. I grab my jeans and yank them on, then snag my shirt from the table and pull it on as well. Calli looks a bit disappointed that I've covered myself up, so I hook a finger under her chin, encouraging her to gaze up at me. "Donnae worry. You'll get an extended view—one day soon, for as long as you like—when we make love."

"You mean when we have sex."

"No." I lean in to press my lips to hers in a sweet kiss. "I mean when I make love to you, because we're going to fall in love. Soon."

She stares into my eyes like she's searching for something there. I imagine she still can't believe I'm serious about the two of us falling in love. Despite knowing she's still married, technically, I want her—for more than sex. Every new moment I spend with her convinces me even more that she is the woman for me.

I drop onto the sofa beside her, relaxing into the cushions, and link my hands behind my head. "Your turn."

"My what?"

With my feet propped on the table, I cross my ankles. "Your turn to undress."

Her jaw crashes down while she makes a soft croaking noise.

"I showed you mine," I say, raking my gaze over her clothed body, "so show me yours. I can tell you want to."

She pulls her knees up and grips them. "I'm not stripping for you."

I cover one of her hands with mine. "It's all right. One day you will. One day very soon. I can wait until you're ready, because once you show me everything, I'll know you're ready for the pleasure I can and will give you." I brush the backs of my fingers over her cheek. "And then I'll be inside you, stoking that fire I see burning in you right now, driving you toward an ecstasy that will leave you spent and satisfied beyond your wildest dreams."

"You're awfully certain you'll rock my world."

"Aye." I look at her with complete seriousness. "Because I will. Because I'll make sure of it. Nothing matters more than ensuring you feel all the pleasure you deserve."

She studies me like she can't quite decide whether to believe me. Maybe she's worrying again, about her almost ex-husband or the fact I live in Scotland. Calli seems to worry about a lot of things.

When she glances at the bulge of my cock, a delicate blush tints her cheeks.

"You're thinking about it," I say. "About sex. With me."

"Maybe I am. Doesn't mean I'll do anything about it."

"Take your time, I'll wait. Unless you're wanting me to go home."

"I don't want that. Having you here is…nice."

I kiss her temple. "Being here is nice."

She clears her throat, straightening her legs to rest her feet on the coffee table. "Would you like to play a board game? The owners left some games behind."

I make a pained face.

"What?" she asks. "If you don't like board games, just say so."

"I like them." I wipe a hand over my mouth. "Erica and Lachlan played Monopoly the day after they met. I know you don't like me to repeat things they did together."

"Right. No board games."

Movement outside the windows catches my attention, and I glance that way. Misty is leaping through the air like she has springs in her paws, flying past the sliding glass doors in midair. She lands and takes off across the yard toward Mandy. The puppies collide and roll, with Misty underneath her smaller sister, both baring their teeth in mock combat.

"Let's go outside," I say. "Get fresh air and play with the puppies."

"Sure."

I give her a sly look. "Maybe you'll roll around on the grass with me. We can take turns being on top."

"Cooking for me is hot, but not quite enough to make me ruin my clothes with grass stains."

"Donnae worry." I stand, smiling as I offer her my hand. "My sister Fiona taught me the secret to removing any stain."

Calli accepts my hand.

I help her up, then we head for the sliding doors hand in hand the way any normal couple might. The fact that she wants to hold hands with me gives me even more hope for us. Maybe I've never tried to make a woman fall for me before, but I will do whatever it takes to win Calli. Not only because she's American. I want her because she is the bonniest, sweetest, most incredible woman I have ever met.

If Lachlan can win a woman's heart, so can I.

Chapter Twelve

A walk with Calli turned out to be the most relaxing thing I'd done in ages. Building my construction business had taken a lot of hard work, which didn't leave much time for fun. Oh, I still found ways to have a good time. But not as much as I would've liked. I hadn't been in any danger of turning into an ogre like Rory, that was for dead sure. Time with Calli, just ambling through the woods while holding her hand, felt better than anything I'd done in longer than I could remember. To have her soft palm in mine...

I wanted to keep doing that forever.

Calli lusts for me. I know that, but she also likes me. The lass can't hide it. She enjoys spending time with me as much as I enjoy being with her. Though I wonder, repeatedly, what her husband did to her, I won't ask. Not yet. She needs to learn how to trust me, and I need to prove to her I'm not a selfish erse. Sounds easy. But I have no illusions it will be.

Still, things keep happening that give me hope.

I make dinner for her again and insist on washing the dishes afterward, like I had last time. Her appreciative smile sends a wee thrill through me. She's not appreciating my body this time, but rather, she's admiring my skill in the kitchen and my desire to do things for her to make her life easier. That kind of appreciation might be more valuable than her lust for me because it means she's starting to think of me as more than a sex partner. I'm not doing these things as a calculated attempt to seduce her. I want to make her life easier—and more fun.

After dinner, I take a shower. Just as I step out of the stall, I wonder if I should do a little something to make sure Calli doesn't forget I want to make love to her. A wee bit of calculation can't hurt. Affectionate calculation. Aye, there is such a thing—because I just invented it.

So, I forgo drying off and wrap a towel around my hips. Then I saunter out of the bathroom and into the living room where Calli is watching television, halting just behind the sofa but to the side of where she's sitting.

Calli glances at me and freezes. Her eyes go wide, but she doesn't blink. Her lips fall open a touch, and her gaze travels down my body, from the drops of water drizzling down my chest to the lump under the terry cloth. "Why are you standing there in a towel? You didn't even use it to dry off."

"Need another towel. Where can I find one?"

"In the bathroom," she says like that was a silly question. "On the towel rack."

"Oh aye, of course." I wink. "Liking the view, eh?"

She glances at my *slat* again and sighs.

I cup my cock with one hand. "You can have this inside you anytime, lass."

Then I walk back into the bathroom.

At ten o'clock, Calli goes into her bedroom and shuts the door. I'm not sleepy yet, so I Skype my sister Jamie. When her face appears on-screen, she moans pitifully instead of saying hello. Her hair looks messy, and her eyes are bleary. "Why did ye wake me up at three o'clock, Aidan?"

"Oh, sorry. I forgot it's five hours later over there."

She yawns and stretches. Her fluffy purple robe covers up her flannel pajamas, which everyone knows she sleeps in every night. The pajamas have kittens on them. Jamie combs her fingers through her hair to tame the mess and gazes at me, virtually, with clearer eyes than a moment ago. "Having trouble with your wife hunt?"

"No, I found the woman of my dreams. But she's not convinced yet that I'm the one for her."

"Don Juan can't seduce a woman? Aliens must have landed in Loch Ness, aye?"

"Not funny. I will have no trouble seducing Calli. It's talking her into falling for me that's the problem."

Jamie says nothing for a moment, her expression blank. "And you rang me for advice? Again? You didn't like what I said last time."

"No, I did not ring you for advice. Well, maybe." I groan and throw my hands up. "Donnae know what the fuck I'm doing."

"Poor Aidan. Finally met a lass who didn't fall into your arms at first sight."

Calli did fall into my arms at first sight. She bumped into me in the club. Since I seem unlikely to get reasonable advice from my little sister, I decide to change the subject. "Tell me what everyone's been doing while I'm away."

Jamie spends the next twenty minutes chatting to me about our sisters, brothers, and cousins. I'm exhausted after listening to her for ten minutes, but once Jamie gets started, it's hard to stop her. She might've been sleepy when I rang her, but now she's wide awake and in top form.

Finally, after twenty-two minutes, I interrupt her. "Jamie, I'm knackered from listening to you. Need to go to sleep."

"Aye, get your beauty rest. Sounds like your lass will make you work hard to win her over."

"She will, but Calli is worth it."

"Maybe I should come to America. See what you and Lachlan love so much about it." Her tone turns sneaky. "Maybe they have sexy American men for me to meet and—"

"No, Jamie. Stay away from this continent." I thought I'd talked her out of that idea last time I rang her, but she's a stubborn lass. So aye, we have nothing in common.

"I see. It's fine for you and Lachie, but not for me."

"Aye. That's exactly right."

She huffs. "You don't run my life, Aidan. I could stay at Erica's house in Chicago to look for my Prince Charming."

"No, you bloody will not."

"Did Rory lend you his caber? Sounds like it's wedged up your erse now."

"Very funny. Good night, Jamie."

"Good night, Aidan."

My sister finally ends our video call, and I yawn and stretch. She won't come to America. Jamie isn't that daft, so she'll change her mind. I suppose I am that daft, but it's different because I'm a man. Aye, that probably makes me a sexist twat. Cannae help it. My baby sister would get herself into trouble for sure if she comes here.

Lachlan and Rory will talk her out of it. Now that Jamie has the idea, she'll tell everyone about it.

Just to be sure, I ring Lachlan and ask him to keep an eye on Jamie. He's not pleased with being woken up in the middle of the night, but he agrees to watch out for our sister.

I shuffle into my room and crawl under the covers, ready for a good long sleep. I've just started to doze off when my mobile rings. *Bugger off*, I want to mutter, but I'm too drowsy to speak. The mobile rings again. And again. I fling a hand out to grab the device off the table and answer the call. "Hello?"

"Were you asleep?" Calli asks. "Didn't mean to wake you."

"Not sleeping." I sit up and yawn. "Just a wee bit tired after Skyping with Jamie. She's got more energy than your puppies."

"Well… I should let you get some rest."

Did she ring me strictly to tell me to rest? I swing my feet off the bed. "Ahm no sleepy. Why are you calling me when you're down the hall?"

"I, uh…wondered if you'd like to…"

"Spit it out," I say. "Unless you want me to come in there and torture it out of you."

Aye, I said that in my wickedest voice. I'm getting the feeling she wants me right now, and that fact makes me suddenly awake and alert. My cock is alert too and ready for action.

She clears her throat. "Remember that thing you wanted to see?"

"Thing? Are you meaning the quilt on your bed? Or maybe the window drapes." I love teasing her.

"You said maybe one evening I'd let you watch. How about tonight?"

I choke and splutter. "Do ye mean—"

"I want you to watch me masturbate."

Suddenly, I'm breathing hard. Did she just suggest what I think she did? I haven't hallucinated it? Calli wants me to go into her bedroom and watch her wank off.

Her voice turns low and throaty. "If you're not interested anymore…"

"Ahm interested," I rasp. "When?"

"Now."

I end the call and race out of my room.

The puppies gallop out of the living room, following me as I burst through the door into Calli's room. Misty and Mandy careen toward the opening, but I clap the door shut in their sweet little faces. "Sorry, wee lassies."

Breathing even harder now, I stand frozen by the door, my gaze glued to Calli. I'm still wearing my T-shirt and my jeans, which are unbuttoned. I'd been too jeeked to bother getting undressed. But I don't feel tired anymore.

Calli crooks a finger. "You can't see anything from way over there."

The puppies whine and paw at the door.

My bare feet make only the slightest sound on the wood floor as I amble to the bed and climb over her legs to lie down at a diagonal to her with my head near her hip. I brace my head on one palm.

"Should I take my nightie off?" she asks.

"Not this time." I stretch my free arm down to rest one fingertip on her ankle, then glide it up the inside of her leg, past her knee, halfway up her thigh. "I like a bit of mystery."

With that one finger, I push the hem of her nightie down to cover her better. When our gazes intersect, she just stares at me.

"Second thoughts?" I ask, scrutinizing her face for signs she's changed her mind. I don't see anything except lust.

"No." She reaches out to skate her fingers over my cheek. "I want to do this, but I've never done anything like it before."

"Take your time, I've got all night. And if you change your mind, you can stop anytime. I willnae complain."

She spreads her hands over her throat, dragging them down to her collarbone, pausing there to gaze straight into my eyes. Hers have grown darker, thanks to her pupils dilating. It means she wants me, really wants me. Christ, I want her too, so badly I think I might have a heart attack from watching her touch herself, but I don't care. I press my lips together, then flick my tongue out to dampen them, imagining what it will feel like to lick her swollen flesh. But I won't do it tonight. This is phase one. Or phase two. Maybe it's three or four, I donnae know for sure.

Calli glides her hands lower until they cover her breasts, and she sighs out an uneven breath. She cups her breasts in her slender hands and flicks her thumbs over the hard nipples while she kneads her own flesh.

I stare at her hands, the way they massage her breasts, and my voice becomes a rough whisper. "I want to be doing that to you. I want my mouth on you, right where your thumbs are."

She pinches her nipples through the satin of her nightie, letting out a wee moan and rocking her hips. My gaze is pinned to her hands, and I track their every movement as she skims her palms down her belly with deliberate slowness. Her hands breeze over her hips and down onto her thighs. The seductress lets one palm hover there, flat on her left thigh, and sweeps the other up and under the nightie's hem. Though I can't see what she's doing under that fabric, I picture her fingers grazing her mound. Her neck arches, and her head tilts back as her eyes flutter shut.

"No," I all but growl, "donnae close your eyes. Please, Calli, look at me while you do this."

She opens her eyes, and our gazes lock onto each other as if they're bound by an invisible force, a power borne of lust and something deeper, something she refuses to acknowledge. But I know what it is. She has feelings for me, whether she wants to or not. Neither of us can stop it from happening, but the difference is that I don't want to stop it.

And I definitely don't want her to stop showing me how she touches herself.

Beneath her nightie, I can see her fingers moving and imagine she must be stroking herself, rubbing up and down her slick flesh. She keeps her focus on me while she moves her hand and her fingers underneath the satin fabric. My mouth falls open, and heavy breaths huff out of me, while she rubs herself harder and faster. My gaze darts to her groin, to where I know her fingers work her flesh though I can't see it. Her hips gyrate, and her legs move in a restless rhythm. I rip my focus away from her groin to watch her face again, though I'm desperate to get a peek at what she's doing to herself. My *slat* is thickening, and my breathing has grown so labored I start to feel almost lightheaded.

"Watch me touch myself," she says. "Please. I'll keep my eyes open and watch your face."

I blow out a heavy breath, nodding, and level my gaze on her hand moving beneath the nightie.

With her other hand, she eases the fabric higher to reveal a glimpse of her rosy, glistening flesh and her fingers whisking over it, while her breaths shorten into sharp gasps.

I suck in a long, deep breath to inhale the scent of her. With my eyes almost closed, I smile with intense satisfaction. "You smell like everything I've ever wanted."

She scrapes her middle finger up her cleft and onto her clit, rubbing the rigid nub with ruthless strength and speed like she's frantic to achieve release. I see the moment it hits. Her back bows up off the bed even while she keeps stroking herself hard and fast, wringing every last ounce of pleasure from her own body. When she collapses onto the bed, her hands slack on her thighs, I can't stop staring at her with slitted eyes, my mouth tight. *Bod an Donais*. Watching Calli make herself come is now my favorite sexual experience ever.

"How was it?" I grind out the words.

"Good," she says between heavy breaths. "But nowhere near as good as when you touch me."

Ducking my head, I shift my hips in an attempt to alleviate my discomfort, but my cock won't be satisfied until I take matters into my own hands. I exhale a shaky breath. "Excuse me."

I scramble off the bed, staggering toward the doorway, almost limping. My cock has never been harder, and it's difficult to walk a straight line in this condition.

"Wait," she says, and I hesitate with my hand on the knob. "Are you running away to relieve your needs in the bathroom? Like you did this morning?"

Body rigid, I growl out a frustrated noise as I glance back at her. "Aye."

"You don't have to leave the room." She pushes up into a semi-sitting position, her legs outstretched and her hands on the bed, holding her up. "I want to watch."

"No, you don't." I tip my head from one side to the other, my shoulders bunching, while I avoid looking at her. "Ye donnae want to see my—"

"Come on, I've seen your penis before."

I growl again, letting my head fall back. "Not that. Ye donnae want to see my—to see me—what happens when I—"

"When you come? I can handle seeing you ejaculate."

"Cannae control it." I shove a hand through my hair, clenching my fingers. "After watching you… Never been this hard before."

"It's okay." She rises onto her knees. "Let me see you pleasure yourself, Aidan. It's only fair, since I let you see me."

Let her watch? No lass has ever suggested that. I twist my head to gawp at her. "Are ye sure?"

She nods, beckoning me with one hand.

I take halting steps back to the bed.

Smiling, she pats the mattress in front of her.

And I settle onto the bed. My erection bulges large and hard inside my jeans, the reddened tip peeking out where the button is undone.

She grasps the zipper and eases it downward.

I haul in a deep breath and let it out slowly while my eyes slide shut. My cock springs free.

"Would you like me to…" She trails off as if she's uncertain of speaking the words.

But I can guess what she wants to say.

"Aye," I tell her, grinning at the lass, "I'd love you to do that. But not this time. We can save that for after we fuck."

"If we do."

"When," I correct.

"Still arrogantly certain, eh?" She sits back on her heels, then thrusts a hand out to grasp the base of my cock. "Sure you don't want some help?"

My grin broadens for only a second before her firm grip on my *slat* makes me contort my face in the best kind of agony.

"Ahhh…" I clench the sheets as she drags her hand up my length. "Calli…"

A drop of liquid oozes out of the head. She bends over my lap to roll her tongue over my reddened tip.

"You win," I hiss. "Have your bloody way with me. But do it quick, I may not last long."

"If I do something wrong, you can tell me."

"Willnae do it wrong. Follow your instincts and do it quick."

She hops onto the floor to kneel between my thighs and closes her mouth around the head of my cock. When she draws me into her mouth in one long thrust, I gasp, and my entire body goes as stiff as my *slat*. She sucks and laps at my flesh with her tongue, then pulls her mouth free only to swallow me again. Her mouth is hot and silky, her tongue agile and greedy. I've had women give me head before, but not like this. Calli seems to revel in doing this to me, her soft grunts and little moans driving me to the edge of reason and beyond. I dive a hand into her hair to cup the back of her head, urging her on with gentle pressure. She consumes me again and again, her mouth alternately devouring and releasing me while the sweetest kind of pressure mounts inside me. A virgin shouldn't be this good at oral sex, but it's her enthusiasm for the task that makes it so bloody hot.

I buck my hips every time she plunges my length into between her lips. I gasp and grunt, my face twisted with a pain that stems from the frenzied need to come with her silky tongue wrapped around me.

With her hand clamped around the base of my erection, she pumps in sync with the thrusts of her mouth, licking and suckling as if she'll die without the taste of me on her tongue.

A throaty shout erupts from me as my body convulses and I explode in her mouth.

"Mm," she murmurs, sitting back and smiling. "You taste good."

I gawp at her, panting, shocked by her statement. "It's not fair. I haven't tasted you yet."

"Oh, you'll get around to it."

Aye, and it will be soon. Cannae wait any longer to taste and touch and push inside that sensual body.

What she just did for me... I owe her all the pleasure I vowed I could give her. And I never renege on a promise.

Chapter Thirteen

fter what Calli did to me, for me, I need a few minutes alone in the bathroom to clean myself up and recover from the shock. I've known since the night we met that Calli has a naughty streak a mile wide, but somehow, I never expected her to go down on me. She said she wouldn't cross the line with me, not even on her "tippy toes." But then she took my cock in her mouth.

Calli Douglas is a very confusing woman.

I return to her room a few minutes later, and we lie down together on the bed, on our sides, so we can face each other. She's tucked under the covers in her nightie while I stretch out on top of the blanket with all my clothes on. I've decided Calli has probably shocked herself too and needs some platonic time with me to help her adjust to how much she wants me and what that lust inspired her to do.

That probably explains the topic she chooses for conversation.

Nestling under the covers, she asks, "What are your brothers like?"

"I've told you Lachlan used to be uptight before Erica. He's still overbearing, but a lot more fun than he used to be. Rory's got a caber up his erse, but women seem to like him." I prop my head up with one hand. "Of course, Lachlan and Rory both used to be more like me."

"Caber up his erse?"

"A caber's a bloody great wooden pole. Scotsmen like to chuck them around to show how manly they are. Not me, but others like Lachlan and Rory. And an erse is…" With one hand, I reach behind her to palm one buttock. "An erse."

"More Scottish-isms. I'm learning a new language." She punches her pillow to get it situated better under her head. "You said your brothers used to be like you. What happened?"

"Lachlan married a right bitch." I screw up my mouth. "Suppose I shouldn't say it, but she wasn't a nice person. Don't know what she did to Lachlan, but he wound up terrified to love anyone else. When he met Erica, he offered her a one-month fling, but vowed he'd never love her and couldn't offer anything more substantial. He couldn't help it, though. He fell for her."

"What about Rory?"

I roll my eyes heavenward, then back to her face. "Ah, Rory. He married three different women who each shoved that caber a bit further up his erse. One left him because he was too boring, being a solicitor and all. The second cheated on him several times. And then there was the third, who left him for another woman."

"Ouch."

"It's no bloody wonder he has no interest in dating anymore." I rub my chin while I consider the issue of Rory. "He does run off on so-called business trips on occasion, though. When he comes back, he's much more cheerful—for a time, at least. Makes me wonder if he's off having one-night stands, to satisfy his needs without risking another disastrous relationship."

"He can't be happy with that lifestyle."

"Clearly not, or he wouldn't have the caber up his erse." I let my lips curl into a mischievous smile. "The man needs a good woman to shag some sense into him."

"An American of his own?"

I hook a finger under her chin and brush a kiss over her lips. "Couldnae hurt, eh?"

"Don't get any ideas. I'm not your key to happiness."

"How do you know?"

"Take my word for it." She slides a hand over my chest. "Not sure I'd want to meet Rory if he's that much of a jerk."

"He's not a jerk," I say. "Sometimes he's the old Rory again, smiling and joking, like at Lachlan's wedding. He helps people with their legal problems even if they can't pay him, and he donates his money and his time to worthy local causes."

"All right, he sounds like a good guy in spite of the caber." She gives me a teasing smile. "What about your sisters? How do they feel about marriage?"

"Not sure about Fiona and Catriona. They don't talk about it. But Jamie..." I roll my eyes heavenward once more, shaking my head. "Jamie wants to fall in love at every opportunity until she finally meets her Prince Charming. Last night, she announced she plans to come to America, stay at Erica's house in Chicago, and look for an American man."

"She's younger than you, right?" When I nod, she frowns. "Not sure a young woman from another country should be alone in Chicago, especially if she's hunting for a man."

"I agree, which is why I tried to talk her out of it. She's determined, though, and she'll empty her bank account to pay for the trip. Since she's between jobs, that doesn't seem like a wise choice."

"What will you do about her?"

"Rang Lachlan last night. He's going to give it one more go at convincing her this is a bad idea."

"If he fails?"

I shrug one shoulder. "Our only idea is I go back to Chicago to keep an eye on her."

"What if," Calli says cautiously, "you didn't have to go away? What if your sister could come here?"

"Here? There are no rooms available in this area."

"I know, but..." She hesitates. "Jamie could stay *here* here, in this house. In the guest room."

I watch Calli for a moment, feeling both baffled and aroused by her suggestion. "If she's in the guest room, where would I be?"

"On the sofa."

My lips pucker, and I nod slowly. "Ah, of course. The sofa."

"Were you hoping I'd invite you to sleep in my bedroom?" She nudges me with her knee. "We're not there yet."

I hope I don't look as dejected as I feel. Aye, I'd thought she might mean for me to share her bed. I'm a dafty, for sure. Of course Calli Douglas, the not-quite-divorced virgin who went down on me, wouldn't ask me to sleep in her bedroom.

Then I realize what she said, and a sly smile comes over me. "Not yet? You're implying we may get there."

"Don't read too much into everything I say." She rolls onto her back, hands clasped over her belly. "I'm trying to keep your sister from getting into trouble."

"And I appreciate it." I sidle closer, my head inches from hers, still braced on one hand. "Tell me, why do you care so much about what my family thinks of marriage?"

"I suffer from an insatiable and inappropriate curiosity."

"Hmm." I study her with keen interest, my eyes narrowed. "You say you won't fall in love with me, but you can't marry me. One is a choice, the other implies an impenetrable barrier. Eventually, you will be divorced, which means you could marry me."

"Yes, I suppose I could." She falls silent for a moment, her gaze aimed at the ceiling. "But you're better off without me. I'm bad news."

I make an irritated noise. "Stop telling me you're bad. I don't believe it, and I never will."

"Stop being so stubborn. Why can't you accept my decision?"

"Because it's clear that's not what you want. I wouldn't be here if it was." I settle a hand on her arm. "Why don't you want to care for me? Am I so frightening?"

"No, of course not. I feel safe with you."

"Donnae understand. Is it your husband who scares you?"

She shuts her eyes, covering her face with both hands and letting them slide back down to rest on her chest. "Not him. It's way too soon for me to share my deepest fears with you."

Neither of us speaks for a moment while the silence stretches on.

Finally, she peeks sideways at me.

I regard her without expression because I have no ruddy idea what to say to her now. We've known each other for five days, but it feels like much longer. Still, she needs more time to decide she trusts me.

"You're exhausted," I say, caressing her arm with light sweeps of my fingers over her skin. "Sleep now, worry later."

Calli curls up against me with her face on my chest. As she drifts off to sleep, I know I won't sleep anytime soon. What frightens her? Why can't she trust me enough to tell me? I've told her about my family, but not about the accident or Seona. Yet I expect Calli to tell me everything.

Damn eejit, ye are, and selfish too.

All right, I will slow down and give her time. Even if it drives me insane.

I'll do anything for Calli.

Chapter Fourteen

We spend the next day at home, playing with the puppies, watching television, and cooking for each other. Calli tells me all about this part of Michigan, which is called the Keweenaw Peninsula. The elderly couple I'd met at the beach had tried to explain some of the geography to me, but I didn't really understand. The Keweenaw is a peninsula on a peninsula, Calli says, since it sticks out of the northwestern section of the Upper Peninsula. She even shows me a map, but I still find it very confusing. This part of Michigan isn't connected to the rest of the state, though it does link up with Wisconsin.

"Then why is it part of Michigan, not Wisconsin?" I ask.

"Because it isn't. Don't ask me why. At one time, there was a movement to make the U.P. its own state or country, but that never took off."

"I see." Maybe I don't really, but the geography and politics of this region aren't of great interest to me. The geography of Calli's body is.

But I don't seduce her. Yet.

In the evening, I have a shower while Calli washes the dishes. She insisted on cleaning up after dinner, saying I'm a guest and shouldn't do all the housework. I can't resist Calli, even when she's urging me to be lazy, so I give in to her command. I have to admit, she is sexy when she's bossing me around. When I emerge from the bathroom, I can see her sitting cross-legged on the sofa.

I saunter into the living room, veering around the sofa, and drop onto the cushion beside her. My hair is still wet since I never bother with girlie things like hair dryers. Besides, I know Calli likes me damp and fresh from a shower. I probably should've walked out in a towel. She'd loved that yesterday.

As I stretch an arm across the sofa's back, I let my fingertips graze her shoulder. "Thought I heard voices."

"Talking to my cousin on the phone."

"How is the wee Tara?"

"Living it up on her Hawaiian honeymoon." She hesitates, seeming uncertain of what to say next. "Tara asked me to give you a kiss for her."

I feel my mouth tighten and curve upward in a half-repressed smile. "Did she now."

"Mm-hm." Calli slants toward me, bringing our mouths to within inches of each other. "Can't let my cousin down, can I?"

I shake my head. *Thank you, Tara.*

Calli touches her lips to mine in a chaste kiss. "That was for Tara. The next one's from me."

Gazing into my eyes, she moistens her lips with two long, slow passes of her tongue. I let my lips fall open, my breathing suddenly labored, excitement rushing over my skin with electrifying effect—all because Calli implied she's going to kiss me. She lays a palm on my chest and urges me to lean back into the sofa, then she climbs astride me and plants her hands on the sofa's back on either side of my shoulders. I let my head fall back onto the cushions.

Leaning in, she hovers her mouth so close to mine that our breaths mingle, and I swear I can taste her. "I really want to kiss you, but I'm afraid things might get out of hand."

"Then maybe you shouldn't have climbed on top of me."

"Fair point. But I'm already here."

I settle my hands on her hips. "I promise not to take any liberties. Unless you beg me to."

"Beg?" She flicks her tongue out to tease my lower lip. "Not going to happen."

"What if I beg?"

Her brows lift, and she tips her head to the side.

"Please," I say, my voice low and rumbly, "kiss me, ahm begging ye."

She brushes her lips over mine, and I experience the barmiest sort of thrill from that simple contact. Why does Calli Douglas always make me so excited for a kiss from her? She nips and licks at my lips, teasing and tempting me, and it takes all my willpower not to seize control and ravish her like the Don Juan she used to think I was. I coast my palms up her back to splay them over her shoulder blades.

And I murmur one word: "Please."

Calli sinks deeper into my lap, rubbing her groin against my cock with only our clothes separating my *slat* from her flesh, which I know will be hot and wet for me. She seals her mouth over mine, our lips fused while our tongues thrust deep, tangling and questing, hot and silken and rife with hunger. *Bod an Donais*, she tastes so bloody good. I explore her mouth with abandon, not even trying to temper my lust, though I move my tongue in slow swipes and languorous glides, taking intense pleasure from sampling every inch of her. With my hands on her back, I urge her to nestle more snugly against me, the hardness of my erection trapped between us. I want her like mad, but I promised I wouldn't take any liberties, which means I can't do what I need to the most. Her rigid nipples scrape across my chest while she writhes on my lap, grinding her body into me.

My mobile rings with the sound of bagpipes and vibrates inside my jeans pocket.

We both freeze, our lips still glued to each other. I peel my lids apart to find Calli already gazing at me. She looks faintly dazed, like I imagine I must too. The last thing I want to do is answer my mobile.

But it rings and vibrates again.

I fumble to get the mobile out of my pocket without dumping Calli off my lap. I keep one hand on her hip while I answer the call with a gruff hello.

"Are you sitting down, Aidan? If not, you should."

"Jamie?" I say.

"Aye, it's me. Your ex-girlfriend rang me. Seona says you're refusing to take care of her the way you promised to do. What's going on, Aidan?"

"She what? Rang *you*?"

"That's what I said. I met her once, and she barely spoke to me. Why is Seona calling me now to tell me what a bastard you are?"

Calli, still squatting on my lap, has no choice but to overhear my part of the conversation. She glances around, shifting her hands here and there like she's unsure of what to do with them. At last, she rests them on her thighs.

"Ignore her," I tell Jamie. "I'll speak to Seona myself."

My gaze falls on Calli, and I pull in a long breath. How am I meant to explain this to her? She doesn't want to share her problems with me, so I don't feel like I can share mine with her even if I want to.

"Don't worry," I tell my sister. "I will handle it, but I have to go now."

"Are you sure you're all right?"

"Yes. Goodbye, Jamie."

I drop the mobile onto the cushion beside me and reach for Calli. Just as my palms land on her lower back and I lunge my mouth toward hers, she holds up a hand between our lips. "Was that your sister?"

"Aye."

"Is everything okay? You seemed upset."

I sweep my hands up her back to pull her closer, with her hand the only barrier preventing me from claiming her mouth. "I'll be fine as soon as I'm kissing you again."

She hurls her body to the side, tumbling off my lap and righting herself to sit beside me with her body turned toward me. "I think we need to share a little bit of our secrets. Not knowing and not sharing is probably giving me an ulcer."

I draw my head back, eying her with disbelief. "You want to tell me your secret?"

"Part of it. The only part I can."

"If you're doing this because you want to know mine, there's no need. I'll tell you anyway."

She braces her head with one arm on the sofa. "That's not why I'm suggesting this. I want to explain what I can to you, but don't ask me why. I have no answer for that one."

"All right." I turn partway toward her, wriggling a little to get settled. "I'll start. Ask me whatever you like."

"Who is Seona? Is she the one who keeps calling you?"

"Yes." I aim my gaze down at my lap, feeling uneasy about telling Calli my secret, but I did say I'd explain, whether or not she tells me her secrets. "Seona Ross is a former girlfriend, if you can call it that. We dated for a few months, but it was never serious, nothing more than a pleasant distraction. You might call it a casual sort of arrangement. We got on well." I flatten my lips, my entire body going rigid as the memories replay in my mind. "Until the accident."

Calli sneaks a hand out to touch my knee.

I aim a grateful smile at her before returning my gaze to my lap. "Six months ago, Seona was seriously injured and spent a long time in the hospital and in rehabilitation. I haven't seen her in about six months. No contact at all. She was angry with me because she bl—" No, I cannae tell her that yet. Maybe it makes me a coward, but I just can't force the words to come out of my mouth. Instead, I scrub a hand over my face and lift my gaze to hers. "She told me to stay away from her, and I did. Had no wish to fash her when she was unwell."

"Makes sense."

"Somehow, she heard I'd come to America and started calling me to ask for money. Ask. No, she's demanding it."

Calli lights a hand on my thigh. "Why would she demand money from you?"

"She's very bitter. And maybe she has a point about me owing her, but I donnae have money to give her."

"Why would you owe her?"

I swerve my attention to the backyard view, though I don't really see anything with my thoughts a chaotic jumble. Aye, I'd convinced myself I was ready to share everything with Calli, but I don't want her to see me as a selfish *bod ceann* who abandoned a lass after… Christ, I can't even think the words. Maybe I am a dickhead. Calli doesn't need to know that about me.

She slumps against the sofa. "You don't have to tell me. I'm not going to tell you my whole story either."

I plow both hands into my hair. "Seona keeps calling me, and now she's called my sister Jamie to enlist her help. Jamie told her no."

"What will you do?"

I bluster out a sigh, my shoulders flagging. "Donnae know."

"I'm sorry, Aidan." Calli scoots closer, caressing my cheek. "You don't have to talk about it anymore. I think it's my turn, anyway."

Considering how long I've wanted to know more about her, I should be happy that she's about to share some of her secrets with me. But I don't feel triumphant. All I want to do is bury myself in her body and forget about everything else for a while. I cannae do that, though. Seducing her now would make me a *bod ceann* for sure.

"You wanted to know why I married a man I never loved."

I nod. "If you want to tell me. Don't feel you have to because I told you about Seona."

"It's okay. I want to tell you." She gives me a quick kiss. "Though it's very sweet of you to give me an out."

I enfold both her hands in my palm, holding them to my chest. "Whatever you feel like sharing, I'm listening. You can tell me anything, and I will keep your secrets. You have my word."

Her lips tremble a touch, but then she sucks in a breath and tells me. "I met Rade in college. He's from Croatia and came here on a student visa. Though he was two years ahead of me, we became friends and spent a lot of time together—but just as friends. His parents had died when he was eight, and he inherited a real fortune. I don't know exactly how much, but it would definitely qualify as stinking rich."

The anxiety in her expression might not be noticeable to anyone else, but I've gotten to know her enough that I can see it. She's uneasy about sharing her past with me. I clasp her hand more firmly, hoping to give her some small measure of comfort.

"Five years ago," she begins, "my parents died in a car accident. My brother Gavin didn't handle it well. He'd left the Marines eight months earlier, after a tour in Afghanistan, and he wasn't completely readjusted to civilian life yet. He's the toughest guy I know, but he basically fell apart after our parents died, and I had to handle everything. There were bills and debts neither of us had known about because our parents had kept their financial problems a secret. No life insurance, they'd stopped making payments on it. No savings. Almost nothing in their checking account. It was a horrible time, discovering how much they'd kept from us, and we couldn't even ask them for an explanation."

I fold my hands around both of hers now, lifting one to place a soft kiss on the backside.

Burgeoning tears shimmer in her eyes. "Rade was very kind during those first weeks after the accident. Two months later, he asked me—" She pauses as if she's searching for the right way to explain. "He asked me to marry him, for reasons I can't explain. I agreed, not because I wanted to be married to him but because I owed him a lot more than I can tell you."

"You don't have to say any more, if you don't want to."

"Thank you." The tears fill her eyes, about to spill over onto her cheeks. She sniffles and tries to wrest her hand free of mine.

I release her hands and wipe the tears away with my thumbs.

"Rade saved me, in a way," she says. "My life was in shambles, and he stepped in to pay bills I couldn't, helped me stay in school to finish my degree and go on to grad school. He gave me a place to stay too, when I couldn't afford my apartment anymore. When he asked me for a favor, I couldn't say no."

"A favor?" I squint at Calli, studying her face. "Marriage isn't a favor."

"Please, Aidan, I can't tell you anything more."

Lips compressed, I watch her for a few seconds, but can't understand this at all. She's told me a big part of her secret, that much I'm sure of, so I can't push her for more.

I exhale a long breath and run the backs of my fingers down her cheek. "I'm sorry. This is not my business, but I don't like the sound of your arrangement with this Rade person."

"I know." She kisses my cheek. "You're a very good man, Aidan MacTaggart."

I stand and stretch, arching my back. Time to forget all this emotional rubbish and get a good night's sleep that will make us both feel better in the morning. So, I offer her my hand. "This has been a tiring evening. To bed with you, Calli."

"You sound like a medieval lord," she says as she accepts my aid in getting up off the sofa.

"If I were, you'd have to obey me."

"Lucky for you, I feel like doing what you commanded. Sleep sounds wonderful right about now."

I walk the lass to her bedroom door, which hangs halfway open. Inside, the puppies have already settled in for the night on Calli's bed, with Misty at the foot and Mandy half on the pillow.

"Sleep well," I say.

"Good night."

I press a kiss to her lips, lingering there for a long moment. Then I turn and stride into my room, pausing on the threshold to glance over my shoulder.

Calli is just shutting her door.

Something changed between us tonight. I'm sure she senses it too and probably feels anxious about whatever this shift between us means. We've grown closer, for sure. I told her some of what happened between me and Seona, and she confessed to me that she married a man she doesn't love for reasons she still isn't comfortable telling me. The fact she shared that much has to mean something. She trusts me. Why else would she confess anything? I confessed to her too, but I still have so much more I need to explain to Calli.

Not tonight. Maybe not tomorrow. I need more time with her before I admit that I'm a selfish bastard. Calli thinks I'm a good man, and I don't want to ruin her opinion of me just yet.

Do I still plan to seduce her into loving me? I shouldn't, but I do.

I think I might already be falling for her.

Chapter Fifteen

Another day with Calli. What can I say? She gets more lovable every day, and more sensual. The lass cannae keep her hands off me, though we mostly hold hands. The occasional kiss involves our lips only. I can't help wishing she would straddle me again and kiss me like she wants to suffocate me with her tongue. I wouldn't mind dying if she's devouring me while it happens.

But we keep it chaste. Bloody hell, willpower is a terrible thing.

In the evening, we sit in the living room with Calli seated on the sofa facing the sliding glass doors while I lounge in an armchair that's positioned perpendicular to the sofa. And aye, I know what "perpendicular" means. Most lasses think I'm a dumb lug since I do construction for a living, but I need to understand geometry to do my job. Calli has never even suggested I might be a thickheaded erse. She seems to assume I have a brain and know how to use it. I love that about her.

She occupies the corner of the sofa with her legs tucked under her, and she keeps eying me like she might want to climb on my lap again. *Please do, leannan.* I haven't called her sweetheart in Gaelic out loud, but all day I found myself thinking the word *leannan* every time I looked at her. Aye, I'm falling for her. The idea doesn't fash me, though I know it fashes her. The remains of our dinner litter the coffee table—two plates scattered with crumbs, two empty water glasses, and two sets of forks and knives. I had insisted on making our meal from scratch.

When I told her that, she said, "You're a total sweetie-pie, but watching you cook makes me so damn hot for you."

Unfortunately, being "hot for" me didn't mean she planned to rip my clothes off. *Damn.*

While I relax in the armchair, I hook one ankle over the opposite knee and rest my hands on the chair's arms. The carpeting tickles my bare feet, but I like the sensation. It reminds me of Calli, for some reason. Aye, I'd love to roll around on the carpet with her. Today, I've been wearing a snug grey T-shirt and low-slung jeans because I love the way she licks her lips when she sees me dressed this way.

I swivel my gaze to her and rub my lips together like I'm starved and imagining the feast I want to devour. "What's for dessert?"

She will be my dessert, if I have my way.

"Nothing," she says. "Sorry, I didn't have time for baking, what with playing referee between the puppies and every object not nailed down in this house. They're always rambunctious, but they love you so much they're insanely happy."

"The pups are adorable, but not half as adorable as you."

"You're pretty damn adorable yourself."

"I'm wicked, remember? Maybe I need to remind you of it."

Rising, I stretch my arms above me and arch my back, knowing full well the action tightens my muscles and pulls my shirt up just enough to give her a glimpse of my abs. "Lachlan sent me a present."

The box had arrived by FedEx overnight delivery, addressed to me care of Calli. No matter how sexily she begged me to show her the contents, I had resisted her and only gave the lass a secretive smile whenever she asked about it.

"Thought you hated his presents," she says while shamelessly gawking at my body.

"Ah, but this one is for you." I amble toward the kitchen. "I stashed it in a cabinet, behind other things."

She cranes her neck to follow my movements. "Do I want to know what this gift is?"

"Something I want to share with you." I give her a mysterious smile, or at least I try to, then I bend down to retrieve the item in question and my head dips below the bar, out of her sight. When I pop up again, I'm holding the item behind my back. "Close your eyes."

"Why?"

"So suspicious," I chide, with humor in my tone. "Trust me."

Calli settles back into the sofa cushions and shuts her eyes.

I come out from behind the bar and approach the sofa, settling my weight onto the cushion beside her. "Open your eyes."

Blinking slowly, she turns her attention to the object in my hand. I have my fingers wrapped around a bottle filled with a golden liquid that almost glows in the lamplight. Confusion tightens her forehead. I rotate the bottle so she can see the label.

Calli reads it aloud, pronouncing the name carefully. "Talisker single-malt Scotch whisky."

I nod and puff up a wee bit, feeling oddly proud of myself for offering her this gift.

"Whisky?" she says. "You know I don't drink."

"Because you've never tasted a drink you like, that's what you said." I wag the bottle. "You'll like this. It's made on the Isle of Skye, off the western coast of the Highlands."

"I've heard of Skye, but I seriously doubt I'm going to like its whisky."

"Not just any whisky." I lift my chin. "Scottish whisky. A single malt distilled on a mystical island where the ancients held their mysterious rituals to commune with the gods."

"How will a history lesson make me like the booze?"

I huff. "Will you not let me tell you about the whisky? I'm trying to paint a picture for you."

"I'm sorry, really. You're creating a wonderful picture for me, but I doubt anything you say could alter my taste buds." She eyes the bottle with sarcastic suspicion. "Are you trying to get me drunk, Mr. MacTaggart?"

"Don't need to get you drunk to have my way with you." I tip the bottle to one side. "Will you try it once?"

She considers the bottle for a moment. "Okay. One sip."

I can't help the grateful smile that curves my lips because this is oddly important to me. I pluck up the whisky glass I'd hidden too and open the bottle, struggling in the effort. Is Talisker always so hard to get open? I've never drunk it before, so I don't know. I'm not picky about whisky, but Lachlan is the only one in the family who drinks Talisker. Finally, I get the bloody thing open and decant the liquor into the glass, filling it with one inch of amber liquid.

I offer her the glass. "Taste the legend of Skye."

She gives me a playful smile. "You're starting to sound like a Scottish tourism brochure."

"Taste the bloody whisky."

"Yes, sir." She lifts the glass, sniffing the drink. Her nose wrinkles. "Smells like bad vinegar."

Mhac na galla. My lips tighten, and I squint at her. Bad vinegar? It's a high-quality single malt. I manage to regain my composure, though, and curl my lips into a sensual expression. "Take a sip, let it slide down your throat, and feel the whisky penetrate your body."

I want to penetrate her body, but right now, I'll settle for watching her experience her first drink.

She dips her nose to sniff again.

I slap a hand over the glass. "Drink, don't smell."

"Okay, okay." She waits for me to remove my hand, then lifts the glass to her mouth. "Here goes."

She takes a dainty sip—and gags.

Calli splutters and coughs and nearly spits out the whisky, but then seems to decide she needs to swallow it to get rid of the stuff. Her eyes flare wide, then she winces as she shoves the glass at me and uses her shirt to scrub her tongue while a coughing fit overtakes her.

I stare at Calli, my face slack, the glass in one hand and the bottle in the other. No woman has ever reacted to whisky that way. I've never fed a lass Talisker, but I have offered them other kinds of Scottish single malt.

As she recovers from her coughing fit, she clears her throat several times in quick succession. Her voice comes out hoarse when she declares, "That's the most awful thing I've ever put in my mouth."

I cannae understand this. Calli hates whisky.

Defeated, I collapse against the sofa, facing forward. The bottle rests between my thighs, but I hold the glass on my lap. How can she hate it? I meant to arouse her with Talisker, but instead, I've probably convinced her I'm the worst eejit on earth.

"Cannae believe it," I mumble. "This worked for Lachlan."

"Was this another thing Lachlan did with Erica?"

"Aye," I admit miserably, rubbing my forehead. "It's how he started his seduction. She loved the whisky."

Calli cringes a wee bit, like she feels bad for hating the drink. "Two days ago, you wouldn't play a board game with me because Lachlan and Erica did that. Why are you back to reenacting their affair?"

"Wanted to do something special, but I couldn't think of anything. Seemed like a good idea until you drank the whisky."

She lays a hand on my arm. "I was kind of obnoxious about that. Can you forgive me?"

"Aye, it's not your fault." I let my head fall back. "I'm the eejit who keeps trying to re-create my brother's affair. I figured if it worked for uptight Lachie, then it has to work for me."

"I'm not Erica, and you're not Lachlan. How about we try being ourselves? You don't need to win me over with liquor and flowery descriptions of an island. I like you, Aidan. I'm here with you, not your brother."

I grumble. "If you met Lachlan, you'd probably like him better."

"Bullshit." She rests her chin on my shoulder, sliding her hand over my belly. "You don't need props to impress me."

I set the glass on the table and swig a mouthful of whisky straight from the bottle, a bit of it spilling onto my lips.

She takes my face in her hands, sits up, and drags her tongue across first my bottom lip, then the upper one. "Mm, it tastes better on you."

My breath hitches, and I lock my gaze on her. The tone of her voice… It was ravenous.

With her hands still bracketing my face, she tugs me closer. Our gazes never diverge, as if a rope binds us to each other. She captures my lower lip between hers and suckles, gently at first, then with more hunger. Though I hold on to the whisky bottle with one hand, I settle the other onto her hip and curl my fingers around it.

She releases my lip.

I'm already breathing harder, and our faces are so close that our breaths seem to mingle. Suddenly, she crushes her mouth to mine.

I make a low noise—part groan, part gasp—and open my mouth to her.

Need pulses through me, straight into my cock that's hardening swiftly. She keeps hold of my face as she thrusts her tongue inside my mouth. I cannae resist coiling my tongue around hers in a slow and seductive movement that drives her to wriggle against me and quest deeper as if she means to lap up the flavor of the whisky I'd swallowed. The texture of her mouth, slippery and soft, heightens my lust, and so does the way she pants into my mouth while her breasts mound against my chest, rubbing her stiff nipples against me.

We're on the verge of fucking. But no, I cannae take her virginity like this.

I surge up off the sofa, leaving her in a dazed heap on the cushions.

Calli blinks up at me like she's struggling to clear the haze of desire and catch her breath.

I toss back a mouthful of whisky, then clap the bottle down on the coffee table. Swiping at my mouth with the back of my hand, I glance down at her. "Best stop."

My cock is throbbing, so aye, we need to stop before I do something I shouldn't.

I stalk around the sofa to the bar where I plant both palms on the surface, leaning into it with my head bowed. Why am I fashed? I think it's because Calli means more to me than she realizes, and I don't know if she ever will feel the way I do. But here, now, I know exactly what I want from her.

Behind me, I can hear Calli's movements when she pushes up off the sofa and approaches the bar. She halts beside me. I don't dare move a muscle, so I keep my head down and my eyes closed while she places one hand on mine. I can't stop myself from tensing up.

"What is it?" she asks. "Thought you liked kissing me."

"I love it," I say in a hushed voice. "But I want more than kissing."

She keeps her hand on mine, her skin warming me just enough that I relax a little. She bends one finger to stroke the back of my hand. "I know. You want sex. I want—"

"No." I pull my hand away, turn, and stalk halfway across the living room. Scrubbing my face with one hand, I sigh. "I want more than sex. You know that."

Peripherally, I see it when she leans against the bar with her elbow braced on it. "Okay, but you said sex would come first."

I face her, forcing myself to stand straight and resolute. "Marry me."

"What?" She almost shouts the word, her eyes wide and her mouth open. "Where is this coming from? You know I can't marry you. Even if I wanted to, we barely know each other."

"Aye, but I know what I want." I take two steps toward her, hesitating a short distance from her. "Please, Calli, marry me. I swear I'll make you happy and you'll never regret this. One day, maybe you'll even love me."

"Do you love me?"

Lowering my gaze, I scratch the back of my head. "Not yet."

"Then why would you want to marry me? What's the rush?"

I hike up one shoulder and stare at the floor while seconds tick by on the clock in my head. Am I insane? What has come over me tonight? Yes, I want to be with Calli for good, but this was not the time or the place for a barmy proposal. Clearly, she doesn't like the idea. I shuffle to the padded chair on the other side of the living room, the one situated against the wall under a topographic map of the Upper Peninsula. I fall into the chair with a groaning sigh, my shoulders deflating, my entire body slumping. With my hands on the chair's arms, I can't make myself look at her, not even when she crosses the room to kneel before me.

"Aidan." She lays her hands on my knees. "Please tell me what's going on with you."

"Ye donnae want to hear."

She shifts her hands to my thighs. "Yes, I do."

I make a pitiful noise that's sure to convince her I'm the sort of man she needs, and I twist my mouth into a tight expression. "Lachlan didn't want a wife, but he found one. Thought if I did what he'd done, I could change your mind about me. But ye still donnae want me, not the way I want you."

"Did Lachlan propose to Erica after one week?"

"No." I fidget in my seat. "First, he broke her heart and left her for two months. Then, he begged her to marry him."

"Uh-huh." She taps a finger on my chest. "Why would you want to re-enact that? Sounds like the Amazing Lachlan fucked it up with Erica and then got lucky when she generously took him back. Is that really how you want things to go with me?"

I roll my eyes up to meet hers, and my lips curl up at the corners. "You said fuck."

"That's what you took away from what I said?"

"No, I understood the rest." I bend one arm to prop my chin on my knuckles. "But I've never heard you say 'fuck' before. Kind of like it, though I'd rather hear it from you when we're both naked."

She sits back on her heels, giving me a sardonic smile. "Getting back to Lachlan…"

"I do see your point," I say. "Lachlan made a mess of things, but I was hoping some of his methods might work for me. This is the first time I've tried to win a wife. No bloody idea what I'm doing."

"Oh, I'd say you're doing fine all on your own."

"You still don't want to love me."

"Sure, but you don't love me either."

"I want to. That's the difference. Deep down, though, I think you want to love me too."

"Give it up, Kilt Boy. I am not falling for you."

Dropping my hand, I let it dangle over the chair's arm onto my lap while I frown. "Then you won't be sleeping with me."

She spreads her palms on my thighs and leans in, pushing between my legs to get closer. With our faces so near each other that I swear I can almost taste her breaths, she meets my gaze head-on. "I've already decided to have sex with you."

My eyes fly wide. "You what? Why?"

Laughing softly, she squeezes further between my thighs until my stiffening cock presses against her. "I like you, Aidan. You're sweet and funny and smart, and you make me feel good." She moves her hands to my chest, toying with the neckline of my T-shirt. "And you're the sexiest man on earth."

"Sexiest? Do I get a trophy for that?"

"No, but you do get a prize." She slides her hands down my torso. "Me."

"But—ah." I flinch as she cups my erection. "You know I want you. Badly. But not like this, I need to prepare."

She plasters her body to mine, running her hands up my arms. "Prepare? I have condoms. Bought them at the store today when you were contemplating the avocados."

"Not that." Her body glued to mine is rousing my *slat*, and I grip the arms of my chair in a vain attempt to short-circuit my lust for her. "Need to set the scene, make it special."

"How long will that take?" She nips at the flesh at the juncture of my jaw.

I suck in a sharp breath. "Might need a day, maybe two."

"A day or two?" She pulls her head back. "You're kidding, right? I offer myself to you, and all you can say is let's wait two days."

"Donnae want to."

She scrutinizes me for a moment. "Is this what Lachlan did with Erica?"

I scratch my cheek. "Aye."

"For heaven's sake." She grasps my head in both hands and speaks in a stern voice. "Stop with the Lachlan and Erica reenactment. I told you I don't want that. I want you. Can you get that through your thick, Scottish head? I want *you*. Tonight. Forget about your brother, forget about everyone else. Do this your way."

"My way would be I carry you into the bedroom and strip you naked right this minute."

"Yes. Please do."

I grin. "You are wonderful."

She rubs her body against my straining erection. "You gonna fuck me or what?"

"Aye." I scoop her into my arms at the same instant I surge up from the chair, then I carry her down the hallway and into her bedroom. When I spot the puppies asleep on the quilt, I tell them, "Time to go, furry lassies."

Misty and Mandy fly off the bed and out of the room. The dog door whaps closed behind them as I kick the bedroom door shut.

"Need privacy," I say, setting Calli on her feet, "for what I'm going to do to you."

Her eyes light up with unmistakable lust and excitement.

I grasp her around the waist, tugging her into me. "I'm about to show you how wicked I really am."

<h1 style="text-align:center">Chapter Sixteen</h1>

I slip my fingers under her shirt, gliding them upward, lifting the fabric as I go. Her flat belly caves in with every exhalation, and I love that her excitement affects her so much. No lass has ever wanted me the way she does, with a depth of hunger that makes me crave her even more. Eyes half-closed, she lights her hands on my chest while her gaze stays bound to mine.

I stop, my fingertips a hair's breadth below her bra. "No, not like this."

She throws her hands up. "What now? If you say we have to wait so you can do whatever Lachlan did—"

"Easy." Aye, she *really* wants me. That knowledge makes me chuckle softly. "I meant not with me undressing you. I want you to strip for me."

"Oh." A slight blush turns her cheeks a delicate pink. "Sorry."

"Don't be." I tip her chin up with one finger. "I like your passion."

"Apparently, I get a little irrational when I'm sexually frustrated."

I kiss her, keeping the contact quick and light. "I'll take care of that soon enough. First, I want to watch you."

Cannae help smirking as I saunter to the bed and lower my erse onto the mattress. It creaks under my weight. I lay my hands on the quilt, but my attention stays fixated on her. I don't think most women understand how much men love to watch them undressing. Calli definitely doesn't understand. I love that I'll be the first man ever to see her strip—and I'll be the last too. Maybe I jumped the gun on proposing, but I know one day we will be married. It's destiny or some bollocks like that.

She stands there, seemingly immobilized like she can't figure out how to start.

"Relax," I say, canting my head as I sweep my gaze down the length of her sexy body and back up to her bonnie face. "Just take your clothes off. I'm easy to please, trust me."

With her, aye, I'm easy in every way. All she needs to do is look at me, and I get hard as concrete. Since I've poured concrete foundations, I know what I'm talking about.

She chews the inside of her lip, fingering the hem of her shirt with her gaze averted to the dresser.

"Look at me," I murmur. "Keep your eyes on me and try to relax. Look like you've got a caber up your erse."

"You have a caber fetish, don't you?"

"I've got a fetish for watching you undress."

She hesitates for only a moment, then takes hold of her shirt and lifts it over her head, tossing it onto the floor.

Her hand flies to her mouth. "Oops. Was that too fast? Should I do it slower?"

"It was fine." I move my hands behind my erse and lean back into them. Then I let the tip of my tongue poke out between my lips, tracing the seam of my mouth, while I contemplate the many ways I want to make her come tonight. "Keep going."

My voice has turned huskier, though I didn't do that on purpose. I think all the blood in my brain has flooded into my *slat*, so I can't think anymore. Calli Douglas is the sexiest lass in the universe.

She unzips her jeans, shimmying out of them while I track every movement of her hands, her fingers, her hips, mesmerized by the vision of Calli stripping for me. When she kicks her jeans away, I swallow hard enough that she must see it. The lass turns her back to me and throws me a teasingly sexy smile over her shoulder.

"More," I growl, breathing harder now.

Calli unhooks her bra and lets it tumble off her shoulders, fluttering down to the floor. She pushes her thumbs inside the waistband of her knickers, and little by little, eases them down while swaying her hips in a seductive rhythm, dragging the fabric over her erse. I breathe even harder, suddenly unable to pull in a full breath, so turned on by her striptease that I cannae move.

Nude at last, she folds her arms around herself, still gazing at me over her shoulder.

I twirl one finger in the air. "Turn, please. Slowly."

She brushes her hands up and down her arms while swiveling her hips, then spreads her palms over them, undulating her whole body as she rotates to face me.

Fuck, that body. I think my mouth falls open. Her breasts look like they'd fit perfectly in my hands, and the tips that jut up make me want to suck them into my mouth right now. The sight of her sweet little belly button draws my attention down her belly to her hips and the curly hairs that nestle between her thighs. I want my face buried in those hairs while I devour her cream. She has shapely thighs and the bonniest erse I've ever seen, but I can't tear my gaze away from her hips. I swear I can smell her lust even from several feet away.

She sashays up to me, lifts one leg, and sets her foot on the bed next to me. The pose reveals her slick, rosy folds, and I'm sure she did that on purpose. I cannae stop staring at her glistening flesh while she drapes her hands over my shoulders. My chest heaves, and I hear myself growling low in my throat like I've transformed into a wild animal. Drops of her juices cling to the fine hairs on her mound, and the sight of it makes me growl again.

"So bonnie," I say breathlessly. "So bloody perfect. Pink and slick and begging to be tasted."

I raise one hand, almost in slow motion, and hover it near her body without contacting her skin. I desperately want to cup her groin, but if I do that, I'll lose my mind and shag her like a lunatic. So instead, I wiggle my fingers to tease those silky hairs.

Her fingers dig into my shoulders.

"Cannae wait," I hiss. Grasping her hips with both hands, I tilt them toward me while I slant closer to her. When I seal my mouth around her clit, she gasps and clutches me so hard it hurts, but I donnae give a toss about that. Her head falls backward as I lick and nip at her nub, swirling my tongue, suckling gently, and then so hard she cries out. Calli tastes so fucking good, like sweet cream and whisky, the flavor of her more intoxicating than any alcohol or drug could ever be. I shift my hands to her erse, holding her in place while she still has one foot on the bed, and I lavish her *brillean* with rough swipes of my tongue, increasing the pace with every pass. Starved for more of her, I rake my tongue up and down, up and down, side to side, up and down, knowing I can drive her wild this way—and I need to make her as ravenous for me as I am for her. I pause briefly until she makes a desperate wee noise, then I consume her flesh again and work her hard nub until she's moaning and thrashing her head, clinging to me like she's afraid she'll fly away into the heavens if she lets go.

Her body goes rigid, and she stops breathing. A look of surprise overtakes her features, then she cinches her face up into the most erotic expression of pleasure I've ever seen. I can't feel the spasms of her climax, but I watch the fierce ecstasy on her face while I keep tormenting her nub and she writhes in my grasp, letting out a strangled scream.

I tip my head back to gaze up at her over her mound. "Ah, Calli, you taste like everything wonderful. I could feast on you all night, but I've got other plans."

She seems a bit stunned as she drops her foot to the floor and steadies herself with her hands on my shoulders. Gradually, the astonishment on her face melts away. She flicks a finger on the neck of my T-shirt. "You're not naked."

"Noticed, did ye? Nothing gets by you."

She slaps my shoulder. "Well, get rid of your damn clothes."

"If you insist." I press my mouth to the sensitive skin just above her mound, eliciting a small shiver from her. "Wanted to taste you since the night we met. Now, I want to make you mine."

"Get naked already."

I chuckle but don't move, because I love the way she gets bossy when she's aroused.

With a sharp huff, she grabs the hem of my shirt and yanks it up. I arch one brow but raise my arms so she can haul the garment off me and fling it aside. The shirt lands on the dresser. She kneels between my thighs, fumbling to undo the button on my jeans, but her fingers have started to tremble, and she can't quite grasp it.

I catch her hands. "Easy, love."

With one fluid movement, I wrap an arm around Calli to pin her to my body, rise off the bed, and with my free hand hurl the covers aside. A puff of air rustles her hair from the sudden motion of the quilt and blanket. The top sheet billows, then settles onto the bed.

And I toss Calli onto the mattress.

She lands with a bounce and a wee yelp. "Hey! What are you doing?"

"Speeding things up." I strip off my jeans and kick them out of the way. Since I never bother with underwear, she now gazes with rapt attention at my nude body. I love the way she looks at me. Though she's seen me naked before, tonight everything feels different between us. I give the lass a moment to appreciate my body while I drink in the vision of Calli nude and aroused, her chest and cheeks speckled with pink.

Her focus lands on my cock, which is now as hard as steel-reinforced concrete.

"But you wanted me to go slow," she says, feigning a pout.

"I'm fickle." I give her a salacious, teasing grin. "Should I leave?"

"Don't you dare."

I plant one knee on the bed alongside her hip, preparing to straddle her, but I stop. For some reason, my lips have compressed, and I feel my forehead tightening into furrows. I've wanted Calli since the moment I first saw her, but now, I suddenly wonder if I'm doing the right thing. She hasn't wanted to have sex yet. Her divorce problem keeps her on edge, I know that, and I might've accidentally pushed her into doing this tonight.

"What is it?" she asks, pushing up onto her elbows, the action hoisting her tits out and up.

Though my lips work, all I can manage to do is stare at her for several seconds. Finally, I summon my voice. "Are you certain you want to do this? If I'm your first, you'll always remember me."

"Hate to break it to you," she says, nudging me with her knee, "but even if we don't have sex, there's no way I'd ever forget you. Even if you'd never touched me. Or kissed me. You are unforgettable."

"So are you." I swing my other leg over her body to straddle her hips, landing on my knees poised above her luscious body. I bend forward to anchor my hands on either side of her head. "Guess you're stuck with me, then, even after you tell me to bugger off."

I pray she never tells me that, but deep down, I know she might. I have as much time as she'll allow me to show her what she means to me and that I will never hurt her. But will any amount of time be enough?

Dipping my head to hers, I tease her mouth with swift brushes of my lips. She dissolves for me in an instant, her body lax and limp beneath me even while I smell how turned on she still is.

"Tell me," I say, "what would ye like me to do first?"

"Anything. Everything."

I laugh softly. "Hard to do everything at once."

"You pick. I—"

Before she can finish that thought, I capture her lower lip with my teeth and release it with exquisite slowness. She squirms and makes hungry wee noises while I rub my *slat* across her abdomen, spreading a drop of moisture over her skin. She glances down at my cock, then moans.

"What are ye thinking?" I ask, with my lips barely touching hers.

She snakes a hand down to wrap her fingers around my erection. My lids shut of their own volition while I let myself enjoy the sensation of her soft, delicate fingers on my flesh. She glides her hand up and down.

"Ah," I hiss, and seize her hand to pull it free of my cock. "Not this time, *mo chridhe*."

I just called her "my heart" in Gaelic, and maybe she is that to me. But I can't tell her what the phrase means, or she'll panic for sure.

My thoughts disintegrate when Calli reaches down, intent on getting her hands on my *slat* again.

My lips twitch with wry amusement as I collar that hand too, pinning both above her head. "Behave."

She lifts her brows as she arches her hips into my erection. "Since when do you want me to behave? You've spent over a week trying to convince me to do the exact opposite."

"Did the job a wee bit too well, eh?" I lower my body onto hers, going slowly, delicately, as the weight of my body presses her into the mattress. I thread my fingers through hers, our hands linked above her pillow, and nibble on her bottom lip.

She lashes her arms around my back and splays her fingers over my skin. "What happened to speeding things up?"

"Easy, lass." I savor her mouth with flicks of my tongue, keeping the touch light and sweet though I can tell it's making her hotter and hungrier for me. "We have all night."

She lunges her head forward to kiss me.

I pull back, grinning, then shake my head. "Uh-uh-uh."

Calli huffs. "Well, dammit, do something."

"Maybe I should take pity on you since this is your first time." I muffle her complaint with my mouth, crushing it to hers with brutal pressure, thrusting my tongue between her lips to forge deep inside. With strong, punishing strokes, I devour her mouth while she devours mine, our teeth clashing, our tongues tangling, our lips fused like nothing short of a crowbar could pry our mouths apart. She clutches me tighter, her nails sinking into my back, and bends her knees to spread her legs for me.

I pull my head back, breathing hard, my lips slick and hot from our kiss. "Guess ye cannae wait, can ye?"

She shakes her head furiously, panting, her hair flapping around her face.

"Well then." I rise onto all fours. "Hell with taking it slow."

She bites her lip so hard it turns white. "Oh yes, please, Aidan."

"Condom?" I ask.

Jerking her head, she indicates the bedside table. "Drawer."

I rip the drawer open, snag a condom from inside, and shut it with a *thwack*. I'm almost wheezing with the effort to catch my breath, and my cock twitches as I fumble to open the foil packet with one hand and my teeth.

Calli snatches the packet from me. With a rough ripping noise, she tears it open with her teeth and hands me the packet.

I gape at her open-mouthed. "Ahm getting the impression ye willnae be passive when I take ye."

"You wouldn't want me to be." She scrapes her nails down my chest in one long, slow sweep. "Take too long and I might fuck you instead."

Laughing, I sit back on my heels to cover myself with the condom. "Ye willnae get the chance. Not this time."

I slant over her again, dropping my head to take one nipple in my mouth. I swirl my tongue around the swollen peak as I close one hand around her other breast, pinching the tip with my thumb and forefinger. I feast on the other breast, consuming the whole areola along with the nipple, and suckle hard enough to squeeze a gasp from her while I knead her other tit. She lodges her heels on the mattress and hoists her hips, struggling to catch my cock but missing.

As her erse drops back onto the bed, I withdraw my mouth from her nipple. "Not one for foreplay, are ye?"

"Maybe next time."

"All right. Have it your way."

I grasp her knees and push them toward her chest, forcing her legs to bend. With her knees drawn up and my weight pinning her, she gazes at me with glossy eyes, already struggling to catch her breath.

"Please," she moans. "Please, now."

"Cannae let my woman suffer." I grip her ankles and lift them, settling her knees on my shoulders. "Donnae want to hurt ye, so tell me if—"

"Now, Aidan. Take me now."

I drive into her with one long, smooth stroke, my cock penetrating deep. Her hot, slick body molds to me like a glove, the silky smoothness of her channel so bloody wonderful that I can't think about anything else, only how badly I need to fuck her.

She lets out a sharp cry, part gasp, part yelp.

I freeze, buried within her body. "Did I hurt you?"

"No," she says, breathless. "Don't stop."

Motionless, unblinking, I stare at her as if I'm seeing her for the first time. Never in my life have I paused in the middle of sex to pore my gaze over a woman and admire every inch of her skin, but I do that now. Calli is an angel, the naughty sort, and I've never wanted anyone more.

"Please," she whispers, clasping my wrists. "Please don't stop."

"Won't." I slip free of her hands and shift her legs off my shoulders. Her soles drop to the mattress, though her knees stay bent on either side of me. Still buried inside her to the hilt, I settle my body on top of hers, braced on my elbows with my hands bracketing her head so I can stroke her face with my fingers. "I would never leave you wanting."

I kiss her sweetly, loving the sensation of her lips on mine, unable to stop myself from gazing at her like she's the sun and I haven't felt her warmth in ages. The brush of my lips on hers transforms into an exquisitely tender kiss, with our lips caressing each other in a questing exploration. Then I start to move inside her, easing out until only the tip of my cock touches her opening, then plunging back in with a long, lazy glide. She arches her hips to meet my thrusts, her hands gripping my biceps. With my full weight on her, I feel connected to Calli in a way I can't explain or describe, and I donnae care that I have no words for how good this feels. The whole time—while I glide my cock in and out, consuming her with deep strokes only to abandon her body again—I keep kissing her, savoring her lips with tiny licks but never plunging inside. Her body grows wetter and hotter while I gradually increase the pace.

"Oh God, Aidan," she moans against my lips. "Please."

"Tell me what you want." The words groan out of me as I push inside her with another measured thrust, marshaling all my willpower not to come before she does. "Tell me."

"More. I want more."

Somehow, I know what she means, what she needs. Plastering my mouth to hers, I pull my length out and plunge my tongue deep at the same instant that I plow into her body with one swift, powerful thrust.

Calli cries out.

I rip my mouth from hers to growl, "More?"

"Oh yes, Aidan, more." She lunges her hips up as I punch into her again. "Yes-yes, oh God, yes."

Pushing up onto my straight arms, hands braced on either side of her shoulders, I piston into her again and again, my hips undulating, every muscle taut while I focus on delivering all the pleasure I'd promised her. An electric current fires down my spine into my cock, and I know I can't wait much longer to come. *Donnae do it yet, ye eejit.* She clutches at my arms while wee cries of joy burst out of her one after another and her body goes rigid, a sure sign she's on the verge of climax. I grunt with every thrust, bouncing her on the bed, and she clamps her legs around me with her heels digging into my erse.

Her body clenches tight around me.

The climax seizes her body, wrenching a hoarse scream from her.

I grit my teeth and fight not to come yet while her muscles grip me over and over and she screams again. Then she goes limp, satiated at last.

My entire body goes stiff now, and I contort my face as the desperate need to unleash everything I have inside her body grows too strong to deny. Spasms rip through my cock, one after another, so fast I can't breathe or move a muscle. Then I let go, and my release pulses through my *slat* while I punch into her twice me, the power of my climax forcing me to spend everything while buried deep inside her lush body.

With a long, deep groan, I collapse onto the bed beside Calli. Shedding the condom, I chuck it into the small rubbish bin beside the bed. Second by second, my breathing slows and evens out while I tug her against me and cradle her in my arms. She nestles her cheek against my chest.

I skim a hand up and down her arm. "Sorry about that."

She raises her head to squint at me. "You better not be apologizing for having sex with me."

"No." I sigh, shutting my eyes for a moment. "I meant to take it slow, make it special. This was your first time."

"It was special." She wriggles until she gets into position to touch her lips to mine. "What you gave me tonight, it was perfect."

I lift one brow. "Perfect? I'm good, but I'm not that good."

"Not actually perfect," she says with a laugh. "But for me, that was the perfect first time. I should be thanking you."

"Are you sure you don't mind having me as your first?"

"Why would I mind?" She studies my face like she's trying to puzzle me out, but I don't think she succeeds. "You are sweet, funny, gorgeous, and incredibly sexy. You make me feel...treasured."

"Because you are." A slight smile tightens my mouth as I slide a hand into her hair, massaging her scalp. "I want you for more than sex. I know you think you don't want me for more. You don't love me yet, but you will."

"You can't make me love you by repeatedly telling me I will."

"Can't hurt." I tap a finger on her sealed lips. "You did vow you'd never have sex with me. And look how that worked out."

"Uh-huh."

I pull her closer, fastening her body to mine.

She snuggles into me with her head in the crook of my neck. The woman I just shagged like mad still smells of sweat and sex and sweet womanly things. With my arms around Calli, her warm body draped over mine, I feel better than I have in a long time, since before Seona and the accident. I'm starting to feel like myself again, only better. Calli gives me this feeling, and I never want to give it up.

I wish I could give her the same gift. One way or another, I know we will fall for each other. It's inevitable. Not because I'm an arrogant *bod ceann*, but because she suits me perfectly and I suit her too. We fit, like two pieces of a jigsaw puzzle.

A realization hits me so hard I almost gasp, but then it melts into something gentler and sweeter, and I realize the truth.

I am in love with Calli Douglas

Chapter Seventeen

I wake up the next morning in the best way possible—covered in warm, soft female bodies. Aye, more than one female. Of course, two of them have fur and tails, and they often drool. Sometime after midnight, the puppies had whined and pawed at the bedroom door, and I got up to let them in. Calli and I had forgotten about the poor pups after our "totally mind-blowing, earth-shattering sex," as she called it. I have to agree with that assessment. Last night was the best sexual experience I've ever had.

This morning, I lie beside Calli with one arm holding her against my body. Misty lies stretched across me with her back end between my legs and her head on my tummy. Mandy is curled up by my feet. Though I know Calli is awake, she seems unwilling to move yet, and I feel the same way. She has her head tucked into the hollow of my shoulder, and I can't help turning my head to feel her silky hair on my face.

Though I've been awake for a while, I've pretended to be sleeping just so I can keep enjoying this intimacy. But it's time to rise and shine so I can make love to her again. I pretend to stir, as if I've just woken up.

She tries to roll onto her back, away from me.

I pin her in place with one arm, and when she pushes against it, I tug her into my body more firmly.

"Morning," I murmur in a sleepy voice that is not an act. I do feel very relaxed, almost drowsy.

"Good morning. How are you?"

I chuckle. "In rude health. And you?"

She nudges me with her elbow. "Being held prisoner by a presumptuous Scotsman."

"Hmm." I clamp both arms around her. "Never had a captive woman before. It has interesting possibilities."

Our movements rouse Misty, who lets out a loud, high-pitched yawn and rolls onto her belly, her front paws on my chest. Her tail thumps on the bed, which awakens her sister. Mandy sits up and wags her tail. I hold on to Calli while both puppies spring up and hop around on the bed while making excited little growling and snuffling noises. They crash into Calli and me to lick and drool on any exposed body part they can reach.

Calli squeals when Misty jams her wet puppy nose into her mistress's ear and Mandy lays a sloppy kiss on Calli's lips. Spluttering, she tries to push the puppies away.

I surge out of bed and hook an arm around first one puppy, then the other. With a canine under each arm, I march out of the room and straight to the dog door, where I dump Misty and Mandy on the floor. They rocket out the door, making the plastic flap go *thwap-thwap-thwap*. Just as I return to the bedroom, Calli swings her legs over the bed's edge, about to get up.

Shutting the door, I stride back to the bed. My erection waves in front of my belly. Calli probably doesn't know about morning hard-ons. Should I explain? Or would that embarrass her? Considering her brazenness last night, I can't see how she could feel uncomfortable hearing about my *slat*, but it's hard to tell with Calli. I decide to play it safe. Instead of pouncing on her for another round of life-altering sex, I stroll to where my clothes lay heaped on the floor and pick up my jeans.

"Hey!" she complains. "You can't get dressed yet."

Fighting to repress a smile, I pause, with the jeans dangling from my hand. "Can't I?"

"No." She crosses her arms over her breasts, but I think that's feigned indignation. "I was expecting a night of hot, sweaty sex."

I swing the jeans from one finger. "We had hot, sweaty sex."

"Only once. You were supposed to have your way with me all night like a proper, wicked sex fiend. I got cheated."

As I toss the jeans aside, I lunge down to crouch before her and settle one hand on each of her knees. Then I give her a look of mock shame. "Please forgive me, my darling Calli. How could I have been so remiss in my seducer duties?"

Laughter bubbles out of her, and she lets her arms fall, her hands coming to rest on her thighs. "All joking aside, I was hoping for more than once."

"Didn't want to hurt you. This was your first time. Are you sore?"

"I'm fine."

I scan my gaze over her, but can't tell anything about her physical state. "I, ah…took you rather hard."

"Think I'm lying?"

"No…"

She clasps one of my hands in each of hers and guides them up the insides of her thighs. "Why don't you test me?"

Calli spreads her legs, moving my hands to her hips and scooting forward until her erse rests on the edge of the bed.

My gaze drops to the slick pink flesh between her thighs. I suck in a breath through my nostrils as my eyes drift partway closed. I allow myself five seconds to revel in the scent of her arousal. Then I open my eyes.

"*Bod an Donais,*" I hiss, nailing my gaze to hers. "You smell like sin, and I want to feast on you."

"Go right ahead."

My focus wanders back down to the hairs between her legs and the sweet cream that awaits me. My tongue pokes out between my lips while I imagine feasting on her again. "Love to, but Lachlan's ringing me in half an hour to talk about Jamie."

"We have time," she purrs, her tone sultrier than ever. "Aidan, I need you inside me. Fucking me like a demon."

I stare at her, wide-eyed. This woman surprises me at every turn, and I love it.

"Ahmno a demon," I say, as I rise up before her, my erection in her face. "But I can fuck ye like a man who hasnae had a woman in centuries. Will that do?"

"Yes-yes-yes."

I crawl onto the bed, moving behind her on all fours, and slide my legs around her on either side. I position my groin against her erse and my hard cock against her back. When I settle my hands on her thighs, she leans back into me. I plant my feet on the floor and ease one hand between her thighs. The second I dive my fingers between her wet folds, she moans.

"Thought you wanted to feast on me," she says, as her head lolls against my shoulder.

"Another time." I pet her folds, keeping my touch delicate. "Do ye trust me?"

"Completely."

I toy with her flesh with my fingers, gliding them around her outer folds and into the inner lips of her cleft. I stroke slowly up and down, and even when she writhes her hips in a desperate plea for more, I touch her everywhere except her *brillean*. I sink one finger inside her, then another, pushing them as deep as possible, coating my fingers with her wetness. The heel of my hand covers her mound, but I wriggle it until I have my palm pressed into her clit.

"Aidan," she moans.

"Shh," I whisper into her ear. "Let me take care of everything."

I rub my hand into her stiff clit with slow and rhythmic strokes while I withdraw my fingers and plunge inside her, repeating the motion as deliberately as I'm rubbing her. She grips my thighs, writhing against me, rolling her hips into my palm and my thrusting fingers. Her orgasm sweeps over her in lazy waves, her body squeezing and releasing my fingers over and over. She whimpers with every pulse of her release and keeps thrusting against my palm even when I slide my fingers free of her body.

I lean around her to retrieve a condom from the drawer, then pull away from her backside only enough that I can tear open the packet and cover myself. Once I've done that, I grasp her hips and hoist her up and onto my lap, impaling her on my cock.

"Oh," she gasps, like she's surprised by the sudden fullness of my *slat* buried to the hilt.

Christ, she feels good, like a hot, silky glove that conforms to my dick. I swear her body must've been made for me, the way every part of her fits every part of me so well.

I strap one arm over her belly and pitch backward, supported on my other arm. Then I start thrusting in smooth strokes that gradually escalate into a pounding rhythm. Her tits flail every time I punch into her with so much force her erse bounces up off my cock, and when she slams back down, my balls slap against her flesh. Every punishing thrust sets off another round of wet slapping as our bodies converge, separate, and converge again. Our fevered cries echo around us, and the musky scent of sex permeates the room.

She comes with an erratic scream, her body still bouncing on my cock.

I thrust one last time, letting out a hoarse bellow while my release barrels through me. Then I collapse backward onto the bed, taking her with me, my softening *slat* wedged inside her.

The sound of puppies barking at last penetrates the fog of our sexual fervor.

"Better see what's going on out there," she says between heaving breaths as she climbs off me.

I groan, sprawled on the bed.

She grins at me. "That's okay, you stay there."

"Thanks." I give her a lopsided smile. "Still feeling cheated?"

"Not in the least."

<h1 style="text-align:center">Chapter Eighteen</h1>

C alli comes back after checking on the puppies and informs me the furry lassies are barking at a squirrel in a tree. The squirrel fled, so now the puppies are quiet again. Not that they stay quiet for long. Misty and Mandy have more energy than any dogs I've met before. Sometimes I could use an injection of their energy.

The lustful American I slept with last night seems determined to exhaust me with her sexual appetites. Aye, it's a tough job, but I can handle it.

While Calli goes into the bathroom to take a shower, I settle onto the sofa to watch the puppies playing out in the yard. They have a stick, and they take turns trying to get the thing away from each other. That entertains me for a few minutes, then I decide to turn on the television and find something to watch. I try three different home improvement shows, but all the people on those shows do bloody stupid things. I guess a contractor shouldn't watch that rubbish. I'm not normally a couch potato, but I can't think of anything else to do until Calli comes out of the bathroom.

My mobile rings, and I see a familiar name on the caller ID. Lachlan is ringing me, right on schedule. I put him on speaker.

"Aidan, what trouble have you gotten into now?" he asks in his annoying big-brother voice, the one that always makes me feel like a wee laddie who got caught doing something naughty. "I had to hear it from Jamie that you've got a girl. When's the wedding, Don Juan?"

"Donnae be calling me that. And there's no wedding." Not yet, but I won't say that to Lachlan.

"If you promise never to call me *that* nickname again, I won't call you Don Juan."

"Sorry, that's a promise I can't keep. It's too much fun calling you Lachie."

"You and Jamie love tormenting the adults in the family."

His mention of our sister turns our conversation to the subject he'd wanted to discuss today—Jamie's barmy plan to find an American man. Lachlan points out that I had a similar plan to find a wife, but I reject the comparison. It's different when the person with the barmy idea is my baby sister. And aye, that makes me a hypocritical erse. Donnae care.

Lachlan pauses in the middle of our Jamie conversation, and he gets a serious tone in his voice when he speaks again. "How are you, Aidan, really?"

"Fine. I'm having a bloody fantastic holiday in Michigan."

"Glad to hear it. But your problems won't disappear because you had a good time. Your company is—"

"I know what's going on with my own company. Donnae need you to tell me about it." Is that me sounding grumpy? *Bod a' chac.* I'm turning into Rory. "Sorry, Lachie, but I don't want to think about that right now."

"You can't ignore it for much longer." Lachlan sighs in the exasperated way he loves to do whenever he talks to any of his siblings. "Let me help. I have more than enough money, and you could call it an investment or a grant if that will make you feel better."

The only way I will feel better about this conversation is if I hang up on Lachlan. I know he means well, but honestly, I'm not a bairn. I can deal with my problems on my own.

Probably.

But even if I sort out my company's problems and somehow resurrect the business, I still have the Seona issue.

I slouch into the sofa, twisting my mouth into a half frown, my gaze aimed in the general direction of the windows overlooking the backyard. Two blurry shapes that vaguely resemble puppies race back and forth across the lawn, slaloming around the cedar trees.

"Don't be stubborn, Aidan," Lachlan says.

I pinch the bridge of my nose with my thumb and forefinger, glancing down at my lap. "I do *not* want your money."

"You're skint," my brother helpfully points out as if I don't know that, "and we can help. There's no shame in letting your family lend a hand."

"It's not a hand," I grouse. "It's charity."

Out of the corner of my eye, I notice Calli skulking up behind me. She raises onto her toes and peeks over my shoulder. I'm sitting here with one ankle lodged on the opposite knee and my mobile balanced on that knee.

"Erica worries about you," Lachlan says, "and she won't give up until I convince you to take the bloody money."

"Cannae say no to your wife, Lachie?" I say with a cheeky tone in my voice as I shake my head at my brother, though he can't see it.

"I know what you're doing, Aidan. Calling me Lachie to fash me, hoping I'll give up. But you know how Erica is when she sets her mind to something."

"Aye, I know," I sigh. "But I've got my pride. No money, Lachlan."

Some kind of noise in the background of the call makes Lachlan grunt. "Erica says to tell you that you're a pigheaded goof, and when you're home she's going to—I'm not saying that, love."

The last bit was aimed at Erica, for sure. My brother doesn't call me "love."

"What are you not going to do, Lachie?" I ask, not even trying to erase the sarcasm from my voice.

He groans out a sigh. "She says she'll whoop your stubborn erse until it shines bright red like Rudolph's reindeer nose."

"Och," I say, chuckling. "I'm terrified. Never coming home now."

I turn my head slightly, arching one brow at Calli.

She winces, then bows her head to eye me from under her lashes. Her sheepish smile is adorable.

That's right. I caught her eavesdropping, and I'll need to think of the right way for her to atone for her behavior. Something that involves nudity.

Calli moves forward, bending down to rest her forearms on the sofa's back on either side of my head.

I slip a hand over one of hers, caressing her palm with my fingertips.

"You have to help me keep my wife satisfied," Lachlan says. "At least let us arrange a better car and hotel for you, and just a wee bit of cash to—"

"No." I slap my free hand on my thigh, but I only stay annoyed for a second or two, then I smirk. "It's not my fault you can't satisfy your wife."

"Aidan." Lachlan's stern tone doesn't convince me. He isn't fed up with me. He's just being bossy.

"Do I need to spell the word for you?" I ask. "N-O."

My neck has started to ache, and I suddenly realize I've hunched my shoulders. My mouth has flattened into a line, and the fingers of the hand on my thigh are bent like claws.

Calli leans in, trailing her fingers down my throat while she whispers into my ear. "Let's make out."

I fidget, casting her a sideways glance. The second she suggested we make out, my cock started to rouse. Not ideal for a phone conversation with my overbearing brother.

Lachlan keeps talking. "Say yes, Aidan, or I'll tell our mother to call you."

Does he think I'm a bairn? Ma doesn't intimidate me.

Calli takes my earlobe in her mouth, flicking her tongue over it.

I hiss in a breath.

She lays her palms over my collarbone and glides them down my chest toward my waistband. Her voice is barely a whisper. "Want to make out with me?"

I swivel my head toward her, our lips grazing each other. "Aye."

"Thank heavens," Lachlan says, with intense relief in his voice. "I'll take care of everything right away."

"What?" My head snaps to the front again, and my eyes go wide. I snatch the mobile from my knee. "No-no-no, I wasnae talking to you, Lachlan."

"Who were you talking to?"

My gaze darts to Calli, and I shake my head with mock chastisement. "I'm with a saucy wench who's trying to seduce me."

"Wench?" Lachlan says with amusement. "Have you become a pirate?"

"Go ravish your wife, Lachlan." I disconnect the call and toss my mobile on the table. Then I twist around to grab Calli by the waist and haul her onto my lap, where she lands sideways. Cupping her face in one hand, I pull her closer. "Now, about your offer to make out."

"Still open."

"Good." I move my hand to her nape, tipping her head back. "You tricked me into taking my brother's handout, which means you owe me."

"I wasn't trying to trick you. Just wanted a kiss."

"Mm." I brush my mouth over hers, and my lips vibrate against her flesh when I speak again. "You're wanting more than a kiss, aren't you?"

"Yes."

Before she can close her mouth, I seal mine over her lips and thrust my tongue inside for a deep, hot kiss.

When I give up her lips, her expression has turned soft and sensual. "Thought you were talking to Lachlan about your sister."

"We talked about her." I drag my tongue up her throat while I close my hand around her breast. "Are you sure you want my sister staying here?"

"If the alternative is you going back to Chicago, yes." She pushes a hand down between our bodies to rub my hardening *slat* through my jeans. "I want you here. Both in the sense of you staying in this house and in the sense of you taking me right here, right now."

"Let's wait a bit for that. I'll feel better when I'm sure you're not too sore."

"If that's what you really want." She clambers off my lap to sit beside me. "Sorry I inadvertently helped your brother get his way."

"Doesn't matter." I let my head fall back on the sofa, my hands slack at my sides. "Lachlan would've gotten his way, eventually."

"I can relate. Gavin is always positive he knows best when it comes to my life."

"Lachlan's the same." I drape an arm across her shoulders, and she cuddles into me. "My family thinks I'm incapable of taking care of myself."

"Your brother said you're skint. Are you unemployed?"

"I like to say I'm between opportunities." I almost smile, but it fades away. "Told you I had a construction company, but the business dried up and now it's gone. I'm bankrupt. My bank accounts are almost empty."

She twists her head around to look at me. "Aidan, I'm so sorry."

"Doesnae matter."

Calli rests a hand on my chest, over my heart. "Um, I hope you won't take this the wrong way…"

"Just say it." I let my hand fall over her shoulder. "Ahmno sensitive."

"Yes, I've noticed that." She hesitates, but then plows ahead. "I'm wondering why you're on the hunt for a wife, with the intention of starting a family, when you're bankrupt and unemployed. If you're looking for a rich woman who'll support you, I have to tell you I'm as poor as you are."

I stiffen, but keep my hand on her shoulder. "I am not looking for a rich woman. And I didnae plan anything. Acted on impulse is what I did." I clench my jaw, averting my eyes. "Begged Lachlan for a loan to finance my trip to America, but I wouldnae take more than I needed, and I insisted on staying at Erica's house in Chicago instead of a posh hotel. Had to give in a little, since Lachlan refused to help me at all unless I flew here in his jet. But I will pay him back for every penny I owe him."

"And I made sure you owe him even more, thanks to you accidentally agreeing to let him do more for you."

I tug her closer, sheltered under my arm. "I told you, Lachlan usually gets his way in the end. Being the oldest, he thinks it's his right and duty to shove his nose into the lives of every one of his brothers and sisters. And he's right, more often than not."

"He isn't one of those greedy people who won't help out their relatives."

"Definitely not. He loves spending money on us. You should've seen how much he spent getting Erica cleared of embezzling charges after her former lover set her up. Lachlan is the most generous person you'll ever meet—except for Rory. They're tied for the title."

She rests her chin on my shoulder. "You love your brothers, don't you?"

"Course I do. Love all my brothers and sisters." I kiss her forehead and tuck a lock of hair behind her ear. "I hope one day you'll tell me what's going on with you, why you're hiding in the woods."

"It's a very long, very tedious story."

"Doubt that." I whisk my hand up and down her arm in a gesture meant to comfort her, and she settles her head on my chest. I murmur, "Nothing about you is tedious."

"You either. But you have to take my word for it that you probably wouldn't like it if you knew everything about me."

I lean my head against hers, my breaths ruffling her hair. "No judgment from me. Made plenty of mistakes, some worse than others."

Silence falls between us for a moment. My curiosity keeps pestering me to ask her more questions, but I don't want to make her uncomfortable. She's convinced I won't want her anymore if she tells me all her secrets, but there's nothing that could ever make me walk away from her.

Calli lifts her head, and her lips curl into a sweet little smile. "Should we take a drive today? I can show you my favorite parts of the scenery."

"I'll go anywhere with you. Anywhere at all." I place a palm over her hand, on her lap, and thread my fingers through hers. "I'm easy to please."

Chapter Nineteen

An hour later, we're preparing to climb into Calli's car when the crunching of tires on gravel draws our attention to the long driveway, where it winds through the deep woods toward the house. The vehicle gradually comes into view as it passes through the deepest shadows and into a stretch of intermittent sunlight, then finally, into the full sun. A blond-haired bloke sits behind the wheel of the red sports car. He parks it alongside Calli's car, which she calls a beater. My hired car is stowed on the opposite side of her vehicle.

The blond bloke shuts off the car's engine, swings the door open, and hops out with a big smile on his face. He turns to me, offering his hand. "Mr. MacTaggart?"

I look at the lad warily, a wee bit confused, but I shake his hand anyway. "Aye, I'm Aidan MacTaggart. Who are you?"

"Billy, from the rental agency."

"From the what?"

"The car rental agency. Your brother called about getting you an upgrade."

"Upgrade?" My confusion crumbles away, replaced by the light of understanding. "Ah, Lachlan said he was going to get me a better car. I almost forgot."

And aye, I wish my brother had forgotten. Lachlan is going overboard again.

Billy hands me the keys to the cherry-red vehicle. "It's a convertible, by the way, perfect for beautiful summer days."

I accept the keys, but my gaze veers to Calli. "Mm, perfect for enjoying a beautiful lass on a beautiful summer day."

"Exactly," Billy says, seeming oblivious of the innuendo in my words.

No, I wasn't talking about making Calli laugh. I mean to shag her in the convertible.

I hook the key ring over my middle finger and flip the keys around it once, making them jangle. "Billy, how are you to get back to wherever you came from?"

"I'll take the other car. The one you rented yourself."

"Of course." I extract the keys to that vehicle from my pocket and toss them to Billy. "Do I tip you? I'm new to this country, and I don't know all the etiquette."

"No tip required, sir. Your brother took care of everything."

My mouth warps downward at one corner, half annoyance, half humor. "Naturally, he did. Lachlan takes care of everything for everyone, whether you want him to or not."

Calli slips her arm around mine, leaning into me. "Brothers. They can be presumptuous, but they do it out of love."

Billy glances back and forth between us, his brows furrowed. "Sure, I guess they do. I should get back to work. Have fun with the car."

The lad all but runs to the other hired car, apparently put off by our conversation. He must've been confused by our interactions, though he seemed oblivious to the innuendo dripping from every word I said to Calli. As the rejected vehicle roars off down the gravel drive, spewing dust and gravel in its wake, Calli rests her cheek on my upper arm and gazes up at me.

"So," she says, "shall we take your gift for a drive?"

"Yes." I straighten, rolling my shoulders back. "I planned to take you for a drive, and I intend to keep my word."

"Actually, it was my idea." She steps away from me to skirt around the front of the sports car, approaching the driver's side. "Cool, it's a Mustang."

"If Lachlan could've hired an Aston Martin, I'm sure he would have."

"Here in the U.P., you aren't likely to find a rentable luxury car, especially not one as expensive as an Aston Martin."

"Lachlan owns two of them." I pucker my mouth. "He keeps trying to give me one."

"Oh, don't be so petulant about it. Your brother's only trying to help." She walks back to me and loops her arms around my neck. "I think it's nice your rich brother wants to help out his family. In my experience, a lot of people who have money don't like to share it with anyone. Or if they do share, it comes with chains attached."

"Chains?" I crook a finger under her chin, tipping her head up until our gazes meet. "You say the oddest things at times. Have you known someone who—"

"Let's not talk about serious things." She tightens her arms around my neck, pulling her body snug against me so I feel her lush breasts crushed to my chest. "Let's take advantage of this wonderful summer's day."

"We will." I peel her hands away from my neck, clasping one of them as I lead her toward the Mustang's passenger door. Then I hold the door open while she climbs inside and settles into the plush leather seat.

She skims her hands over the upholstery. "Ooh, this is nice. I could get used to the high life."

I can't stop myself from frowning. "Guess Lachlan should be dating you."

Before she can respond, I slam the door shut and stalk around the front of the vehicle, hurling the driver's door open, and throw my body into the seat. I yank the door shut with a huff.

Am I being petulant? I suppose I am, but I have good reason. My brother can give his wife anything she wants, and I have nothing to offer Calli. Now Lachlan has paid for a much nicer car for me—and he's giving me money too, despite the fact I don't want his help.

"Oh come on," Calli says. "You have to get over this aversion to being pampered. Are you jealous of Lachlan? Because I'm here with you. I invited you to stay with me, not your brother. I'm sleeping with you, not your brother."

"If you met Lachlan, you'd probably prefer him. Or maybe Rory." I jam the key in the ignition, jerking it to start the engine. It grumbles to life.

And I feel like grumbling too. What an erse I've become.

"Is Rory well off too?" Calli asks. "Because if he is, I'm starting to see a definite pattern."

"He's got money. Not as much as Lachlan, but at least fifty-fold more than I've got." I shift the car into reverse, fling an arm over the back of her seat, and crane my neck to glance behind. "And of course there's a pattern. They're successful, and I'm a failure."

"That is not true."

I swerve the car backward in a semicircle, so fast she's thrown forward. Since she hasn't done up her seatbelt yet, she has to thrust her hands out to stop from crashing into the dashboard. She yelps.

And I hit the brakes hard, which flings her backward into her seat.

"Jesus Christ," Calli hisses, "if this is how you drive, you can forget me going anywhere with you."

I drop my face into my hands briefly, then look at her. "I'm sorry. That was childish and stupid, and I could've hurt you. It will never happen again."

"Damn straight it won't. If it does, I'm out of here, and you can sleep in this car."

"I'll be more careful, I swear it." I point at her lap. "But you should still do up your seatbelt."

"Oh, yeah." She secures the belt and rests her arm on the center console. "By the way, you are not a failure. Everybody has bad times, and that does not make you a failure in life in general."

I grunt, then shift the car into drive and ease it down the gravel road. Cannae believe I behaved that way, all because she asked if my brothers are rich. I'm skint, which she knows. Of course she didn't mean anything by her questions, but I seem to have developed a thin skin lately. My brothers might have more money than I can ever dream of having, but Calli is with me, not them. She wants me.

What am I complaining about? I have the perfect woman.

Sighing, I relax into driving and even manage a satisfied smile. "Where should we go?"

"What are you in the mood for? Secluded or crowded?"

"Secluded." I glance at her sideways, letting my smile heat up. "I have plans for you that might be illegal in public."

She sinks into her seat, her smile soft and warm and full of sensual promise. "Take a left at the end of the driveway. We're heading north, into the wilds."

Chapter Twenty

The Mustang hugs the asphalt as it flies up the winding, two-lane highway through the woods toward the summit of Brockway Mountain. Calli told me the name of the mountain. It's the highest point in Michigan, and I have to admit the view is magnificent. I'd rolled the top down so we could enjoy the scenery with a three-sixty panorama. I love the way the wind whips through Calli's hair and her lips curve into a relaxed smile like she's completely content. I keep my hand wrapped around hers on the center console, our fingers entwined, while I drive with one hand draped over the wheel. I feel relaxed and happy too, because I'm with her.

My outburst of bloody stupid macho rubbish didn't ruin our road trip. I'm grateful for that.

"There," I announce with great conviction, pointing at a turnout along the side of the highway. "We'll stop for a bit."

"Okay, but it's just a view of trees."

"It's secluded." I glance in the rearview mirror. "And we have no company at the moment."

Naturally, I want privacy so I can do wicked things to her. My idea of a road trip with Calli involves her screaming my name—and not because I'm rocketing down the road at ninety miles per hour. I haven't driven *that* fast.

The side mirror shows no cars behind us either. Perfect.

I slow the Mustang, pulling off into the turnout. It's a dirt patch situated at the edge of the mountainside, hemmed in by a wooden railing. I stand up and step out of the car over the top of the door, strictly to show off. Why not? I love making Calli smile.

She watches me stride around the front of the car to swing her door open. "You have something against using the driver's door?"

"With the top down, I don't need it."

"Uh-huh." She accepts the hand I hold out to her and lets me help her out of the vehicle. "I've never seen anyone get out of a car that way. Got to admit, it's kind of sexy."

"Kind of? Is that all?" I feign a scoff. "Must've done it wrong. You should've been weak with desire after witnessing my stunning display of masculine prowess."

She laughs and leans in, lifting onto her tiptoes to peck a kiss on my lips. "I was very impressed. Does that count?"

I pretend to consider her question. "I suppose I'll accept it."

The lass laughs again.

Folding my hand around hers, I shut the car door and guide her toward the railing. We admire the view for about a minute before I tell her, "Back to the car."

"Don't you want to absorb the scenery a little longer?"

"Ahmno interested in trees or water at the moment." I throw an arm around her waist, pulling her tight against my body, and dip my head close to hers. "I have other ideas."

I slide my hands down to cover her erse, massaging her flesh through her jeans, and I can tell it's arousing a fire deep inside her. Since meeting Calli, I've learned all her responses, from the way her eyes turn softer and darker to her habit of biting down on her lip when she wants me. I tug her forward and upward, pressing my erection into her groin. Her breaths quicken, and her gaze flies to my mouth as her tongue sneaks out to glide across her lower lip.

Aye, that's another sign of her lustful intentions. I've memorized that one too.

I growl low in my throat because this woman always makes me feel as randy and possessive as a wild beast. I grip her erse more firmly, sinking my fingers into her flesh.

She moves to kiss me.

Clucking my tongue, I pull my head back. "Not yet, my impatient angel. Ye cannae have me until I've had your pleasure."

The sweetest little irritated noise squeaks out of her. She flings her hands up to grasp my face, intent on dragging me in for a kiss.

I capture her wrists in my hands, shift them behind her back, and secure them there with one hand. My free hand I move in front of me, rushing it down between our bodies so I can cup her groin through her clothes, slid-ing my palm lower until the heel of my hand rests on her mound and my fingers stretch between her thighs. I can feel the heat of her arousal. She sucks in a sharp breath. While I rub my fingers up and down her cleft, she rocks her hips, silently urging me to rub harder and faster.

Chuckling, I stop moving my fingers. "Easy. No need to rush."

"Why the hell not?"

I graze my lips across her mouth, flicking my tongue out to tease the seam. Against her lips, I murmur, "I want to drive you wild until you beg me to take you. And you will, that's a promise."

I punctuate that promise by scraping my fingers up and down her cleft three times in rapid succession, though her jeans keep me from feeling her slickness. She whimpers, her knees wobbling like they might buckle. I release her wrists to clamp my arm around her back, pinning her to my body and trapping my hand over her groin. I rub and rub, fast and then slow, faster again until she clutches at my shoulders and throws her head back, abandoning herself to the pleasure. Her body tenses, and I know she's close to climax. But I don't want her to come just yet.

I remove my hand and step back, then grasp her hips to keep her from tumbling to the ground.

She gapes at me, panting so hard I doubt she can speak.

With my hands still on her hips, I rotate her toward the view and back her up toward the car. When her erse bumps the passenger door, I set her hands on top of it where the window would be if we didn't have the top down. "Hold on."

I kneel before her and rip the zipper of her jeans down to dive my fingers inside the waistband of her knickers. I yank both her jeans and her underwear down over her hips, all the way to her ankles. She gazes down at me with the bonniest expression of dazed lust, but my focus veers to the hairs between her thighs that glisten with hints of her wetness. I pick up one of her feet, moving it to the side, spreading her legs for me.

Calli follows my every movement while I part her slick folds with my fingers and blow on her flesh.

She whimpers and slumps against the car.

I thrust my tongue deep between her folds and drag it up toward her clit. Within millimeters of that hard nub, I withdraw my tongue.

Her head falls back. "Please, Aidan."

Bod an Donais, I want her right now, but I need to show her all the pleasure I can give her. It's never been this important to me before, and I know that's because she means more to me than any other lass. So, I skim my tongue along her outer folds—up one side, down the other—over and over until her knees start to tremble. Then I grip her hips to hold her up and roll my gaze up to hers. "Please what, *mo chridhe*?"

"Take me, Aidan, please."

I seal my mouth over her clit and suck hard.

Though I can't feel her orgasm, I know when it grips her. She goes rigid, breathless, and her knees buckle. Her body is held up solely by the car and my hands.

And my cock is throbbing.

I flip her around and lay her hands on top of the door again. "Are ye ready?"

She nods.

One more thing to do before I take her. I unzip my jeans and dig a condom out of my pocket, ripping the packet open, and roll it on. A relieved breath gusts out of me.

With both hands, I take hold of her hips again and tilt them up and back, all while kissing the tender skin of her neck. I plow into her in one long, powerful stroke. Then I freeze, clutching her to me.

"Okay?" I ask, my voice rougher than usual. Shagging Calli always does that to me.

"Uh-huh," she responds.

That's all I need to hear. I drive into her again and again while my cock plunging into her sheath creates a wet sucking sound and my *bagais* slap on her erse with every thrust. She throws her head back, her fingers clenched over the door frame. I grunt every time I push inside her, every movement growing harder and faster, and I lift her hips into my thrusts while my fingers dig into her flesh. I feel her body tightening around my cock, gripping me like a vise as she comes again. Her fingers grip the car so hard her knuckles turn white, and her body clutches me with the same desperate need that spurs her to scream my name and buck her hips up to take me deeper inside her.

Calli's cries echo off the trees.

I punch into her twice more until my release forces me to shout to the heavens, my entire body stiff as steel while my cock pulses. I relax gradually, breathing hard, loosening my fingers on her hips. Then I lean forward to seal my mouth over her ear. "Now that's how to enjoy the scenery."

"The scenery?" she says breathlessly. "All you saw was my ass."

"And your sweet, pink flesh."

I tug her underwear and jeans back into place, zipping them up. Then I do up my own jeans.

She staggers in her attempt to turn toward me.

I scoop her up and deposit her in the passenger seat without bothering to open the door. After hooking her seatbelt over her, I march around to the driver's side and vault over the door to land in my seat. With a flick of my wrist, I turn the key in the ignition, then I navigate the car back onto the road.

"You really are sex incarnate," she says.

"I'm what?" I ask, with a hitch of laughter in my voice.

"When we first met, I decided you were sex incarnate. You radiate sensuality like it's a part of your essence."

I cast her a sidelong look, my brows raised. "I've never been called sex incarnate before."

"Never? Haven't you done this sort of thing before? To other women, I mean."

"No. Only you."

I focus on the road now as we rush down the two-lane highway again, heading for the summit of Brockway Mountain. Sex incarnate? I love that Calli is the kind of clever woman who thinks of things like that, and I love that she sees me that way. She is sex incarnate too. Her passion surprises me again and again.

With my eyes hidden behind my sunglasses, I peek sideways at Calli. Her hair is whipping around her face while she wears the bonniest look of contentment.

She sneaks a hand out to squeeze my thigh.

I smile but keep my focus on the road as I steer the Mustang around a sharp curve. Aye, her passion knows no bounds. Maybe that's why I've fallen in love with her, because she's more like me than either of us could've guessed she would be.

Well, I've heard the myth of the sexy librarian. But now I've met one—met, kissed, and shagged.

She rakes her nails up and down my thigh until I lay a hand over hers to halt her movements. "Which part have you done only with me?"

"Most everything I've done with you is new for me."

"Why are you different with me than with those seven other women?"

"Because *you* are different. It was always casual before, but this time I want it to be more." I curl my fingers around hers on my thigh. "I want everything with you."

"You know I can't give you what you want."

"I know you think you can't—or think you don't want to." I lift her hand to my lips and pepper kisses over her knuckles. "We could be happy together, I know we can. Please let yourself think about the possibility, instead of dismissing it out of hand."

Pulling in a deep breath, she exhales it slowly. "I'll consider your request."

"That's all I ask."

I set her hand on her leg and return both of mine to the steering wheel.

Peripherally, I see her gazing at me with a dreamy smile on her lips, like she's more content than ever before. She deserves happiness, and I want to be the one to give it to her if she'll let me.

But I don't know if she will, unless I can convince her to share all her secrets with me.

I spend three days on the road with Calli, letting her choose the destinations because she knows this area much better than I do. I'm a tourist. She lives here. I couldn't have asked for a better, or sexier, tour guide than Calli Douglas. Every evening, we return to her house for dinner and rest.

Twice during our adventures, Seona calls to harass me about why I haven't sent her any money yet. Twice I tell her to sod off, though not in those exact words. I still can't make myself speak to a woman that way, even when the woman in question is acting like a harpy.

I know I'm at least partly to blame for her problems, but I have no money to give her. Christ, I'd borrowed money from Lachlan to pay for my holiday in America. I am bankrupt. Seona will need to find another way to get what she wants. After every brief conversation with Seona, I feel uneasy and on edge, though I try not to let Calli see it. She probably notices anyway. The lass is very clever and perceptive.

Our road trips take us to waterfalls, inland lakes, state parks, Lake Superior beaches, historic copper mines, and wee museums that celebrate the rich history of this region. Every morning before we leave the house, she spends an hour sitting at her desk in the corner of the living room, doing something on her computer. I want to know what she's doing, but I decide it's best not to question her right now.

Aye, I'm a coward who's afraid of what she might say.

During our outings, I find every secluded place where I can shag Calli. We do more than have sex, though. We laugh and explore and have a bloody good time. When we had reached the summit of Brockway Mountain on our inaugural day trip, I'd marveled at the panoramic view of the tip of the Keweenaw

Peninsula. Lake Superior stretched along one side of the view, while a shuttered gift shop behind us gave the location a rather melancholy air. Still, Calli smiled as she pointed out every item of interest, from ore boats on the lake to bald eagles soaring above our heads.

Leaning against the concrete wall at the cliff's edge, I had informed her, "This view is nice, but it can't compare to seeing Loch Leven from the top of Beinn a' Bheithir."

"You're not speaking American, are you?"

I winked and grinned. "Gaelic. It's the name of a mountain near Ballachulish."

"Do you climb mountains?"

"No, I—" A memory crashed through my mind, of falling rocks and screams and jumbled limbs. I turned my face away from Calli, swallowing hard. "Not anymore."

She lifted my hand to settle my arm over her shoulders. Tucked against my body, she slipped her arms around me. "I didn't mean to bring up bad memories."

"Not your fault." I wrapped my arms around her, burrowing my face into her hair, drawing in a long breath to inhale the sweet, soothing scent of her. "Why marry a man you didn't love?"

"Why does Seona expect you to pay her off?" When I said nothing, she tilted her head up to look at me. "See, we both have secrets. I don't expect you to tell me all of yours."

"And I'd be a hypocrite if I expected you to answer my question. You're right. No more questions about your marriage." But I wanted to know so badly it made me anxious. Instead of demanding an answer, I kissed the top of her head and smiled. "Why don't we get back to our drive?"

After that, we avoided talking about our personal issues. Instead, we focused on enjoying our sightseeing tour.

On the morning after our last day of road trips, I walk out of the bathroom and into the living room, where Calli sits at her desk typing furiously on the keyboard. She's so focused on her task that her tongue pokes out between her lips in the way I've come to recognize as Calli Douglas deep in thought. She is absolutely adorable.

And of course, I want to shag her. Right now. On that desk.

Maybe I want to shag her every time I see her, but that's beside the point. Her concentration makes me want her even more. Considering how deeply she's focused on whatever she's doing on the computer, I can't resist giving her a wee surprise.

I sneak up behind her chair and bend over to place my head alongside hers. "What are you doing?"

She yelps and jerks, twisting her head around to look at me.

Aye, I love teasing her—and surprising her.

"Don't sneak up on me," she says, and lightly slaps my arm. "You scared me half to death."

"At least it was only halfway."

"Not funny." She grumbles out a sigh. "Why are you spying on me?"

"You seemed absorbed by whatever you're doing."

"And scaring the shit out of me sounded like a good plan?"

"Didn't mean to frighten you." Surprise her, yes. Terrify her, no. I did too good a job of it, I guess.

She swivels her chair sideways to the desk, laying one arm on the desktop.

I stay right here, bent at the waist, my face a foot from hers. I might also be giving her a wry smile. "You can tell me. Whatever it is. I'm good at keeping secrets."

She gazes at me with her eyes wider than usual, though not enormously wide. For a moment, neither of us says anything. The silence goes on for so long that I can't stay quiet anymore, especially when she bites her lip. I place the pad of my thumb on her lower lip and press down. Her lip pops free of her teeth.

She sits up straighter, clearing her throat.

"Don't be anxious," I say. "I won't think less of you, no matter what it is."

Calli glances at the computer, clicks a mouse button to bring up a website, and faces me. As she drums her fingernails on the desktop, she bites her lip again. I reach out to touch her mouth like I had before, but she releases her lip a second before my thumb would've touched her.

I withdraw my hand.

She groans in resignation. "I've been looking for a job. I'm unemployed and have been for months. My savings will run out very soon, and I have zero prospects for employment."

"That's your shameful secret?"

"It's not a secret. I hadn't gotten around to telling you is all. 'I'm an unemployed pauper' isn't something I tell everyone I meet."

"You don't need to be ashamed of having no money."

"I'm not ashamed of being poor. Not being able to find a job, that's another thing altogether." She drums her fingers on the desk. "I have a master's degree in library science, but I've never had a job that required it, even when I worked in a library. Today, I'm considering a part-time secretarial position in Alaska. It's nobody's fault, but it sucks and it's demoralizing. Not the kind of thing I'm dying to share with the world."

I drop into a crouch beside her. "I know how you feel."

"Guess you do."

"Why not ask your family for help? Surely, they'd be glad to step in."

"The man who balked at accepting his brother's help is encouraging me to accept the aid of my family."

"I'm twice a hypocrite, eh?" I shrug and sigh. "Donnae mean to be. But you did trick me into taking Lachlan's charity, so…"

"I owe you a personal humiliation of my own?" She puckers her lips, struggling not to smile. "We sure have a strange relationship, don't we?"

"But it works for us, doesn't it?"

"Suppose it does."

I stare at her for a few seconds, feeling rightfully stunned by what she just said. "You called this a relationship."

"No, I—I meant in the general sense, not like we're *in* a relationship."

"Ah, of course." My gaze flicks to the computer screen and back to her. "The job search seems to be making you tense."

"Duh."

I rest a palm on her thigh, skating it up to her hip. "I can ease that tension and make you very relaxed."

"Um… Thanks, but I need to focus on my job search right now. I can't keep living here past next month unless I find work. You'd be better off hunting for a financially solvent American girl."

"Don't care about money." I move my hand to her inner thigh. "I'm bankrupt, remember? We have more in common than I knew."

"Oh great. Two broke people." She clasps a hand at her nape, almost wincing. "Listen, can this stay off the MacTaggart grapevine for the time being?"

"I won't tell. You can trust me."

"You know I do."

I lean in, my face near hers, close enough that I could kiss her with the slightest movement. "My offer to distract you is an open one. Take me up on it anytime."

"Maybe later."

"Aye, later. I'm always ready for you."

"Likewise."

I trace a fingertip down her jaw. "Feel free to sneak into my room in the dead of night."

"Since you've been sleeping in my bed, that's pretty much a certainty."

"Tonight, I'll sleep in the guest room." I skim a fingertip across her lips. "Just so you can sneak in and crawl under the sheets with me. We've never made love in the dark."

Her breasts rise and fall as she begins to breathe more heavily, and her lips turn a deeper shade of rose.

"You like the idea," I say.

She sinks into her chair. "Oh yeah, I really do."

"Then I'll be waiting for you tonight." I skate my lips over hers and straighten. "I'm having a shower. Care to join me?"

She squirms in her chair. "Not this time."

"My sister's coming tomorrow, so this may be our last chance to rattle the house."

"As much as I'd love that, I can't. Gotta continue the fruitless job search."

"You'll find something, eventually." I kiss the top of her head. "I believe in you."

"Thanks."

I head for the bathroom. Just as I shut the door behind me, I hear the doorbell ring in the living room. Maybe it's another extravagant gift from Lachlan, delivered by someone he lavished with money to make sure they would bring the whatever-it-is right away.

While I shower, I think about Calli—but not in an erotic way. I think about her reaction when I said I believe in her. She'd seemed surprised and almost embarrassed. I gather no one gives her compliments like that, certainly not the men she's known. Since she's trapped in a marriage she doesn't want, I wonder if she's dated anyone in the past five years.

She gave her virginity to me. That must mean something. And she called this a relationship.

Aye, she just might be falling for me the way I've done for her.

Chapter Twenty-Two

After my shower, I intend to head back into the living room. But the second I open the bathroom door, two furry wee bodies fly at me. I kneel to babble nonsense to them, ruffle their hair, and let them lick my face. It's hard to stop these two from licking every inch of visible skin or shoving their noses into my erse—when I'm wearing clothes. Even I'm not daft enough to let a dog do that when I'm naked. I don't mind their enthusiasm. They're sweet pups, though not as sweet as their mistress.

I bet Lachlan and Rory would never let puppies jam their noses into their erses. Can't picture Rory letting a dog lick his face either, or even his hand. Not that he hates animals. He just isn't the sort to get within licking distance of a puppy. Maybe he was different as a laddie, but considering our eleven-year age difference, we weren't exactly best mates—and he was out of the house and at university before I turned eight.

Once I've satisfied the furry lassies, I make my way toward the living room and the human lass I want to satisfy in a different way. That's why I've put on my jeans but not a shirt, not yet. I'm also holding a towel in one hand because I didn't finish drying myself off. I want to see that lustful look on Calli's face when she sees me half-dressed and still somewhat wet.

Halfway down the hall, I pause.

Calli is talking to a man I've never seen before. She snags his arm and tries to pull him toward the front door, but he resists, his expression full of granite-hard stubbornness.

"Please," she says, "let's go outside and talk. It's a beautiful day."

His gaze narrows on her. "What don't you want me to see?"

Could this be her brother? The overbearing one? That would explain their behavior toward each other. It reminds me of Lachlan and Rory when one of our sisters does something they disapprove of and refuses to see it their way.

I, of course, never behave like that. A perfect angel, that's me.

The time has come to let Calli and her brother know I'm here. Maybe I could be more subtle about it, but that's not my style. I saunter out of the hallway, holding my towel in one hand.

When Calli sees me, she clamps her lips between her teeth and winces.

Oh aye, the stranger must be her brother.

The man turns around, coming face to face with me, though we stand several arm's lengths apart. His gaze is flinty, and his eyes narrow to slits as he zeroes in on me. If he means to intimidate me, he will fail. If I can withstand Rory's steely glare, I can handle this bloke and whatever expressions he wants to throw at me. His fingers tense and curl toward his palms, just enough to convey his desire to throttle someone. Probably me. Or maybe Calli.

He must know about us.

"Hello," I say, giving the man a friendly, wide smile. I'm not pretending. I do want to be friendly with the brother of the woman I plan to marry.

The man clenches his jaw. His gaze darts from me to Calli.

I lift my towel to scrub my head with it. I swear this is not an act. I honestly am not intimidated by Calli's brother.

The bloke lodges his hands on his hips. "Who the hell are you?"

"Aidan MacTaggart." I move closer to him and hold out a hand. "And you are?"

He glances at my hand, his lip curling a wee bit. "I'm the Marine who's about to kick your ass from here to Mexico."

Calli stomps between the two of us and rounds on her brother. "Stop acting like a caveman. Aidan is not the enemy, and I can take care of myself, thank you very much." She leans toward him and whispers, "Remember who took care of you after Mom and Dad died."

She must've meant for that to be heard only by him, but I heard it too. Since Calli had told me about her brother's breakdown after their parents died, I don't know why she feels the need to whisper about it. Well, I suppose she doesn't want her brother to know I know.

The anger evacuates his body. He pinches his forehead with his thumb and forefinger, sighing as if the weight of the world resides on his shoulders alone.

"Should I leave?" I ask, running a hand through my hair to comb it out. "Seems like the two of you have things to discuss."

"You don't have to leave," Calli says, casting me an over-the-shoulder glance. "This is my brother, Gavin."

I smile again, gazing at Gavin with curiosity. "Your brother? That does explain it."

"Explain what?" Gavin asks.

"Why you're concerned about her welfare. I have three sisters, and I wouldn't like to find a man I'd never met staying in any of their homes. Especially not my younger sister."

Gavin's face goes blank. He doesn't move or speak for a moment. Then one side of his mouth ticks up as he looks at me. "Maybe I should go move in with your little sister."

"You could try," I say, "but Jamie lives with my older brother Rory at the moment. He's not as friendly as I am."

Grasping the back of his neck, Gavin frowns. "I still don't like this, but...Calli's an adult. She can do what she wants."

I gather they had a lengthy conversation about the topic of me before I got out of the shower.

Gavin takes a step toward me, bypassing his sister, and offers me his hand. "Might as well make peace, huh?"

"Aye." I shake his hand.

"Just so you know," Gavin says, "I was in the Marines, and I served in Afghanistan. Not only could I kill you with my bare hands, but my buddies from the Corps would help me dispose of your body so no one will ever find it."

"I don't doubt it." I sling the towel over one shoulder. "I would never hurt Calli or let anyone else hurt her."

"Damn straight. If she gets hurt, I'll hunt you down and take you out."

"You could try."

Gavin stares at me for a long moment, then slaps my shoulder. Hard. "I think we understand each other, don't we?"

He and Rory would get on well, I think. They both like to threaten violence and potential murder to cow the men their sisters want to date. So aye, I'm used to that sort of rubbish.

Calli waves her arms as if to get our attention. "Your bromance has begun, congratulations. Should I leave you two alone?"

Gavin's mouth twists into an exasperated expression. "Real funny, see. But you and me still need to have a serious conversation."

"There's nothing to say. Aidan's staying here, you don't like it, I don't care, end of discussion."

Did he say "see" or was he calling her "C" as an abbreviation of her first name? I think he meant it that way, since the word see didn't fit with what he said.

I start for the hall, tiptoeing away to give them privacy.

"Where are you going?" Calli asks.

Gavin snorts. "I hope he's going to put on a shirt."

Calli covers her face with her hands.

Aye, overbearing big brothers can make any of us drop our heads into our hands in resignation.

I return to the guest room and shut the door, then finish getting dressed.

Just as I'm walking out of my room, I hear Gavin tell Calli, "Going to get my stuff. Back in a tick."

His stuff? Is he staying here with Calli and me? That would mean I have to move into her room since Jamie arrives tomorrow. Maybe I won't mind so much if Gavin wants to stay here.

I can handle Calli's hostile brother, but I know she will be panicking, at least on the inside.

The door has just clicked shut behind Gavin when I reach Calli. Her shoulders slump. When she sees me, the rest of her body slumps too.

I nod toward the door. "Gavin is staying, I gather."

"Yes." She almost moans that word, though not in a sexy way. "This could be a huge disaster."

"No, it'll be fine." I hook an arm around her shoulders and give her a gentle squeeze. "I'm used to bossy older brothers. And I donnae mind at all sharing a room with you. We've been doing that anyway, unofficially."

"Gavin is staying in the hunting shack that's about two hundred feet away from the house."

"And you want me to stay in the guest room." And tomorrow, I'll be sleeping on the sofa.

"Yes, please. This is complicated enough without Gavin figuring out we're sleeping together."

I try very hard not to smirk. "Think he's already figured that out, *leannan*. I did walk out of the bathroom wearing only jeans. Even the most thickheaded eejit would understand the situation."

"Oh great," she whines, though it's partly sarcastic. "How do you prepare for thermonuclear disaster?"

Giving her another light squeeze, I kiss the top of her head. "Relax, Calli. This won't be as bad as you think. I'm quite charming, you know, so I should have your brother eating out of my palm in no time."

"Gnawing on your carcass is more like it."

The front door swings open, and Gavin lugs his bags over the threshold, halting when he sees us.

I still have my arm around Calli.

She warps her entire face into a pained expression.

And I squeeze her again.

Gavin drops his bags on the floor and kicks the door shut. "What the hell are you doing with my sister?"

"We're dating. Haven't you heard of that? It's when two people—"

"I know what dating is. But C never mentioned you, which makes me wonder what's really going on here."

Calli makes no move to pull away from me.

I lift one brow at Gavin. "Your sister is very important to me. That's all you need to know because the rest is private, between me and Calli."

"Uh-huh."

Though he's glaring at me, his attitude doesn't fash me at all. I should introduce Gavin to Rory. Watching one overbearing man glare at another who's just as overbearing might be entertaining. Maybe they'd thrash each other with cabers.

Aye, Rory can pull out the one that's wedged up his erse and batter Gavin with it.

Calli finally wriggles out of my embrace and waves for Gavin to follow her. "I'll show you to the hunting shack. If you're sure you want to stay out there with no electricity."

"After a tour in Afghanistan, I think I can handle living in a shack in the woods."

Calli flashes me a apologetic look as she leads her brother out the sliding glass doors.

Well, at least I won't have Gavin glowering at me every time I walk out of his sister's bedroom after we've had a poke.

Chapter Twenty-Three

I wake up the next morning in the best way possible, with Calli's warm, supple body molded to mine and her erse tucked against me. She's lying on her side, facing away from me, and I've got one arm draped over her hips. Aye, the lass had sneaked into my bed last night—but only to sleep nestled in my arms while wearing a satin nightie. The slippery fabric feels good brushing against my skin, but not as good as her nude body would feel. I slept naked, of course. Always do. I informed Calli of that fact when she asked if I'd really expected us to have sex after spending the whole day with Gavin.

"Sleep naked every night," I'd mumbled. "Not trying to have a poke at ye."

"Is 'poke' a strange Scottish term for sex?"

I'd mumbled again, but produced no meaningful words.

Gavin and I had circled each other all day, taking each other's measure in hopes of winning the argument about our opposing ideas of what Calli should do. I advocated for letting her decide for herself, but Gavin insisted he knew what was best for his sister. We did reach a kind of truce, I think, though we are in no danger of becoming best mates. I cannae understand why some blokes insist on butting into the lives of their siblings.

At one point, late in the evening, Gavin had even made jokes at my expense the way tough men like to do, which Calli insisted meant he'd accepted me provisionally. By that time, we were all too jeeked to keep up the odd bonding rituals. Luckily, Gavin retreated to the hunting shack, though not before commenting that he was within earshot of the house.

Donnae care if he hears me shagging his sister. We're both adults.

I had worked hard to make Calli's brother feel better about our living situation, and I think it worked. Despite the rocky start to our acquaintance, things have thawed a bit, and I know Calli is glad for that.

Lying here with Calli tucked against me, I feel so relaxed and content that I fall back asleep.

The bed jostles a touch just as I'm drifting off.

Has Calli gotten out of bed? I was hoping to make love to her before we faced the big-brother inquisition again.

Sometime later, I rouse because the bed has begun to rock like a boat on rough seas. The mattress bounces, and I hear panting and chuffing noises. Peeling my lids apart, I look into the eyes of a grinning puppy. Before I'm awake enough to stop her, Misty slavers a sloppy kiss over my mouth. Spluttering, I push up into a sitting position.

Mandy leaps on me, planting her front paws on my shoulders to get close enough to give me a puppy kiss. Fortunately, I see it coming this time and block her with one raised hand. The furry lassies bark and jump around, rocking the bed again.

What else can I do? Saying no to adoring females has never been my forte. So I pull them both against me, one puppy under each arm, and babble to them while rubbing their chests.

After a few minutes, I crawl off the bed and get dressed, choosing khaki trousers and a blue button-down shirt. Though I donnae care what Gavin thinks of me, I'm trying to make a better impression on him, for Calli's sake. Walking into the living room while half-naked and wet wasn't the best way to introduce myself.

Halfway down the hall, I'm waylaid by the puppies again and kneel to scratch behind their ears. I don't mean to eavesdrop, but it's hard not to hear the voices coming from the other side of the living room, where the bar separates it from the kitchen. Calli stands in front of Gavin, who sits on a stool.

"Yep," Gavin says in a knowing tone, "that's right. You moon over him, and I'm guessing you don't even realize you're doing it. Man, you've got it bad, don't you?"

Calli has it bad for who? Me, I assume. Though I love the idea that she might "moon" over me, I doubt she appreciates her brother's comment.

She clamps her lips between her teeth and shifts her gaze to the kitchen cabinets.

Gavin laughs softly, not mocking his sister, just expressing a growing understanding of the situation. "At least promise me if you marry him, you won't move to Scotland."

Her attention snaps back to her brother. "I'm not marrying Aidan."

A knot tightens in my gut when I hear her say that. Does she have to sound so positive it will never happen?

"No?" Gavin says. "You say that like there's no way in hell you'd even consider it. You always wanted to get married. I remember you acting out fake weddings between your Barbie and Ken dolls."

"That was a long time ago."

"What's happened to you, C?"

I've wondered the same thing ever since I met Calli. I know her anxieties revolve around her husband, but there's more to it. I'm sure of that.

"Whatever's going on with you," Gavin says, "you can tell me."

She opens her mouth, clearly about to speak, though I recognize the panicked look in her eyes.

And I decide to rescue the lass from a conversation that's fashing her.

I amble into the living room, straight to the bar.

Gavin smirks at his sister, probably because she's gazing at me with an expression that I can best describe as "moony." I've never used that word before, but it seems appropriate now.

"Good morning," I say, smiling at Calli's brother. "Are you joining us for breakfast, Gavin?"

"Sure," he says while still smirking. "You guys must be starving after all that…driving."

Calli shoots her brother a sharp look.

I had told Gavin about our road trips yesterday, but he must've guessed our activities involved more than sightseeing. Hardly difficult to suss that out, given the way Calli looks at me. I must look at her the same way.

Gavin's lips warp as he struggles not to laugh.

"Better have a quick breakfast," Calli says. "We have to pick Jamie up at the airport."

Mhac na galla. I'd almost forgotten about Jamie.

Gavin and I begin discussing breakfast options while Calli heads for her bedroom to get dressed. Gavin isn't such a bad bloke once he eases up on the deadly Marine thing. I understand a man feeling protective of his baby sister, but there is nothing Gavin could do that would make me walk away from Calli.

She might be afraid to marry me—and she technically can't, not yet—but Gavin is right about one thing. She can't hide her affection and desire for me. It shows on her face every time we look at each other, and I'm sure my feelings for her are obvious too.

What will happen once Jamie gets here? Will she approve of Calli? I hope she gives up the idea of landing an American man.

My gaze shifts to Gavin, where he's standing at the stovetop, about to start making breakfast. He is American. I suppose women find him attractive, and some might even like his hard-as-nails attitude. But no, Jamie won't set her sights on him. He is not the sort of man she likes. Is he? Not sure I know enough about my sister's preferences to say for sure. What if she does like Gavin?

She won't. They're strangers. I'm being paranoid, that's all.

But Calli and I were strangers on the night we met, when we kissed and came very close to shagging right there in that velvet-covered booth.

What if Jamie and Gavin…

No, that will never happen.

Chapter Twenty-Four

I throw the front door open, and my sister tumbles into the house while oohing and ahhing as she spins in circles, traveling across the floor without paying any heed to the obstacles in her path. That's Jamie. Carefree and impetuous, which means she's nothing like me. No, nothing at all. When she veers toward the end table, I take hold of her shoulders to bring her to a stop. Her long, golden-brown hair falls over her shoulders.

All right, maybe Jamie and I do share a few traits in common. But I'm much more mature and levelheaded than she is. It's not like I waltzed into an underground club and followed a lass I didn't know, one who asked me if I wore a G-string under my kilt.

Christ, I hope Jamie doesn't do anything like that.

With her mouth open and her hazel eyes wide, she speaks in a hushed voice. "This is beautiful. Can't believe I'm in America. I want to see it all, every bit of it."

"Easy," I say, trying to sound tolerant, but I can't help feeling slightly amused too. "You just arrived, Jamie. Give yourself time to adjust to the jet lag."

"But I want to see everything." She spins again while the sunshine streaming through the windows flashes over her.

Maybe I'd expected Jamie to be nervous about her first trip to America, but she has dived in with all the enthusiasm of a lass having a great adventure.

An explosive thwap announces the arrival of Mandy and Misty, who rush at my sister. Misty slaps her big paws on Jamie's tummy, struggling to stretch up tall enough to slather wet kisses on her face but unable to reach that far. Meanwhile, Mandy licks Jamie's ankles, bared by her sandals and knee-length skirt.

My sister giggles. "That tickles."

Calli moves to shoo the puppies away, but Jamie shakes her head.

"Don't worry," she says, "I love animals. Dogs are my favorite."

She kneels to let the furry lassies maul her with their tongues and climb all over her.

Then Gavin enters the house through the sliding glass doors at the back. He halts a few feet inside, watching the spectacle taking place on the floor with a bewildered expression.

Calli seems amused by the situation, but she's not as happy as she was earlier. Someone had rung her while we were at the airport waiting for Jamie's luggage. Calli stepped away from us to take her call in private, but her body language and facial expressions had told me everything I needed to know. It must've been her husband, the *bod ceann* who refuses to give her a divorce. She had said something to him, then placed a palm on her forehead while she squinted her eyes. After another exchange with the bastard, she pulled the phone away from her ear and frowned at it, then stuffed the device into her purse.

I'd wanted to ask her what was wrong, but it isn't my place. Not yet.

"You can love me more later," Jamie tells the puppies. She straightens, smoothing out her skirt, and turns toward Gavin. "You must be Calli's brother. I'm Jamie, Aidan's sister."

The second Gavin lays eyes on my sister, he grins like a bloody moron and hustles over to shake Jamie's hand. "Hey. Nice to, uh, meet you. I'm Gavin. Douglas. Calli's brother, Gavin Douglas."

As much as I don't like him mooning at my sister, I do sort of enjoy knowing he's not immune to the charms of a bonnie lass.

Calli smiles with her lips sealed, seeming quite pleased with this turn of events. I think she's probably plotting all the ways she can rub this in Gavin's face.

Jamie's cheeks dimple, and she giggles again. "Nice to meet you too, Gavin."

Suddenly, I'm afflicted with a powerful need to keep my sister away from Calli's brother. He's eight years older than she is, which means he's seven years older than Jamie. Do I want him seducing my baby sister? No, never in a thousand years.

Aye, I'm a hypocrite. So what?

I grasp Jamie's wrist and tug her hand free of Gavin's. "Let me show you to your room."

Though she allows me to haul her out of the living room, she glances back to smile at Gavin, who grins at her like a numpty.

When Jamie and I emerge from the guest bedroom, returning to the living room, Gavin is gone. I have no illusions that he's flown back to wherever he lives, but at least his hunting shack is separated from the house. I feel like battering someone or breaking a piece of furniture, but Jamie seems quite cheerful and pleased with herself.

"Sooo," Jamie coos, "we should get to know each other, Calli. Since you're going to be my sister-in-law."

I raise my hands, mouth open, and shake my head at Calli. "Didnae say a word to her."

Jamie studies us both with her lips quirked. "Didnae have to, Aidan. I have eyes, and I'm not an eejit. Besides, you told everyone you were coming to America to find a wife like Lachlan did."

Since I can't think of a bloody thing to say, I aim a pleading look at Calli. As if she can save me from my sister's nosiness.

Calli takes pity on me and refrains from telling my sister she insists she'll never marry me. Instead, she tells Jamie, "It's a bit early to think about that."

"Aye," Jamie agrees, "but Aidan has a way of convincing women to do almost anything."

"Does he now." Calli arches her brows at me.

I hike up my shoulders, showing her my palms. We both know I've already convinced Calli to do a lot of things she swore she'd never do, like sleeping with me. But I donnae like hearing my sister announce I do that. What if Calli decides I'm a Don Juan again?

"Where's Gavin?" Jamie asks, glancing around as if he might be hiding behind the bar.

"He's staying in the hunting cabin out in the woods," Calli says. "We'll see him again at lunch."

Does Jamie seem disappointed by the news? My need to beat something or someone to a pulp returns, but I try to stay calm.

"Mind if I have a shower?" Jamie asks. "Airline travel makes me feel grimy."

"Go right ahead," Calli says, gesturing toward the hallway. "Bathroom's on the left."

"I know, Aidan showed me." She starts to turn away, then looks at Calli. "Thank you for letting me stay here."

"No problem."

Jamie disappears down the hall.

When the bathroom door clicks shut, I approach Calli and slip my hand into hers as we face each other. She laces her fingers with mine, and I feel myself relaxing because of her touch. For a moment, I just gaze into her eyes, wondering if she will ever admit she wants to be with me as much as I want to be with her. Maybe when pigs fly.

I should go buy a herd of the beggars and install them in the backyard, then glue wings to their backs. Aye, because pushing Calli to love me won't backfire at all.

Giving up on my musings, I sigh. "Quite a full house, eh?"

"Definitely." She tips toward me a wee bit. "Your sister and my brother seem rather smitten with each other."

"I'd like to tell Gavin to stay away from my sister, but I suppose that would be, ah…"

"Hypocritical?"

"Yes."

She rises onto her tiptoes to peck a kiss on my lips. "You MacTaggarts are a gorgeous bunch. Can't blame us mere mortals for falling to our knees before you."

"You haven't gone on your knees before me." I slide my free hand around to the small of her back, tugging her into my body. "But it's an intriguing idea."

Calli flattens her palm on my chest and gazes into my eyes. "Have you forgotten? I dropped to my knees and took you in my mouth."

A slow, naughty smile curves my mouth. "So you did. I have some other ideas for getting you on your knees, though, ones I'd love to try out tonight."

"Sounds good." She glances toward the hallway. "We have two visitors within earshot of our screaming orgasms. How do we keep them from hearing?"

I chuckle. "Jamie won't care how much noise we make."

"I care. I like my privacy."

"Don't worry." I skate my fingers across her cheek. "We can be quiet."

"Not sure I can manage it. Not with you driving me out of my mind."

I move my hand in lazy circles on her back, bending my head to skim my lips over hers. "Trust me, I can make certain no one hears your screams."

"No gags, please."

I shake my head slowly. "No gags. I wouldn't do anything like that to you. But I will swallow your screams with my mouth on yours."

"That sounds…good." She eyes me with a touch of suspicion. "But you can't cover my mouth the whole time. How else do you plan on keeping anyone from hearing us?"

"You'll see."

Releasing her hand, I wrap both arms around Calli and lift her onto her toes. I seal my lips over hers, exploring with light sweeps that grow firmer the more I kiss her. She flings her arms around my neck and thrusts her tongue between my lips, moaning deeply. I coil my tongue around hers while letting out a moan of my own. A manly moan, of course.

I pull back, frowning, because an unpleasant thought has occurred to me. "I brought my sister here to keep her out of trouble. And what happened? The minute she arrived, she found an American man to captivate."

"Poor Aidan." Calli feathers her fingers over my cheek. "You can't catch a break, can you?"

Cannae help the devious gleam I'm sure twinkles in my eyes. I run my tongue across her lips. "After a day with your brother and my sister, I will be needing some physical therapy." I drop one hand to cup her erse. "A lot of it, in fact."

"Here to serve."

As we begin to kiss again, I let myself imagine that one day soon I will be married to this woman.

Chapter Twenty-Five

I collapse onto the bed on my back, right on top of the covers, with my arms spread wide and my head on one of the pillows. Eyes closed, I groan. "No one should have that much energy, bouncing around like a little bird. It's no wonder your dogs love Jamie, she's as energetic as they are."

Calli sits on the bed's edge, with my hand near her hip, and pats my chest. "Oh, poor Aidan. You have a sweet, happy sister who adores you. Must be awful."

"Hmm." I crack one lid open to peek at her. "Thought I'd get more sympathy from you. After all, your brother was turning you into a bampot."

"You called me that in the club. It means crazy?"

I nod. "You're not literally insane, but sometimes you act like it when you're stressed."

"I don't mind if Gavin makes me a little crazy. I'm glad to see him having a good time. After the way his wife left him, I didn't know if he'd ever show interest in a woman again."

Her statement piques my curiosity, and I lift my head. "What did his wife do?"

She grimaces. "Sorry, that shouldn't have slipped out. I doubt Gavin would want me telling you the story, but I'm wiped out and my brain filter isn't working properly."

I drop my head onto the mattress with a grunt. "I'll have to ask your brother."

"You wouldn't."

"No?" I roll my head to the side, giving her a mischievous smile. "Maybe I would. Or you could tell me, and I'll keep it a secret so he'll never know I know."

"Oh, you are wicked. Devious and canny, in bed and out."

I walk my fingers up her hip. "I'm in bed at the moment."

"So you are." She crawls on top of me on all fours, her hair feathering around her face. "Wouldn't you rather have sex than hear about my brother's failed marriage?"

Aye, normally I would. But I rub my eyes with my thumb and forefinger and say, "At the moment, no. I'm exhausted from spending an entire day with Jamie and Gavin. Siblings are a right trial."

"But we love them anyway, don't we?" Calli lowers her head to nibble on my lips.

"Mm, aye." As much as I'd love to have a poke, I literally can't do it right now. Even my *slat* wants to sleep. I insert a hand between our mouths to thwart her seduction. "I'm genuinely exhausted."

She falls onto the bed beside me and rolls onto her side, cuddling into her pillow. "Aidan MacTaggart is too tired for sex. Does this mean the world is spinning backwards?"

I pull her closer, tucking that sexy body under my arm. "Maybe I am ravenous, but it's your fault. I've never needed to make love to a woman this much before. Cannae get enough of you."

"Likewise. I'm addicted to the feel of you inside me."

"Thought it was the earth-shattering orgasms that had you hooked."

She slides her arm across my chest as she nestles her cheek against it. "That too. I've got it so bad, I'm giving serious thought to offering to try whisky again if you'll have sex with me right now."

"Are ye now." I chuckle. "Can't let ye suffer, can I?"

"It would be rude of you." She nuzzles my chest again, her lips forming a soft, sweet smile. "I've loved every minute with you."

I bury my face in her hair, inhaling deeply. "I loved every minute of it too. Plan to keep on loving every minute with you."

The puppies come barreling into the room and leap onto the bed with us, cuddling up to me. I have no idea why Calli's dogs prefer me, but she doesn't seem to mind. Lying here with a sweet lass tucked against me on one side and two warm puppy bodies stretched out along the other, I start to drift off.

"Want the door closed?" a hushed voice asks.

I open my eyes just enough to see Jamie in the doorway, seeming uncertain, as if she's disturbed us during an intimate moment. In a way, she has. Calli and I are curled up together on a bed—though fully clothed and half asleep.

I wave a hand at my sister. "Best shut it. Otherwise, the pups will paw at your door and whine until you let them in."

"Yeah," Calli says, "and then they'll assault you while you're vulnerable."

Flashing us a bright smile, Jamie laughs. "Good night."

We offer our good-nights to her, and Jamie retreats, shutting the door with a soft click. I fall asleep quickly, but much later, I wake up because I need the bog. After relieving my needs, I sneak back into the bedroom and lie down with Calli again. The puppies have moved to the foot of the bed, so I carefully settle in and pull Calli close against my side. Her cheek winds up on my shoulder, and her gentle breaths tickle my neck.

She's so bonnie and sweet when she's asleep. Well, she's bonnie and sweet all the time, but I especially love watching her sleep. She seems at peace, like all her worries have evaporated. Though I've learned a lot about her, I know there's more to find out. Most of all, I want to know why she can't force her husband to give her a divorce. She did say Michigan has no-fault divorce, which means she will be free eventually, but her husband can drag things out.

No wonder she gets anxious whenever I talk about our future together. Does she think I might trick her into marrying me and then refuse to let her go even if she begs me? No, she cannae believe that. Haven't I proved I care about what she wants, not just my own desires and needs?

For several minutes, I lie here wondering if there's anything I can do to help her. No, there isn't. Not unless she tells me what horrible secret prevents her from telling her husband to sod off. What hold does he have on her? Aye, she feels beholden to him because he helped her during a terrible time in her life, but that can't be all it is. Calli is too clever to let a man hold that over her for years. What else could tie her to him? They don't have children. For a moment, I consider the idea that he might be blackmailing her, but I cannae think of any way that could happen. Calli is a good person who would never do anything so awful that a *cacan* like her husband could use it as leverage.

Carefully, I roll onto my side so I can gaze at her sleeping face. I sweep hair away from her eyes.

Please let me help you.

Though I plead with her in my thoughts, I know she won't let me in, not all the way. She says she trusts me, but she won't tell me everything. Maybe I haven't shared the whole story about me and Seona, but I want to tell Calli all about it. If I do, will she finally open up about her problems?

I touch my lips to her temple.

Doesn't matter if she tells me or not. I will never walk away from her. I cannae do it. One day, the secrets between us will be exposed.

Chapter Twenty-Six

The next afternoon, Calli walks into the house through the sliding glass doors and pauses just inside the threshold. She eyes me with her brows wrinkled, then takes in the whole picture, her confusion growing.

I'm lounging on the sofa, one ankle crossed over the opposite knee, and I have one arm draped over the sofa's back. When I glance at the television, I can't help smiling a wee bit. On the screen, a black-and-white movie plays. The two stars of the film spin around on a dance floor in perfect synchronization, seeming to float in each other's arms. Lovely music weaves a spell around them, just the way I want to entrance Calli.

This is not a calculated plan. I'd been watching the movie while I waited for Calli to come back from visiting her brother in the hunting shack. But the movie did give me an idea.

"Jamie and Gavin are taking the puppies for a walk," Calli says, coming up alongside the sofa. Her gaze flicks to the television screen. "Do you like old movies?"

"I like good movies. Don't care about the age."

"Me too. I like good movies, I mean."

I watch her for a moment, trying to gauge her mood, then rise and stride around the sofa to her. I offer her my hand, palm up. "Dance with me."

"Now? Here?"

"Yes, Calli, now. And here in the living room."

"Why?"

"You're here and I'm here and there's music." I wriggle my fingers. "Give it a go. Please."

She places her hand in mine.

I draw her closer, holding one palm on the small of her back and the other cupped around hers while I raise our joined hands. With my palm on her back, I urge her to move closer until our bodies are molded together, snug and intimate. Her body feels warm against mine, and we fit so well that I get a barmy idea in my head—that fate made us for each other, and we would've met one way or another even if I hadn't gone to that club and she hadn't mistaken me for a stripper.

"The last time we danced," I say, "you wore a bonnie green dress. You're even sexier now, wearing everyday clothes and smelling of soap and honey."

"It's my shampoo."

Lifting her off her feet, I twirl us in a circle.

As her feet touch down again, she swallows hard enough I can see it, and her gaze gravitates to mine. "Don't think this is regulation ballroom dancing."

"Forget regulations." I begin to sway my hips and shuffle my feet, encouraging her to do the same. "We're moving together, that's all. Casual, not formal."

Stiff and awkward, she shuffles along with me as we make our way around the open expanse of floor behind the sofa. Her feet bump into mine, and she tenses up.

"Relax," I say, aiming for a patient tone, though I can't erase the affection and humor from my expression or my voice. "I want to dance with you, nothing else."

"Nothing else?" One corner of her mouth crimps. "We've gone more than twenty-four hours without sex. How long can you hold out?"

I comb my fingers through her hair. "I like having you in my arms, with or without sex. So please, take that steel rod out of your spine and tell me what's bothering you."

"Sorry. Didn't mean to ruin the moment." She hauls in a deep breath and releases it little by little, though that doesn't seem to relax her at all. "Hard to melt steel, though."

"Close your eyes."

She stares at me like she's hunting for the secrets of the universe in my gaze. I wish I had the all-knowing ability to give her the answers she wants and seems to need, but I've never been a god. Might be nice if I could achieve omnipotence. Then I'd have the power to free her from that *bod ceann* Rade. But I don't have godlike insight or power, so I have no idea why dancing with me makes her so tense.

Sighing, Calli shuts her eyes and gives in to the rhythm of our movements, her muscles finally softening. Her lips curve up at the corners, just a touch, and I wonder if the soothing melody of the movie music has eased her anxiety.

I start to hum softly. Donnae mean to do it, but the music is so lovely that I find myself humming along with it.

Calli rests her cheek on my chest. Her entire body seems to melt into me as if she has, at last, let go of her worries—at least for the moment. I hold our hands to my heart, near her face. She barely seems to notice when we stop moving across the floor, our feet now stationary but our bodies moving as if we still glide over the wood beneath our feet. She nestles into me, slipping her hand out of mine so she can wrap her arms around me.

If I were really up myself, I might think dancing with me freed her from all her anxieties. But I'm not arrogant enough to believe that. I'm glad that she's more relaxed now, and I want her good mood to linger even after we separate our bodies.

I comb a hand through her hair again, keeping the touch feather-light and, I hope, soothing.

A breathy moan whispers out of her. "You're so nice."

"Nice?" I say with a hint of laughter in my voice. "Thought I was wicked."

"You are wicked, but you're also nice. And sweet. You're all of it."

"Don't spread that rumor, please. I have a reputation to maintain."

She raises her head, her chin propped on my chest. "I want to tell you everything, but there's a chance you could get in trouble if I do. Legal trouble. You might become an accessory or something."

My heart stutters, and my breath catches. Did she say… Aye, I'm dead positive she just offered to share all her secrets. "Tell me. You're worth any risk."

Snuggling her cheek against my chest, she squeezes her eyes shut—and then she unloads that burden she's lived under for too long.

"I told you the basics about Rade and me," she says. "I mentioned how kind Rade was after my parents died. He offered to go with me to the funeral home, the probate lawyer's office, whatever. I was grateful for the offer, but I couldn't let him do it. He'd never met my parents and… well, I felt I needed to do it on my own. Still, he was there to keep me company and bring me food, little things like that. But when he proposed marriage, he offered me a kind of help I couldn't turn down. I should have, I realize that now. But I was grieving, and I made a horrible decision."

I spread my hands over her lower back, stroking with my fingertips. "What sort of help?"

She hauls in a deep breath and exhales it. "Remember I said my parents had hidden their financial problems from me and Gavin? I'm sure they were embarrassed and thought they were protecting us, believed they'd get back on track and we'd never have to know. After they died, Gavin and I had to shell out our own money for the funeral expenses and neither of us had much to start with. What little was left of their estate went to paying their debts, and we had to sell their house to pay off the mortgage since neither of us could afford the monthly payments. I'd gotten student loans to pay for college, and Gavin was fresh from the Marines, trying to find a job while recovering from the things he'd been through in Afghanistan. Our parents' deaths hit us both hard, but him more so than me. We were wrecked, emotionally and financially."

"Calli…" I brush wayward hairs off her forehead with my free hand, while my other hand remains entwined with hers. "I'm so sorry."

"Believe it or not, that isn't the worst part." She swallows visibly, her expression tight. "Two months after my parents died, I had to cut back my college classes to part-time and get a job to stay afloat. This meant my student loans would become payable in six months' time. No way could I get back on my feet before that happened, and I couldn't afford the payments either."

"Your good friend intervened, I'm guessing. With an offer."

"Rade said he would pay off my student loans and give me the money to finish college. He knew I wanted to go to grad school to study library science, and he offered to pay for that as well. If I did him a favor."

My hands freeze on her back. We've completely stopped moving our bodies, though we linger in each other's arms.

"He'd help me out of my jam," she continues, "if I helped him out of his. Rade's student visa was running out. He wanted to stay, he had plenty of money he inherited when his parents died. I could have my financial problems wiped out in one fell swoop—if I married him."

I make a noise somewhere between a huff and a sigh. "He wanted you to marry him so he could stay in the country."

"Yes. A green card marriage, so to speak." She hugs me tighter like she's desperate to cling to something, anything. "I was still reeling from my parents' deaths, and Gavin was still a mess. I was frantic about the money problems. What Rade offered me sounded like a generous, compassionate offer. And when he told me about his parents, how they died and he was devastated, how he understood what I was feeling…I agreed to marry him."

I circle my palms over her back, hoping the gesture soothes her.

"You have to be married for three years," she says, "before the non-citizen spouse can apply for citizenship. Rade swore once he got his citizenship, we'd wait six months for good measure and then get divorced. It's been five years. He got his citizenship a year ago."

Though I say nothing, I'm sure she can see the question on my face.

"Rade promised to file for divorce," she tells me. "Kept saying he'd do it soon, he was busy, just be patient. Two months ago, I realized he'd never do it, and I filed myself. Couldn't afford a lawyer, so I did it on my own and paid all the fees. Then I had to pay a process server to deliver the papers to Rade, but he manages to always be gone when the server shows up at his house. I can't afford to pay the server anymore."

Can't stop myself from scowling. "Why won't this *bod ceann* let you go?"

She raises her head to look at me. "*Bod ceann?*"

"Dickhead."

Calli almost smiles—almost—but can't quite do it. "Rade claims he wants to have a real marriage, asked me to move in with him. After all these years of sticking to our agreement, suddenly he wants to change it. I don't understand. We lived separate lives by mutual agreement. I can count on one hand how many times I've seen him in all these years. Sure, he sent me flowers and cards on my birthdays. I thought he was being polite, being a good friend and all. Now I'm not so sure, but I can't figure out what he wants."

"This has some bearing on why you don't want to love me, I gather. Confused about how, though."

She buries her face against my chest, sucking in a breath. "Too many people have turned out to be the opposite of what I thought they were. My parents deceived me by not talking about their problems, leaving a mess when they died. Gavin and Tara married people who changed later on. And my husband is suddenly singing a different tune after years of promising to set me free."

I rest my chin on top of her head. "All I want is you, however I can have you. And I willnae give up because one bastard has a hold on you."

"Rade's not a bastard. But you'd be better off going back to Chicago to find another American girl."

"Cannae." I exhale, and the gusty breath ruffles her hair. "I want you."

Why can't she see how much she means to me? It's more than sex, more than companionship, more than anything I've ever felt before. But if I tell her that, she might panic again. Donnae know how long I can wait to share my feelings with her. How long should I wait? There's no manual for how to deal with a wounded lass who can't trust anyone.

"You haven't wanted to tell me," I say gently, "but it would help to know what happened with your cousin and your brother. With their marriages."

"Tara's first husband seemed like a decent guy, but he turned out to be emotionally abusive, putting her down all the time and making her feel worthless. She left him after fourteen months."

"And Gavin?"

Calli pulls away from me, hugging herself. "His wife up and left one day for no good reason. Said she was bored and needed to find herself in

New York. He was like a zombie for weeks after. Leanne seemed like a nice enough girl, but she betrayed Gavin."

I settle my hands on her upper arms. "You worry I'm not what I seem. That later, after we're married, I'll change into a selfish prick or I'll keep important things from you."

She hunches her shoulders. "That's the problem. I can't know if what I see now is the real you. I've known you for twelve days, Aidan. *Twelve days.*"

"Asked you to give me four weeks."

"Even that isn't enough. No amount of time will be enough."

My grip on her arms tightens, no more than a wee bit but enough to reveal my frustration, though I hadn't meant to let it show. "You can never be certain of another person. I wish I could promise you nothing will ever change, but it would be a lie. I won't lie to you. All I can promise you is that I will do everything in my power to make you happy and keep you safe."

She studies my face like she had a moment ago, still searching for answers I can't give her.

I tug her a little closer, maintaining a gap of a few inches between our bodies, and glide my hands up to her shoulders. "You can ask my sister what kind of man I am. Or call Lachlan and he'll tell you. If you need references outside my family, I can give you the names of a dozen people who'd be happy to tell you I'm not a bastard."

"That's not necessary." She shuts her eyes for a moment, silent and perfectly still as if she's struggling to understand herself so she can explain it to me. "The problem is inside me. In my head and my heart. There's nothing you can do to fix this."

"I know," I say, not at all surprised that I sound resigned.

When I drag her into my arms again, she doesn't fight it. She lays her head on my chest and sags against me. I settle a hand on her head and begin to caress her hair while my other hand cradles her back.

"You remind me of Rory in certain ways," I tell her, "since he doesn't want to fall in love either. But I won't give up on you because you're afraid. I'll fight for you, Calli."

And I will, no matter how long it takes or how many times she panics and tries to chase me away.

I stroke her hair with my fingers, keeping one hand on her back, and wait for her to relax into me. It happens slowly, like she's fighting two impulses—one that wants her to give in and trust me, and one that feeds her fears. Her lids slide half-closed, then flutter open. She softens against me but keeps trying to stop herself from letting go of her anxieties, even for a moment. But her eyes drift shut again, and she peeks up at me through the ever-narrowing slit of her eyelids.

"Someone needs a nap," I announce, and I sweep her up into my arms to carry her down the hall to our bedroom.

Ah, the room we're sharing. Sort of. Not officially. I doubt she'd like to know I think of it as "our" room.

I set her on her feet, pull back the covers, and pick her up again to deposit the lass on the mattress. Then I tuck the covers over her. "Should I undress you?"

"No, but thanks for the offer."

"Anytime." I straighten. "I'll leave you to it, then."

"Stay. Please."

Though her request surprises me, I don't waste any time analyzing it. I amble around the bed to crawl across it and snuggle up behind her. Draping one arm over her belly, I press my face to her neck. After everything she just shared with me, I know I can't give up on her—on us.

But one question haunts me. Can she overcome her fears and let herself love me?

Chapter Twenty-Seven

The next afternoon, the four of us—the Douglases and the MacTaggarts—sit around the picnic table in the backyard while finishing up the last remnants of our meal. Calli and I had escorted Gavin and Jamie on a tour of the local area this morning, which mostly involved visiting gift shops where Jamie could pick out souvenirs for our siblings and our parents. I told her she didn't need to buy me a gift, and though she balked, I finally won the argument. Gavin helped her choose gifts for our brothers while Calli and I observed the pair's flirtatious interactions.

Jamie kept giggling, smiling, touching his arm. Calli rarely giggles, but she does smile and touch my arm.

Do I want my sister to date Calli's brother? Not sure it's good for my sanity.

I splay a hand over Calli's thigh under the picnic table, drawing her attention to me, though she doesn't look this way. But I know she's focused on what I'm doing. I can see it in her eyes, especially when I massage her flesh in a gentle, seductive rhythm.

Her breaths quicken when my hand skims higher.

Bod an Donais, do I need to shag her.

"Calli and I are going for a drive," I announce. "Alone."

Maybe I could've been less obvious about my intentions, but I don't care if Jamie and Gavin know I plan to ravish his sister. After all, Gavin is trying it on with *my* sister.

When I had confided my escape plan to Calli while we prepared lunch, she agreed by saying, "Oh God, yes, please. As soon as possible."

Two full days without feeling her warm, silky flesh around my cock have driven me to the brink of madness.

Gavin aims a hard look at me. "I'm watching you."

The slight twitch of his lips belies his vague threat. Not that any of his threats fash me. I have two older brothers and an army of male cousins. No amount of glaring or threats will chase me away from Calli.

I remove my palm from her thigh so I can clasp her hand. Then I glance at my sister before returning my gaze to Gavin. "Got my eye on you too."

Aye, the way I squint my eyes conveys more humor than menace. I'm not a naturally threatening man, though I do have my moments. If I ever meet Calli's husband, I might turn into Rory and aim a hot, steely glare at the man right before I batter him.

I lead Calli across the yard and through the house, out to the convertible waiting for us in the driveway. Lachlan's gift convertible. I've made my peace with my brother's need to overindulge when it comes to gifts for me. Before Calli has time to ask about my specific plans, I whisk her away on a mysterious drive down the highway. Aye, she has no idea exactly what I have in mind. I'd told her we should get away for a while so we could shag, but I hadn't shared the details of what I want to do with her. To her. For her. Over and over and over.

As the scenery races by and her hair whips around her, she gazes at me with an expression I can only describe as adoration. "I'm all for a sex getaway, but where exactly are we going?"

I can't help infusing my smile with smug satisfaction. "It's a surprise."

"Since you're new to the area, do you even know where you're going?"

"You doubt me?" I feign taking offense. "I researched it online. And I've got supplies in the boot."

"In your boot?" She leans over to peer down at my feet. "You're wearing tennies."

I roll my eyes. "Not in *my* boot, in the car's boot."

"What's the boot?"

"The trunk." I hook a thumb over my shoulder, toward the rear of the car. "What are tennies?"

"Tennis shoes. Sneakers." She gestures at my feet. "Those."

"Ah."

Calli relaxes into her seat with one arm on the center console, the other on the door's armrest. "Guess the culture clash has hit us at last."

"No, it hit us when I spoke naughty Gaelic to you."

"Oh yeah, how could I forget that?" She smiles at me, the expression rife with sensuality. "You can talk dirty to me in Gaelic again if you want."

"Best wait until I'm not steering a fast-moving vehicle." I throw her a sidelong glance, complete with a suggestive smirk. "Talking dirty to you tends to get me excited."

"Doesn't seem to take a lot to get you excited."

I wink. "You either, *mo chridhe*."

"Three times you've called me that. What does it mean?"

"My heart."

Her face goes blank.

I probably shouldn't have admitted to what that Gaelic phrase means, but I don't want to hold back with her. Still, I expect she will panic now that she knows I think of her in such romantic terms.

Calli recovers from the shock swiftly, and we go back to talking and laughing—and teasing each other with sexy innuendo. At least she didn't have an anxiety attack this time when I expressed tenderness for her. We pass the remainder of our trip in casual discussions of our respective siblings, the scenery, cultural differences, and countless other things. After two hours, we reach our destination.

She surveys the motel while I park the car. "This was your great plan? A motel?"

"Told you I wanted you alone so I could have my way with you."

"Sure, but I kind of assumed there'd be romantic gestures involved."

"Why?" I give her my best impression of a clueless man. "You said we're not dating and you won't fall in love with me. Why would I bother with courtship?"

Maybe I keep up the clueless act a wee bit too long, because the change in her expression suggests she might be starting to believe me. Time to make the farce clear.

I grin and kiss her cheek, then I purr into her ear, "We're here because I wanted privacy. Your surprises are in the trunk, remember."

"Surprises? Plural?"

"Aye."

Hopping out of the car, I jog around to her side to open the door and usher her out, offering my hand. She lets me lead her to the motel's office, where we check in—I'd made a reservation this morning—and then we head for our room. It's situated at the far end of the long, one-story building. I guide her into the room, then hurry off to move the car since I left it parked by the office.

When I come back, I'm carrying an insulated cooler bag and a plastic grocery sack filled with items Calli won't be able to see. She considers the bags like she's trying to deduce what they contain. I set both on the table near the window. Closing the curtains, I drop down onto the bed beside her, buttressed with one arm on the mattress behind her erse. Then I lean in close.

"Your surprises," I say, "come in stages. Just like you will."

"What does that mean?"

"Means I'm going to make you come for me over and over, harder every time."

"Will any part of this plan involve me on my knees? You did promise."

"And I keep my promises." I curl my tongue around her earlobe. "But I'm not giving anything away. You'll need to be patient, *mo leannan*."

I haven't told her what *mo leannan* means, and I think I'll put that off until later. My cock doesn't want to wait much longer to have a poke.

Kicking off my shoes, I lie back on the bed, propped up on my elbows. "Strip."

"Excuse me?"

"Strip, Calli." I rake my gaze over her, feeling everything inside me heat up into a smoldering fire. "It means take off your clothes."

"I know what it means. Not used to being commanded to undress."

"You like it when I command you."

She slides off the bed and starts to undress. "You've seen me strip before. This is hardly a novel experience."

"But I love watching you unveil that luscious body."

I can't tear my focus away from her, and I find myself licking my lips while I track her every movement. By the time she gets down to her underwear, a lump has started to swell inside my jeans. When Calli sheds her bra, I reach down with one hand to stroke my cock through the denim. I need to fuck her so hard for so long that afterward, she won't have the energy to tell me we can't work as a couple.

Calli shimmies out of her knickers.

I let out a ragged breath and stroke my cock more firmly while it swells even more. Only this woman can make me so hard so fast.

The irresistible lass kneels between my knees and unhooks the button on my jeans, then she grasps the zipper. Her hand brushes against mine. I move to push her hand away but hesitate while I consider what she seems determined to do to me. I'd loved it the first time she went down on me, but I have plans for us that don't involve me going off before I've even pushed inside her body. Still, I never can resist anything she wants to do to me. So, I withdraw my hand to support my body on both elbows.

She drags the zipper down with exquisite slowness, and the rough and strangely erotic sound makes my *slat* throb. Her nipples have gone hard. I swear I can smell her cream too, and the scent makes me suck in a sharp breath.

"Christ," I all but growl, "I want to suck those little nipples until you shudder."

"My turn first." She spreads the flaps of my jeans, freeing my dick. She closes her fist around the base and pumps me slowly while my breaths grow shallower and quicker. Seemingly emboldened by my response, she pumps harder and faster, her palm gliding up and down my cock while I watch every movement of her fingers and the pressure to come builds. She works me with even more vigor, bending to lap the moisture from my crown. When I gasp, she grins. "Mm, I do love the way you taste."

I stare at her, in awe of the woman crouched between my thighs. "Calli Bethany Douglas, you are a goddess."

"You've earned your Viking name." She presses her lips to the head of my *slat* while she milks me with her hand. "You are magnificent."

Letting out a long and resonant groan, I fall backward onto the mattress. My fingers clench the bedspread.

With her hand still on my cock, she sweeps her tongue over the tip in one long lick.

Bod a' chac. I cannae stand it anymore.

I spring up, hug her tight, and flip us both over so she winds up on her back beneath me. Breathing hard, my face pinched, I gaze at her for several seconds while I catch my breath and the pressure inside me eases up just enough that I won't *caith* all over Calli before I've even taken her body. She seems unable to look away from me, just like I cannae look away from her. But I have to sever our eye contact because I need to possess her. I crush my mouth to hers, compelling her to open for me, and I plunge my tongue inside to invade her mouth with demanding thrusts until my cock throbs again and the scent of her lust envelops me.

I jump to my feet.

She gasps.

Cannae wait. I strip off my clothes in a rush, then drop to my knees beside the bed, wedged between her legs. With both hands, I grasp her hips and pull her closer until the edge of her erse lies on the bed's edge. I frisk my hands down to her inner thighs and push her legs apart.

"My turn," I say, surprised by the lust in my voice. Why am I surprised? Calli always turns me into a sex maniac. I shift my hands to the bed on either side of her legs and angle in until my mouth hovers millimeters from her sex. "Taking it slow this time. You'll beg me to hurry up, but I willnae."

My mouth descends on her clitoris, and I seal my lips and tongue over that taut bud. I suckle with such gentleness that she tenses like she might be on the verge of climax already. But when I lap at her clit, she gasps again and fists her hands in the sheets. I glide my tongue in leisurely strokes, loving the way she whimpers, and nip at her clit. With one finger, I find her opening and tease it, then slide my finger along her cleft with aching slowness, only to drag it back down at the same speed.

"Aidan," she whimpers. "Faster, please, faster."

I groan against her flesh, my cock pulsing like it wants me to give in to her plea. Rather than speeding up, though, I pull her clit into my mouth to lick and suckle it even more slowly than before. Her knees draw up to her chest, seemingly on their own, as if a wire running the length of her body has been pulled tight. I rasp my tongue over her flesh in a ferocious lash, and she thrashes her head with her hands fisted in the covers even more tightly and her breaths shortening into sharp, desperate noises. I shove a hand under her erse and boost it up. The angle gives me better access to the part of her body I'm not done with yet, and I scrape my tongue up and down the length of her cleft once, twice, before I thrust my tongue inside her.

The lass's entire body goes rigid as steel, and she seems to have stopped breathing.

I flick my tongue inside her, tormenting her body while I devour the taste of her.

Calli's back arches, and she lets out a wailing cry.

I withdraw my tongue, scraping it up her slick, swollen skin. Just as I cover her nub with my mouth and my tongue lashes it fiercely, I dive two fingers inside her.

And she comes.

Her body shudders and convulses under me. She shouts and whimpers, clearly overpowered by the climax, while her body clutches at my fingers in undulating spasms. When at last she collapses onto the bed, limp and satiated, I sit back on my heels to drink in the vision of her.

I slide my tongue over my lips, which glisten from her wetness. "You taste so good I could feast on you all night. But this was only stage one."

She gapes at me, panting from the release I've just given her. "You'll make me come harder than that?"

I smile with devilish hunger, my chuckle dark and full of erotic promise. "Yes. I. Will."

Chapter Twenty-Eight

O n your knees," I say. Though I tried to sound commanding, the way my lips tick up at the corners probably ruined the effect. Doesnae matter. Calli loves my naughty sense of humor. I turn one hand palm up and lift it in a get-up gesture. "Donnae lie there, love, being lazy and satisfied. We're not done yet."

She pushes up onto her elbows and sticks her tongue out at me.

I gesture for her to rise. "Knees. Now. Or do I have to spank you?"

"Like to see you try."

Aye, that sounds like fun, but I have a plan that I will enact—if the cheeky lass will let me. I give her thigh a playful slap. "Get up."

She obeys. On her knees on the bed, inches from the edge, she reaches out to explore my chest with those soft wee palms.

I wave my hands, silently commanding her to back up.

Calli dutifully waddles backward on her knees until I hold up a staying hand.

Then I retrieve a box of condoms from the plastic shopping sack I'd brought. I rip open the box and pull out a single foil packet. Her nipples are stiff, the surrounding skin pebbled, and I want to palm those tits while I claim her body. That's part of my plan, but I have more in mind for her. With my gaze nailed to her body, I stalk around the foot of the bed and climb onto the mattress on my knees, jostling the bed as I come up behind Calli.

She draws in a shaky breath, like she cannae wait for me to take her.

I slip my hands around her waist, skimming them up her flat belly, pausing when my fingers graze the undersides of her breasts. "Turn your head."

She turns her head to the right, toward the wall.

"No," I say, with laughter in my voice. Laying a hand on her cheek, I gently encourage her to look the other way. "See us."

When she turns her gaze toward the mirror attached to the dresser, I glance that way too. The mirror provides a full view of us on our knees together, our naked bodies separated by a matter of inches, my erection almost brushing her backside. She draws in another ragged breath and catches her lip between her teeth, releasing it slowly.

I push the hair away from the left side of her neck, feathering my lips over the skin at the hollow of her throat. "I want you to watch while I take you. Watch yourself come."

She starts to breathe harder, which makes her breasts rise and fall, and her lips part as she traces her tongue over the bottoms of her upper teeth. Then she tips her head back a little, silently begging me to touch her more, touch her everywhere. When my cock nudges her backside, she tips her head back against my chest.

"Will you watch?" I ask.

"Yes."

With her head still on my chest, she rolls it to the side far enough that she can glimpse the mirror.

I see her reflection, but I see myself too—and just like I want her to watch herself in the mirror, I cannae resist following my own reflected movements while I roll the condom on. When I catch her looking at me, at my cock, I give my length a slow, sensuous stroke.

She's breathing even harder now. Calli is so bloody beautiful when she's aroused.

I grasp her waist with both hands, rock my hips back, and plow into her with one fluid thrust. Her heat surrounds my cock, and her flesh wraps around me, the sensation so exhilarating that I realize I'm holding my breath. The air bursts out of my lungs while I consume her body, penetrating so deeply that she gasps. We both gaze at the mirror, transfixed by the sight of us—my intense and determined expression, the need and pleasure on her face, those bonnie breasts quivering every time I rock my hips into her. I find a strong, measured rhythm and sink my *slat* deeper inside her lush body, but I nearly *caith* when she shudders and exhales a breathless wee cry like she loves what I'm making her feel. I splay a hand over her belly, cradling her to me while my other hand coasts higher to cup and squeeze her breast. She arches against me, her mouth falling open on quick, shallow breaths.

Despite the intensity of our passion, the only sounds in this room are the murmurs of our breaths, the faint creaking of the bed, and the brushing of skin against skin. Calli focuses on the mirror again, observing with rapt attention while I pinch her nipple between my thumb and forefinger, stunning a gasp from her.

Our gazes connect in the mirror.

There in her eyes, I glimpse my raw lust reflected in those shimmering emerald irises. More than passion, though, I feel an aching tenderness in my chest, a deep yearning for more than a physical bond. Aye, I love shagging her. But I want so much more with her. And in her eyes, reflected in the mirror, I swear I see the same longing, the same tender and almost painful need for connection.

I tear my gaze away from the mirror to dip my head to her neck, nuzzling her slender throat and grazing my teeth over her skin as I thrust my cock harder and deeper.

She flings her arms over her head, locking both hands at my nape, but she seems unable to wrench her focus away from the mirror. I cannae stop watching it either. The need to come inside her body mounts higher, the pressure building in my cock, spurred by the image of our writhing bodies and of my length sliding out a few inches only to slam back into her. It takes all my willpower to keep my thrusts measured, but finally, I cannae hold back any longer, and my thrusts escalate into a pounding that makes her tits bounce.

In the mirror, her gaze travels to my face. I turn my head toward hers, which means I cannae see our reflections anymore, but I caught a glimpse right before I looked away. So, I know my expression is full of a longing I cannae hide, a need that makes my chest ache even as I feel her body tense in anticipation of release. Her body grips me in pulsating waves, and she unleashes a wild cry that echoes off the walls. Even as I feel her orgasm fading, she clings to me while I punch into her frantically and, at last, spill myself inside her hot, slick flesh. I throw my head back, plowing into her one last time.

I pull out reluctantly, panting, and hold her to me with my hands linked over her belly. This time felt different. Not only because of the mirror, but because it felt more intimate than ever before.

"You did it," she says. "You made me come harder than the first time."

"Mirror helped, eh?" I murmur against her throat as I trail light kisses down her skin.

She glances down at my hands on her belly and blinks like she's fighting off tears. I can see her eyes shimmering with moisture. Why is she about to cry? Calli must be worrying again. About us. About me. What else can I do to prove I will never leave her or use her?

I sweep a fall of hair away from her face, my fingers grazing her cheek. "What is it? You look about to cry."

"Tears of sexual pleasure," she says in a breezy tone that doesn't fool me. "You give me such incredible orgasms, I can't help but weep from the sheer bliss of it."

"Bollocks." I turn her face toward mine. "What is it?"

"I got a little overwhelmed by the intensity of this. I like being with you. A lot. I'm—I'm glad you're not leaving yet. That's all."

"You like being with me?" I caress her cheek with my fingers. "Sounds personal and…intimate."

"I meant I like having sex with you."

Oh no, she will never convince me that's what has her off balance. And I can't stop my lips from stretching into a triumphant smile as the truth hits me. "You like me. A lot."

"No," she says, elongating the word as if that will make her denial sound more believable. "I do like you, but not that much. Don't get all excited and misinterpret what I said to mean I'm in love with you. I'm not." She scoots away from me to flop onto her back atop the covers. "I couldn't fall for someone I met a couple weeks ago."

"Never said you were in love with me. But you must be afraid you might love me, else you wouldn't have said it." I discard the condom in the little rubbish bin by the bed and settle onto my side next to her, my head supported by my raised hand. "If you like me a lot, that's enough for the moment."

"You can't hold me to statements I make right after experiencing a brain-scrambling orgasm."

"All right, I won't." I spread a hand over her belly, just below her breasts. "But I like you very much too. And it's not coming inside your exquisite little body that makes me feel this way."

She wriggles and twists her mouth into a strange expression, then glances around. "What happened to my surprises?"

"Ah, those." I jump off the bed to retrieve the plastic sack and insulated bag. Both items I place on the bed beside her while I perch on the edge. "First, something to remember me by."

She sits up, tucking her legs under her cross-legged.

From the plastic sack, I produce a mug emblazoned with bold, red letters that spell out "Scots do it better." I set the mug on her knee.

Laughing, she picks up the item and turns it in her hand. "Where did you find this?"

"Had it made special, by a shop in town. Picked it up this morning."

"So that's where you disappeared to for ten minutes when the rest of us were browsing souvenirs."

"I slipped away to a shop down the street." I smile with my lips closed, probably seeming prouder of my secret shopping than I should be, but I like surprising Calli. And I love making her smile.

She deposits the mug on the bedside table. "Jamie said you were in the restroom."

"She was my accomplice." I toss the empty sack onto the floor and unzip the top of the rectangular, insulated bag. Reaching inside, I pause to look at her. "I've pulled together a kind of picnic for you, but I was limited to the items available in your kitchen."

"Then I'm sure I'll like whatever it is. Seeing as it's my food."

"One item was not from your kitchen." I bring out a plastic travel cup with a straw sticking out of it, filled with a light-brown liquid. "Try this? You said you would if I gave you sex."

"Uh… What is that?" she asks, eying the liquid askance. Then she seems to remember what we'd talked about the other day, and her brows furrow. Her lip curls up slightly too. "Whisky?"

I sigh, offering her the cup. "Don't curl your lip. Ahmno giving you poison, and this is Atholl Brose, a blend of whisky, oatmeal, honey, and cream. Give it a go is all I ask." I slide my tongue out to moisten my lips with one long, sensual stroke, just to make her cheeks turn pink—which they do, of course. "Though not even Atholl Brose can compare to the intoxicating taste of you."

Unscrewing the cup's lid, I show her the contents. The creamy liquid sloshes inside the cup, its white color tinged with a rich shade of caramel.

She rolls her gaze up to mine. "Well, I did promise."

"Do you trust me?"

"I do."

Reattaching the lid, I tilt the cup so the straw angles toward her mouth.

Calli closes her lips over the straw, taking a tentative pull. Her expression brightens. "Mm, this is good."

"Maybe whisky isn't so horrid after all."

"Not when it's drowned in cream and honey."

"I know, you still hate whisky on its own." I bend forward to steal a swig of the rich concoction. "But you like Atholl Brose, and you like me. I'll settle for that."

She gets a suspicious look on her face, and I can guess what she's thinking.

I warp my mouth into a rueful smile. "You're wondering if Lachlan did this with Erica. I can see it on your face."

The lass hunches her shoulders, her lips trying to kink up but not quite succeeding.

I rummage in the insulated bag, my gaze focused on the items inside it. "No, Lachlan did not feed Atholl Brose to Erica. This was my idea."

"Good. That's probably why I like it."

"I have more for you." I extract a plastic, sandwich-size container and set it on the bed, then continue my rummaging. "Glad I redeemed myself with you. I was supposed to be the MacTaggart who seduces the lasses, and Lachlan is the uptight one who cannae be romantic if his life depends on it. I was starting to worry I'd lost my touch."

"No chance of that." She takes another sip of her drink, which I know because I hear her slurping. "But I don't think this is genuine sibling rivalry. Ever since you told me about Seona, I've had an inkling you feel guilty about something, and I think that's the real reason you feel like a failure."

I slump my shoulders, shifting my attention to the bedspread. "You're a clever lass. Should've known I couldn't hide the truth from you for long."

"Guess the question is do you trust me enough to tell me."

I swing my gaze up to hers. "I trust you. Completely."

She takes a long pull on her straw, then clears her throat. "Are you going to tell me?"

"Aye." It's time to confess, but I feel a wee bit queasy when I think about telling her. Anxiety is a relatively new experience for me, and that's my only excuse for shoving both hands into my hair and scratching my scalp furiously, like I can shake the unease out of myself. With a groaning sigh, I give up and just tell her. "I told you about my casual-dating arrangement with Seona."

"You were sleeping with her."

For some reason, I can't look at her while I explain, so I glance away and nod. "Six months ago, she invited me to go rock climbing with her. I've never been interested in sports, though Lachlan and Rory like to do the Highland games. Hammer throw, caber toss, anything to impress the lasses."

"You don't care about impressing us females?"

"I'd rather prove my manliness in other ways." I almost grin when I say that, but then I remember what I need to tell Calli, and I can't smile anymore. "But Seona, she did all sorts of extreme things like rock climbing. I agreed to go with her. I'd done a bit of climbing with my brothers, so I understood the risks and the basic techniques."

Calli settles a hand over mine where it rests on my thigh.

I pull my hand out from under hers and move it to my knee. "She took us to Beinn a' Bheithir, a mountain near Loch Leven not far from Ballachulish, and we set out along her favorite trail until she found a spot she liked for climbing. The terrain is difficult and not for casual hikers, only for people who want a challenge. We didn't get around to scaling the cliffs. I donnae know what happened, but all of a sudden the ground came out from under us, and we were falling." I squeeze my eyes shut against the memory, but it still flares in my mind, as vivid and real as when the accident happened. "Next thing I remember is waking up in hospital."

"How bad was it?"

"I got off easy. Cracked ribs, dislocated shoulder, various cuts and bruises. Seona… Her injuries were more severe. Besides broken bones, she hit her head on a large rock. She blamed me for the accident."

"Why? Did anybody figure out what happened?"

"There had been rains the day before, and as best as anyone could tell, that softened the mountainside enough to make part of it come loose. Our weight must've triggered it. No one's fault, they said, nothing but a freak accident."

"But you still blame yourself."

"I was in front, with Seona behind me. Maybe I could've spotted the danger if I'd been paying more attention. But I was too busy flirting with her."

"That doesn't make it your fault."

"She blames me, and I can't help agreeing."

Calli moves her hand like she wants to touch me, but then seems to realize I don't want that. She folds her hands on her lap. "Why does Seona keep calling you and demanding money?"

"For her pain and suffering." My fingers dig into my thighs as I clench my jaw, remembering the spite in Seona's voice every time we've spoken lately. "She seems all right overall, but she's become fixated on the accident and very bitter about the fact I wasn't injured worse."

"Aidan, I'm so sorry. No wonder you feel guilty, with her hammering it into your head."

I slide over to the side of the bed, swinging my legs off it to set my feet on the floor. Cannae look at Calli, not while I keep talking about Seona. "She'd always been hotheaded, but now she seems to want revenge on me. I can't understand it. I may feel guilt over the accident, but I don't have the money she wants. Spent it all on coming here, finding you."

"Guess that makes it my fault she's hounding you."

"Not what I meant." I knife a hand into my hair. "I wasted money on this trip because I was desperate to change my life, to stop being selfish and settle down to start a family. Be responsible."

She scoots across the bed to sit beside me with one leg tucked under her, turned partway toward me. With my hand still shoved into my hair, my arm blocks my face from her view. She grasps my forearm, gently urging me to lower my hand. After a few seconds of struggling to resist her tenderness, I give up and let my arm drop.

"Aidan," she says, laying a palm on my cheek, "regret is pointless. It was an accident, and you can't know why it happened, no matter what Seona says. You have to let it go. Stop giving her that kind of power over you."

"Power?" I finally look at her, because her statement confuses me. Maybe it shouldn't, but it does.

"Yes." She clasps both her hands around mine. "She's using your guilt against you. You know she has problems, and she's obsessed with you. Why are you accepting it's all your fault just because she keeps telling you it is? The woman is trying to extort money from you. Nothing she says can be believed."

For a long moment, I let her jewel eyes entrance me. But I can't avoid responding to what she said, not for much longer. "Maybe you're right, but it's not so easy to get rid of guilt. Or fear. You should know about that."

"I have an idea," she says. "Why not have Lachlan or Rory—maybe both of them, actually—go and talk to Seona? They can find out what she's really after."

That's not a completely rubbish idea. I consider it for a moment while we both sit here in silence, then I give her an appreciative nod. "You are very clever, *mo chridhe*. Seona lives in Ballachulish. I could ask Lachlan or Rory if they'll have a talk with her. Lachlan might be best. He could bring Erica along as a buffer."

"Sounds like a plan." She raises her brows and smiles. "You're going to ask Lachlan for help? I seem to recall a certain someone refusing any kind of assistance from—"

"Aye, well, I've changed my mind. You convinced me." I warp my mouth into something like annoyance and humor fighting for control of my expression. "Don't need to remind me I'm fickle."

"You're not fickle. You finally wised up to the fact overbearing brothers can be useful on occasion."

I turn toward her, bending one knee and reaching for the sandwich container. I offer it to her. "Let's have our picnic in bed and forget about the rest until tomorrow."

"But you'll call Lachlan?"

"In the morning." I tap a finger on her nose. "Happy?"

"Yes." She accepts the plastic container, pops the lid off, and gazes down at the sandwich nestled inside the wee box. She takes a quick peek inside the insulated bag. "Ham and cheese? And potato chips?"

"The selection in your kitchen was rather limited."

"But I was kind of expecting something Scottish."

"Couldn't find haggis around here." I grin when she wrinkles her nose. "So, you don't want Scottish food after all, eh? Turn your sweet little nose up at my whisky, and now you look fit to vomit from the mention of haggis. I think I should be offended by your disrespect for my cultural heritage."

"I do love plaid," she says, probably trying to soothe my wounded Scottish pride, then she leans in until our faces are a breath apart. "Especially when you're wearing a kilt."

"You like my legs."

She slides a hand down my naked thigh and back up to my hip. "Among other things."

I sneak my tongue out to graze her lips, which taste faintly of Atholl Brose. "Why donnae we put off the picnic for a wee bit longer?"

"Oh yes, please." She shifts her hand to my swelling cock. "And I can think of something Scottish I'd love to devour.

Chapter Twenty-Nine

We arrive back at the house around ten the next morning, both of us feeling relaxed and satisfied like we've spent an entire afternoon and evening giving each other intense pleasure. Oh, that's right. We *did* do that. No wonder I feel so good this morning. Telling Calli everything about the accident and Seona had made me anxious at first, but then the anxiety crumbled away as I realized I have no more secrets from Calli. And sharing my guilt about Seona lifted a weight off my shoulders, one that had crushed me for far too long.

Calli freed me. And I showed my appreciation in the best way I know how—by giving her orgasms that she called "soooo beyond earth-shattering." Aye, I felt bloody fantastic after she said that. That's why I didn't complain at all when she reminded me I'd promised to ring Lachlan this morning to ask him to visit Seona. My brother agreed without hesitation.

Hand in hand, we walk up the path to the front door. Calli glances at me just as I glance at her, and we both grin like eejits.

Beyond the window beside the door, something catches her eye. The curtains hang slightly parted to reveal a sliver of the interior, though I can't see through the gap from where I'm standing. Calli leans forward, squinting at whatever she glimpses inside the house. She blinks quickly, as if she's startled.

"What is it?" I ask.

She shuffles backward a step. "Why don't we go for a walk? The puppies must be in the backyard playing, so if we go around the outside of the house we can—"

"What don't you want me to see?"

"Nothing," she says, her voice pitched a little higher than usual. She crimps her mouth and swings her arms like she's pretending there's nothing to see inside the house.

Aye, now I'm dead sure there *is* something to see.

I lean over her shoulder to peer through the gap between the curtains. My jaw tenses, and I feel a muscle ticking there. Eyes narrowed, I let out a wee noise that sounds almost like a growl.

Because there on the sofa, Calli's brother is mauling my sister. They sit side by side facing each other. Gavin has one arm stretched across the sofa's back while he kisses Jamie. Passionately. With tongues. She has one hand thrust into his hair, cupping the back of his head as they ravish each other's mouths.

I didnae need to see that.

Does that scunner think he can debauch my sister without getting a thrashing?

"Calm down," Calli says, turning around to lay her hands flat on my chest in a vain effort to push me away from the window and the house. "They're adults. If they want to—"

I grasp the knob and shove the door open.

Jamie and Gavin jump. Her hand flies to her mouth, but he adopts a look of confused innocence.

Oh aye, that expression seems completely genuine. If I were a numpty with mud for brains.

Calli rushes inside, shutting the door, and seizes my arm to stall me as I stomp toward the sofa. I halt, eying her sideways.

"Let's not overreact," she tells me.

But I snort out a breath anyway, like a rampaging bull.

Gavin pushes up off the sofa. "Hey, didn't think you'd be back so soon."

He cannae believe we'll have a casual conversation after what I just saw him doing to my baby sister.

"Duh," Calli says. "Figured you wouldn't be sucking face with Aidan's sister if you thought he was about to come home."

My gaze rotates toward her again. I mouth, "Home?"

"You two are living together," Gavin says. "I knew it."

Calli bites one corner of her mouth, her gaze flitting from Gavin to me and back again. "Not the way you mean. He sleeps here."

"With you."

"Honestly, we've already had this conversation." She tugs at the hem of her shirt. "Aidan is not my boyfriend."

I'm not? That's news to me since she called this my home too and we've been sharing the same bedroom.

Jamie, Gavin, and I all smirk and snicker at Calli's barmy claim.

With her hands on her hips, she tries to scowl at us, but her indignation seems to crumble away. Slumping her shoulders, she lets her arms go limp at her sides.

Jamie hops up and aims her bright, dimpled smile at Calli. "Gavin's not my boyfriend either, then."

Calli sighs. "Are all you Scottish people so snarky?"

"You like it," I say, slipping an arm around her shoulders. Then I murmur, "From me, at least."

She relaxes into me, apparently giving up her fruitless battle to convince the rest of us.

"Would you mind," Jamie says to Calli, "if Gavin was my boyfriend?"

I grumble because I can guess what Calli is thinking—that she can't say no without sounding like a hypocrite. I have the same problem, so I say, "It's all right. Let them have their fun."

Gavin raises a brow at me. "Fun? I like Jamie a lot. It's more than fun. Not like you and my sister, having sex while she says you're not her boyfriend. At least I'm upfront about it."

"Upfront?" I say. "You snogged my sister while I was away."

"You want I should do it in front of you?" Gavin has a mischievous gleam in his eye. "All right, I will."

He pulls Jamie into his arms and mashes his mouth to hers. What does my sister do? She sags into his embrace, despite the audience of two watching them. Despite *me* watching them.

I push away from Calli, scowling at Gavin. "Why donnae ye just tear her clothes off right in front of us?"

He releases Jamie with a look of self-satisfaction on his face.

Jamie's cheeks flame bright red.

And I fist my hands.

Calli hurries around the sofa to Jamie, placing a protective arm around her shoulders. "Both of you, stop harassing the poor girl. Gavin, quit trying to annoy Aidan. And you, Aidan, let your sister live her own life. At least she's not in Chicago trolling the clubs. My brother is a good man." She throws Gavin a chastising look. "Most of the time."

Gavin and I both lower our gazes to the floor, suitably chagrined. Though I do feel bad for behaving like a *cacan*, Calli's stern tone makes me want to toss her over my shoulder and carry her into the bedroom so I can shag her while she talks to me in that commanding tone.

Jamie murmurs something into Calli's ear, though I can't hear what she says. Calli glances away, toward the far wall, seeming almost embarrassed.

I return my gaze to the floor, but I can't take the silence for more than a couple of seconds longer. Then a breath gusts out of me as I raise my head. "I'm sorry. Won't happen again."

Gavin looks up as well. "Me too. Sorry."

"I suppose," she says, "we will accept your half-assed apologies."

"We will," Jamie concurs.

Gavin glances at her, then at his sister, a question in his eyes.

Calli waves a hand. "Go. Take Jamie to dinner, make out with her in the car, whatever. You're adults, and we" —she shoots me a pointed look—"will not interfere. Will we?"

"You have my word."

Gavin turns to the lasses. "Calli, I am sorry for being such a jerk."

"I know."

He takes Jamie's hand, guiding her toward the sliding glass doors. As the doors whisk shut behind them, Calli approaches me and slips her arms around my waist.

"What shall we do now?" she asks.

The dog door whacks open as Mandy and Misty blast through it. They swarm around our legs, leaping and licking and whimpering with glee.

I hug Calli closer, glancing at the puppies. "Take the furry lassies for a walk, it seems."

Chapter Thirty

We wander back from our walk in the woods, tired puppies trotting alongside us with their tongues lolling. Calli holds Mandy's retractable leash while I grip Misty's, a task that requires strong muscles given Misty's tendency to pull with all her considerable strength. When I had convinced Misty to walk without almost yanking me off my feet, Calli declared that I had achieved the impossible. Though I think she's exaggerating, I accepted the compliment because she spoke it in a sensual tone that I know means she wants to shag me.

As the house comes into view behind the trees, an odd noise catches all of our attention.

Mandy and Misty prick their ears, canting their heads in the direction of the hunting cabin.

Trees screen the cabin from our view, where it lies a few hundred feet away. The noise originating from that direction sounds farther away than it likely is. Calli had told me how the trees absorb sounds and trick a person into believing the noises are more distant than they are. The keening sound grows louder and quieter in a steady rhythm, and I notice another, less obvious sound beneath it, a noise that resembles grunting.

"Is that a fox?" I ask, squinting in the direction of the noises.

A throaty, wordless shout reverberates through the woods. The keening escalates into a high-pitched scream.

Calli winces. "No, that's not a fox."

"What is it…" I trail off as, a second later, a louder shout echoes through the forest.

A female voice screams, "Gavin!"

My eyes fly wide. "He's fucking my sister, the bastard!"

The puppies start barking and pulling on their leashes.

"We better go," Calli says, "before they hear the dogs."

I try to frown, but it winds up as a rueful smile. "Guess this is my punishment for seducing you."

She pats my cheek. "Your sister's an adult, this was bound to happen sometime."

"Would've rather not heard it."

"You'll get over the trauma." Clasping my hand, she leads the way back to the house.

The noise from the cabin ends with another scream as Calli and I enter the fenced yard. We release the puppies from their leashes, and they take off, racing around the yard while barking and jumping. Soon, a squirrel high up in a tree snags their attention. The puppies crouch at the base of the trunk, their gazes locked on the creature beyond their reach.

"They'll be occupied for a while," Calli says.

I can't stop staring in the direction of the cabin. Or maybe I'm scowling.

"Don't torture yourself," she says. "They had sex, it's not the end of the world."

I turn away from the fence and what lies beyond it, hidden in the woods. "I understand how your brother felt when he found us living in the same house."

"Gavin's not sleeping with your sister as revenge. He wouldn't do anything so petty and sleazy."

"I know he wouldn't." I fold an arm around her shoulders, hugging her to me. "Jamie wasn't a virgin. She'd been engaged a few years ago and sometimes sneaked back into our parents' house in the early morning, getting caught a few times. That's why she lives with Rory at the moment, for privacy. I don't think she's been with anyone for a good while, though."

As we amble across the yard toward the house, Calli loops her arm around my waist and leans her head against me. "I was a virgin when I slept with you, but Gavin had no idea about that. We don't talk about sex."

"I only know about Jamie because I saw her buying condoms." I clear my throat. "I may have gotten slightly upset about it. She threw the box at me and said she hadn't been a virgin since she was nineteen."

"She wouldn't have told you if she hadn't been ticked at you?"

"No. I don't talk about sex with my sisters."

"You talk about it with your brothers?"

I pull the sliding doors open, and we enter the house. Without letting go of Calli, I push the door shut and turn us both until we face each other. "I talk about sex with my brothers, but I don't share details."

"No kiss and tell?"

"Absolutely not." I twist my face in fake disgust. "I don't want to hear about the adventures of Lachlan and Rory and their women."

She links her arms around my neck. "Enough about our families. I'd rather talk about what you're going to do to me."

I grasp her buttocks in both hands, tugging her into my groin—and my hardening *slat*. "Tell me what you want this time."

"I have an idea, but it might be silly."

"Got no problem with silly." I grind my erection into her. "Say it and I'll make your fantasy come true."

"I know you will." Boosting up onto her tiptoes, she levels our gazes. "Even though it's daytime, I want you to go into the bedroom, take your clothes off, and get into bed with the lights off. Oh, and shut the curtains too. Make it as dark as possible in there."

"You want to crawl into my bed in the dark and have your way with me."

"Because you invited me to do it." She coils locks of her hair around her fingers, toying with the strands. "And it's my bed, technically."

"Our bed. We both sleep in it."

"True. Our bed, then."

I step backward out of her arms, whip off my shirt, and toss it onto the sofa. "Be waiting for you."

Heading for the hallway, I glance back at Calli one last time until I've gone too far around the corner to see her anymore. The bedroom door makes a soft click when I shut it after me. Once I've gotten naked, I close the curtains and pull the quilt off the bed, then flip the sheet and blanket aside. The lamp is still on, but once I'm lying on the bed, I shut that off too.

And I wait.

Maybe I should've left the door open a wee bit. I jump up and ease the door open several inches, just enough that muted light from the living room leaks inside. Back on the bed, I lie down to wait again.

Someone knocks on the front door.

I can tell it's the front one and not the back door because I hear the distinctive sound of a fist rapping on wood. Glass sounds different. Then I hear a click, as if Calli has opened the door.

Though I have no intention of eavesdropping, the voices out there make their way back here. The house isn't large, so it's no surprise I can hear what they're saying, especially since they speak in raised voices.

"Calli, I've missed you," a man says. It sounds like he has an accent.

"What do you want?" she asks.

"May I come inside?"

"Tell me what you came here to say. And make it fast, I've got things to do."

She only has one thing to do—me. But the anxiety in her voice ensures I stop thinking about sex.

"As you wish," the man says, then he speaks in a softer voice so I can't hear his words.

"Us?" Calli says sharply. "Spit it out, Rade. What exactly are you suggesting?"

They both start speaking in softer voices this time, and I can't understand what they say.

Finally, Calli says in a firm, louder voice, "Might as well give me the divorce because I'll never be with you."

More hushed words. I swing my feet off the bed, experiencing a strong urge to go out there and support Calli, but I think that must be her husband. She might not want me interfering. So, I get back on the bed and pull the sheet over my lower body.

The front door shuts.

Calli shambles into the bedroom. She eases the door further open, steals inside, and shuts the door. The curtains, though thick, allow a hint of sunlight to filter into the room, so she can probably see the shape of me on the bed.

I switch on the lamp, and golden light spills over the bed. I'm lying here with one leg outstretched, the other bent so the sheet has slid off to expose my entire leg up to the hip. The sheet covers my groin and drapes over my other leg. I swear I didn't adopt this pose deliberately in hopes of arousing Calli, but despite the emotional conversation she seems to have just had with another man, she can't seem to stop herself from admiring my body. I link my hands behind my head, gazing at her with a tight expression. My casual pose is bollocks, and I'm sure she's figured that out, but I feel an odd need to pretend I don't care what she and that man said to each other.

"That was your husband," I say.

She nods. "He claims this time he'll accept the divorce papers. I've decided to believe him and let the process server try one last time."

"What makes you think your husband will keep his word?"

"He seemed sincere." She shuffles to the bed, perching on its edge, angled toward me. "Rade said he loves me and wants a chance to win my heart."

I drop my arms onto the bed. "What did you say?"

"No, of course. I don't love him, and I never will. He's done a lot for me and I'm grateful, but gratitude isn't enough to make me feel that way about him."

I study her, unmoving, unblinking.

"There's a bigger reason I can't love him," she says, scooting further onto the bed. "I'm in love with someone else."

"Who might that be?" I'm not being sarcastic. I need to hear the answer and know for sure. My hope that she means me might be nothing more than arrogance.

She crawls across the bed on hands and knees to crouch beside me. "I love *you*, Aidan."

For a moment, I can't move or speak. Did I imagine she said that? Or did she tell me what I think she told me?

A smile stretches across my face, widening and brightening until I'm fair certain I'm beaming. "I love you too, Calli."

She gives my arm a half-hearted slap. "Why did you say nothing for so long? I thought you were going to reject me, and I'd have to sick my vicious puppies on you."

"Rather get a tongue bath from you." I pick up her hand, splaying it on my bare chest. "Didn't pause to make you worry. I was in shock. After two weeks of working hard to seduce you and make you love me, I finally succeeded."

"Oh, poor Aidan. Two whole weeks you had to wait." She pats my cheek. "Think of it this way. Lachlan needed an entire month to get Erica to love him."

"You're right. I outdid Lachie."

"Sure did." She leans in to whisper in my ear. "Turn off the lamp. It's time for your tongue bath."

When she sits back, her gaze darts to the sheet that's tented over my groin.

Calli clambers off the bed while I shut off the light. I watch the shape of her, disguised by the false twilight, as she strips off her clothes and slithers under the covers with her head beneath the sheet. She finds my legs, running her hands up and down my thighs. *Bod an Donais*, this woman is the sexiest lass in the universe.

And she loves me.

"There's a succubus in my bed," I purr. "Will ye drink the life from me?"

"Mm, I think I'll leave you just enough to keep this hard." She closes her fist around my erection. "I've got plans for it."

Positioned between my legs, she takes my cock in her mouth, working it with her tongue and hands. I writhe beneath her, not giving a toss that I'm making desperate noises deep in my throat. Not even the toughest man on earth could stop himself from making those noises when a woman like Calli has him in her mouth.

But I'm the only man she's ever tasted. And I love that.

She releases my *slat* and laves her tongue over the damp head.

"Fuck," I growl.

"Oh no, we haven't gotten to that yet." She flings the sheet off us. The fabric billows and settles down at the foot of the bed with a soft rustling sound. "Condom?"

"What?" I sound drunk, which is entirely her fault. Not that I'm complaining.

"Hand me a condom, please." By the way the mattress moves, I can tell she's rising to her knees and walking forward on them. Then she stops, and the dark shape of her kneels astride me. "Unless you want to keep lying there fully aroused and on the verge of coming."

I seize her hand, flipping it upside down. Then I grab a condom off the bedside table and slap the packet into her palm.

"There," I grumble. "Hurry, love."

"Feeling pressured?"

"If ye donnae hurry, I'll lose my—"

"Verve?" A ripping sound tells me she has torn open the packet, then I feel her rolling the condom onto me. "Can't let you suffer, can I?"

"Bloody hell, would ye—"

She plunges her body onto my cock. Seated astride me, with the full length of my erection buried within her, she slants forward to spread her palms on my chest. I've slouched down onto the silky sheets with my head elevated on a thick pillow. Feels like the perfect position for letting the sexiest woman in history fuck me.

I let out a groan of such depth, such intense relief, that it resonates in my chest. My hands find her erse, and I grip it firmly. "Please, *mo leannan.*"

"I love it when you beg."

With her hands on my chest, and her body anchored to me by my palms clamped on her erse, she lifts her hips and slides back down onto my *slat*. I cry out, the sound hoarse and sharp. She rocks her hips, riding me at a leisurely pace while the friction of our bodies melding and separating creates a wet sucking sound and a slapping of flesh on flesh. The darkness makes it more intense, like electricity is arcing through the air and enlivening our bodies like never before. Her noises grow sharper and hungrier, and she rides me with mounting vigor, her breasts bouncing in my face, though all I can see is the shadowy outline of them. I thrust up every time she slams down onto my cock, our movements in sync. My pulse thunders in my ears and beats so fast I have trouble catching my breath.

"Aidan, oh God!"

I splutter something in Gaelic, not sure what, and flip us both over with her pinned beneath my body. I can smell our sweat and her cream while I piston into her even faster and shove my hands under her hips, hoisting them up so I can drive into her with frenzied force and speed. The squeaking of the bed mingles with my grunts and her strangled cries. I see the outline of her body as she clutches the rails of the headboard.

Calli tosses her head back, her spine arched, and screams. "Yes-oh-God-yes!"

The world seems to vanish, here in the dark, while I feel her come with convulsive force, her inner muscles squeezing me over and over while she flings her legs around my hips to ride out her climax. I punch into her again, so hard and deep that I feel like we've joined more than our bodies. She lets out a whimpering cry, her release pulsating on and on, her flesh squeezing me with every spasm. With one more thrust, I explode inside her, bellowing from the ferocity of my release.

Her breaths come so hard and fast she seems unable to speak.

What we just did robbed me of breath and the ability to speak too. I collapse beside her with a thud that rocks the bed. Then I nuzzle her ear, my breaths blustering over her skin and ruffling her hair, which I can tell because the strands tickle my skin. "Are ye mine?"

"I'm yours, always."

"Ahm yours too, *mo chridhe*. Yours forever." I hook an arm over her belly. "That was the best sex I've ever had. And I thought making love to you couldn't get any better."

"Same for me. I love having sex with you almost as much as I love *you*."

I chuckle, enfolding her in my arms here in the twilight of our room. We lie like that for several minutes, silent except for our breathing, our heartbeats slowing with every passing second. The rest of the world seems to have vanished as if aliens abducted everyone except me and Calli. All right, that's a strange thought. But somehow, the idea makes me even more relaxed because it means I have her all to myself forever.

A noise rouses us both from our shared trance. It sounds like bagpipes. Distant bagpipes.

"My mobile," I mumble. "Forget it."

"It might be important. Maybe Jamie needs you to rescue her from my ravenous brother."

Sighing, I heave my body off the bed, switch the lamp on, and root around on the floor until I find my jeans. I dig the mobile out of a pocket, answering with a groggy hello.

"It's Lachlan. We need to talk about Seona Ross."

I jerk ramrod straight, my eyes wide. The tone of his voice tells me it's not good news. "What happened?"

Though I listen to Lachlan's words, my brain can't interpret any of them. I need time to digest it all, but fate has not given me any leeway. I glance sideways at Calli, and I suddenly feel sick—in my stomach, in my heart, in my soul. What Lachlan is saying, it can't be true. This cannot happen. Not when I've just found the woman of my dreams, and she said she loves me too. Am I cursed? Or just a bloody moron for thinking this could never happen to me?

I respond to everything Lachlan says with grunts and the occasional half-growled "aye." But I'm not really understanding what it all means. Not until we say goodbye, and my mind has nothing to focus on except what my brother told me.

Disconnecting the call, I hurl the phone onto the table. It clacks on the wood surface.

"Everything okay?" Calli asks, pushing up onto her elbows.

I scrub my face with both hands, then drop onto the bed on my back. The mattress bounces, and the frame squeaks. All I can do is stare up at the ceiling. "Lachlan and Erica spoke to Seona."

"Okay." Calli rolls onto her side facing me, braced on one elbow. "Did it not go so well?"

This can't be happening. Not now. I've got my life on the right track and then this…

"She told them why she wants money," I say, my voice flat. "She needs it for the bairn."

"The what?"

I cover my face with both hands again, letting them slowly slide down. The anguish that has me in its grip infuses my voice, but I can't look at Calli when I say the words. "A bairn's a baby. She's pregnant, and she says it's mine."

Chapter Thirty-One

I swear the weight of the entire universe has slammed down on top of me, like every moon, planet, and asteroid has targeted me for annihilation. Cannae move. Cannae think. Am I really the father of Seona's bairn? How could I have cocked it up and forgotten to use a condom? I never forget—as far as I know. Can I be sure of that? Right now, I'm not sure of anything except that I love Calli.

With shaky arms, she pushes up into a sitting position, though she seems as incapable of speaking as I am. She looks shell-shocked, and I feel the same way.

Seona has dropped a bomb on us, one that might blow apart everything Calli and I have built together. It's more than sex between us. It's… everything.

"They're sure," Calli finally says. "Lachlan and Erica are sure it's true. Seona is really pregnant."

"Yes." I wish to hell it was a lie. With my gaze glued to the ceiling, my hands pressed flat on the bed, I lie stiff and motionless except for the rising and falling of my chest. "Seona is very pregnant. Hard to tell for sure, but Erica guesses maybe six or seven months along."

"Is that—Does the timeline match up?"

"Sounds like it. The last time I slept with her was the night before the accident, about six months ago. I was sure I used a condom."

Calli scratches her arms, eying me with a pained expression. "She could've slept with someone else, couldn't she?"

I pinch the bridge of my nose and squeeze my eyes shut. "I suppose so. We were casual, not exclusive."

"You didn't ask her if she was with someone else."

"Calli." I swivel my head toward her, and I'm fair certain I look as agonized as I feel. "How can I ask that? If she says it's mine, I have to take her word unless I find out otherwise."

"What will you do?"

"She nearly died, and for all I know, it was my fault. If the bairn's mine, I won't leave her out in the cold. I'll take care of them both."

"You'll marry her."

"Donnae know." I should've said absolutely not, but I won't lie to Calli. Though I don't love Seona—never have, never will—I can't abandon the mother of my child. If the bairn's mine.

Calli gets a look on her face that I know well. It's the one that means she's sorting through the facts and analyzing the possibilities. After a moment, she turns her attention to me. "She didn't admit she's six months pregnant until today? That woman's been harassing you for money but failed to mention the baby. Doesn't that seem suspicious to you?"

"Donnae know."

She pulls the sheet over herself as if she's cold. "Did you ask for any kind of proof it's yours?"

"That's why I'm flying home tomorrow. To find out." I lever myself off the bed, sitting here with my arms limp at my sides and my body slumped forward. "Any sort of paternity test will take time. If she fights it, I suppose I'll have to try for a court order."

Just the thought of getting the courts involved makes me nauseous and tense. I have a cold pit in my stomach, one that will never go away until I get some answers. Calli's right about one thing. Why did Seona fail to mention the baby until now? She's been trying to extort money out of me, yet she didn't mention her pregnancy until she realized I would never pay her off the way she wants.

Why is this happening now? Am I being punished for my treatment of women? Aye, I've never used a woman. I'm always upfront about what I can offer, but Seona decided to reinterpret everything I told her to remake our casual arrangement into what she wanted. I don't believe she loves me. Seona needs to get psychological help, not money from me. The accident has warped her mind.

I've had slightly more than two weeks with Calli. It's not enough. I need a lifetime with her, but I have no idea what will happen to us now.

"I need to talk to Jamie," I say. "She's coming home with me, whether she likes it or not."

While I stand and collect my clothes, Calli watches me with an expression I've never seen on her face before. She looks...defeated. That's how I feel too, like everything that's happened over the past two weeks means nothing now, like the course of my life is no longer mine to chart. Calli sits immobile on the bed while I dress and head out the bedroom door. I stagger down the hallway and through the sliding glass doors.

I know I'll find Jamie in the hunting shack with Gavin. How will I explain this to her? How will I explain it to any of my family? Lachlan said he'll send the jet in the morning. That gives me a little more time to… Fuck, I don't know what I'll do.

Tomorrow I'll go home. Will I ever see Calli again?

The next morning arrives and flies by like time has sped up to an insane speed and the world is a spinning blur around me. Afternoon comes before I know it, before it feels like it should, and it's time for me to fly back to Scotland without Calli. She has become as stoic as my brothers, speaking only a few words now and then, none of those words meaningful. I donnae know what to say to her either.

My bonnie, sweet, clever, passionate lass. I'm walking away from the only woman I've ever loved.

Aye, Lachlan had walked away from Erica. He did it out of fear, though, not because a greedy woman tried to ruin his life. Maybe Aisley did do that, but it's not the same situation at all. I don't want to leave Calli, and the woman who wants to ruin me has no legitimate claim—unless the bairn is mine.

How many times over the past two weeks have I fantasized about having children with Calli? None of my dreams matter anymore.

Now I'm gathering my things and stuffing my clothes into my suitcase while Calli lies on her back on the bed, fully clothed, staring at the ceiling. The puppies are curled up at the foot of the bed, observing me with solemn faces as if they sense something bad has happened. Animals can be very intuitive that way. I wish I could stay here with Calli and the puppies, but I need to settle things with Seona once and for all.

The zipper of my suitcase makes a *zzzt* sound when I pull it shut, and the noise seems to snap Calli out of her semi-trance. She blinks rapidly. I slouch on the mattress near the bedside table, morose and silent, my gaze on the blank screen of the mobile in my hand.

Silence yawns between us. Silence and an invisible barrier that stretches across the distance.

"I'll pack you a snack," Calli says, "in case you get hungry at the airport."

Crawling out of bed, she hustles down the hallway with the puppies trailing after her.

And I sit here glaring down at the floor. Several minutes tick by before I can summon a single thought. Half a thought, actually. Whole ones are beyond my reach right now. A few more minutes elapse before I force myself to get up and go check on Calli. I drop my bags off at the front door on my way to the kitchen.

She's standing in front of the refrigerator, staring blankly at the food inside it. She sniffles, then sucks in a breath through her nostrils and swipes at her eyes, no doubt because tears have gathered in them.

I'm the cause of her tears. The realization stabs a hard pang into my chest.

"What's wrong?" I ask.

She jumps and shuffles around to face me across the bar.

I rest my hands on the back of one of the stools and note the redness in her eyes.

"Nothing's wrong," she says, but her voice is strained. "We don't have much time left."

"Aye." My posture slumps, and I can't help the weariness in my voice. "I… don't want to go."

"You have to. It's time."

Another, even sharper pang pierces my chest. I stifle a gasp at the sensation, though I know it's not real pain but only a ghost of my tangled emotions. "Do I have to leave? We could be together. If you come with me."

"I can't marry you."

"Not yet." I lean forward, desperation tightening my features and infusing my voice. "Stay with me. Live with me. I donnae care about the circumstances as long as you're with me. We can marry after your divorce comes through."

"I have to be here for that."

"You can fly back when the time comes."

"Aidan—" She freezes for a moment, then confusion wrinkles her brow. "What do you mean if I come with you?"

"Back to Scotland."

She scuffles backward a step. "You assume I'll go with you? Why don't you stay here?"

"Do you want me to?"

"If I did, would you do it? Would you stay here to be with me?"

"You know I have to go home to see Seona." I lower my gaze, unable to keep looking at her, my mouth cinching into a tense line. "Besides, I don't belong here. Scotland is my home and I want to share it with you. I know you'd love it."

"You know? How, exactly?" She raises her hands. "Let me get this straight. You assumed from the start that if you could make me fall for you, I'd happily trot off to a foreign country and leave my whole life behind."

"What life? You've got no job, no money—"

"I have a brother and a cousin I love."

"Gavin lives in Minnesota, and Tara's in Chicago. You hardly see them."

Calli fists her hands at her sides, staring at me like she's never seen me before.

Mhac na galla. I've said the wrong thing again, haven't I? Since I have no bloody idea how to explain my feelings to Calli, I have no way of sorting this mess I've made.

She backs up to the counter, grasping its edge with both hands. "If Seona's having your baby, this is all moot anyway."

"We can still be together, even if the bairn's mine."

She stuffs her hands under her armpits and shakes her head. "You're not the kind of man who could do that. You'll marry her."

"I want you, that's all I know right now."

"You want a wife. Why does it have to be me? Seona can give you a family right off the bat. Why do you still want to marry me?"

"Donnae love her. I love *you.*"

She's trembling, but not because she's cold. "You wanted an American wife, and I was handy. It was an accident we met, you were only interested because you found me in the same stupid club where Lachlan and Erica met. Why marry me?"

I open my mouth to speak, then shut it and study her with more intensity than I've ever done before with anyone. Though I know what she's doing, I can't think of a way to talk her down. Calli has latched onto all her fears about being trapped again the way that Rade bastard did to her, and she's transferring those anxieties onto our relationship. I know I can't change her mind right now. There's no time.

Telling Calli I love her hasn't worked. She asked why I want to marry her, and I have only one answer I can give her today.

"Not for a bloody green card," I say, with a bitter edge to my voice, "that's for certain."

"I didn't mean…" She seems to have forgotten what she meant to say mid-sentence.

Straightening, I march around the bar into the kitchen, straight to her, where I halt right in front of her, no more than a foot away. "I'll do it. I'll stay here. To keep you in my life, I'll do anything."

"What about Seona?"

My features contort as I hiss, "Shit."

"Right, you have to go home and see her." Calli rubs her temple like she's getting a headache. "Besides, you just said Scotland is your home and you'll never belong here. That means you won't be happy here, so if you stay, you'll resent me for making you do it."

I hadn't meant it that way. Had I? Christ, I donnae know anything right now.

Leaning forward, I bracket her body with my hands beside hers on the counter. My breaths bluster over her face. "What do you want of me? I will do whatever you say, if you'll only tell me what I have to do to make you happy."

"Aidan, go home. Take care of Seona and the baby."

I duck my head and scrape my lips across hers. "Donnae want to go. I love you. I need you with me."

"Doesn't matter what we want." She sucks in a breath, her eyes glistening with unshed tears. "This was never meant to be. It's time we face the truth."

Not meant to be? That's rubbish. Besides, we can make our own fate if she will ever give up her fears.

I've lived with too much guilt for six months, but here in this kitchen with the only woman I've ever loved, I suddenly realize the guilt holds no sway over me anymore. Whatever happens, I will find a way to get Calli back. I can't just let her go. She means everything to me.

But I know she needs time to come to terms with what's happened—not just the baby news, but also the fact she loves me. Memories of our time together flash through my mind, and the truth hits me so hard I almost gasp.

My mouth still hovers close to hers, but now it's stretched into a tight scowl. "You're wrong. We are meant to be. I went to that club because it's what Lachlan did, yes. But you mistook me for someone else, like Erica mistook Lachlan for her blind date. I didn't make that happen. We took a road trip, which was your idea, and I didn't realize that's what Lachlan and Erica did too. Lachlan only told me a few days ago. Erica had legal problems and so do you. Erica had a dog and you've got puppies."

"What's your point?"

I splay a palm over her lower back, drawing her nearer. "I didn't do any of that, couldn't have planned it if I tried. Fate brought you to me, and me to you. We belong together."

She turns her head away, making my lips brush across her cheek. "I don't believe in fate. This is a crock of shit, and you know it."

I place one finger on her chin, compelling her to look at me. "I will come back for you."

"You seem to be forgetting one important part of the Erica and Lachlan story. They broke up. We had a fling, like they did, and it's time for you to go home."

"Not a fling." I rub the pad of my thumb over her lips. "And you're forgetting Erica and Lachlan got back together."

"Then I guess you'd better leave it to fate to decide what happens to us."

Bloody hell, is she stubborn. I stare into her eyes, my thumb on her bottom lip, while the silence stretches on and on, broken only by the muted barking of puppies outside. At last, I lower my hand. "I love you, Calli. I always will."

I press my lips to hers, softly exploring them. She holds perfectly still, though her lips yield to mine.

There's nothing more I can do to convince her, not today.

Stepping away from Calli, I turn and shamble to the front door where my bags wait for me. I pick them up, and with one hand on the doorknob, I hesitate.

"I know you're afraid," I say, glancing over my shoulder at her. "I understand why. And honestly, I have no idea what's going to happen with Seona. All I know is I don't want to live the rest of my life without you. Maybe that's why I believe in fate, because it's my last hope for a happy ending with the only woman I've ever loved."

I walk out the door. The click of it shutting sounds much louder in my mind.

Movement inside the window by the door makes me roll my eyes in that direction.

Calli stands there with tears streaming down her face while she peeks between the curtains to watch me go.

Jamie and Gavin wait by the Mustang, holding hands. When they see me, Gavin gives Jamie a quick kiss and says something to her, his expression so affectionate and tender it makes my chest hurt again. At least my sister is happy.

Jamie and I pile into the hired car with our luggage. I slide in behind the wheel and jam the key into the ignition, twisting it. The engine growls to life.

In the rearview mirror, I see Gavin heading for the house. At least Calli won't be alone. Her brother will take care of her.

While the car roars down the gravel driveway, dust pluming up behind it, Jamie reaches out to lay her hand over mine on the wheel. "It will work out, I know it will. Have faith, Aidan."

"I do, but Calli is…stubborn."

"So she's nothing at all like you, eh?"

"Not in the mood for jokes right now."

Jamie kisses my cheek, then switches her attention to the scenery racing past us.

I will get Calli back. Somehow. Even if it takes the rest of my life.

Chapter Thirty-Two

achlan's jet is waiting for us at the airport, waiting to carry me away from Calli. Though I've resolved to get her back, I still have nothing resembling any sort of plan for how to accomplish that feat. I need to give her time, but not too much. She worries about everything, which means she could brood about things for a very long time before she realizes how pointless that is.

Jamie sleeps for most of the trip home. I guess Gavin wore her out.

And thinking about that makes me want to batter him, but only for a few seconds. Then I remember how happy my sister has been since she met Gavin, and all I want is for the two of them to feel like I had when I was with Calli, until the world came crashing down on us. My eyes water and sting. When I swipe away the wetness, I tell myself I was not about to cry. I…had grit in my eyes.

Bollocks. Now I'm deluding myself. Of course I'd been about to cry. I just left the woman I love, for pity's sake, so I have no reason to feel ashamed of shedding a few tears.

When we land at the Inverness airport, the pilot offers to carry our luggage for us. Jamie and I clomp down the stairs and onto the tarmac.

Our entire family is waiting for us, including several of our cousins.

Ma and Da hug me and tell me things will work out in the end, but then, parents are meant to say that sort of rubbish. Aren't they? My parents do, though I probably shouldn't call it rubbish. They mean every word they say. Niall and Sorcha MacTaggart have the kind of relationship I've always wanted to find with a woman. Now I have found it, but I may not get my fairy-tale ending.

Not that I ever thought about fairy tales. That's bollocks wee lassies fantasize about.

While our parents waylay Jamie, Lachlan comes over to slap me on the back. "Glad you're home, though I was hoping your lass would come with you."

"I just found out Seona is pregnant, possibly with my child. Why would you think Calli might come home with me?"

"Aye, of course. Sorry. Just want you to be happy, that's all."

"Donnae worry about me. I'm getting Calli back, one way or another."

"Of course you will." Lachlan throws his arms around me and thumps me on the back. "If there's anything I can do to help, just ask."

He heads for Jamie.

And I stand here mute and dumbfounded. My brother just hugged me. Lachlan has never been the kind of man who does that with his brothers, but he just did do that. In front of everyone.

Bloody hell. I must seem even more pathetic than I realized if Lachie's hugging me.

Rory approaches me next, but he doesn't hug me. "Welcome home, Aidan. As soon as you're settled in again, we need to talk about our next move."

"What move?"

"You need to demand a court order to force Seona to submit to a paternity test."

"Oh. Aye, that." The last thing I want to think about right now is the legal rubbish associated with Seona's claim that she's having my bairn. But I know I need to deal with it. Cannae get Calli back until I've sorted the Seona mess. "Maybe I should come to your office right now, so we can get the ball rolling."

"Are you sure? We can wait until—"

"Let's do it now. Can you give me a ride home after?"

"No, Aidan, we'll take care of that problem tomorrow. Tonight, enjoy being home with the family." Rory lays a hand on my shoulder. "We will resolve the Seona issue as quickly as possible. You have my word on that."

As if I need Rory's word. He's my brother, which means I trust him implicitly. We might have our differences, mostly to do with how uptight he is, but I love my brother. That's the MacTaggart way. We support each other no matter what.

My sisters, Fiona and Catriona, approach me next. They both hug me and kiss my cheek.

Then my cousin Iain comes over to greet me. He's about twenty years older than I am, but I've always had a good relationship with him. Though Iain is a strange man, everyone knows why that is. Angus, Iain's father, has been known to, ah, borrow things that don't strictly belong to him. Borrow them permanently. I don't think he's done that in a long time, though.

Iain sets his hand on my shoulder the way Rory had done a moment ago. "Listen carefully, Aidan. I'm about to give you sage advice."

"All right."

"Donnae let her get away. I made that mistake a long time ago when I let my pride keep me from running back to Rae. It's too late for me, but not for you."

Why is it too late for him? Not sure I believe that, but it isn't my place to say so. Everyone knows Iain met a lass in America when he was teaching at a university there, but that something happened to tear them apart. Iain never talks about the details, only that he lost her. More than a decade has gone by since then.

No, I won't wait that long. If Calli doesn't come to her senses in two weeks, I will fly back to America and kidnap her. All right, maybe I won't kidnap her. But I will make full use of my stubborn side to prove to Calli we belong together. She loves me. The lass told me so, and that means I cannot give up on her.

"Thanks for the advice, Iain," I say. "But I don't plan on letting Calli go."

"Good." He claps me on the shoulder. "Now, let's enjoy the celebration."

"What celebration?"

"The one to welcome you and Jamie home."

I groan, sounding too much like Rory when I do that. "Can it wait? I'm jeeked."

"You know how the family is. Once they've planned a party, there's no stopping that runaway train." He leans in to whisper, "Donnae worry. It's a garden party at Dùndubhan, not a rip-roaring do that will end with all of us having no memory of the night before when we wake up in the morning."

"How can we have a garden party? It's nighttime."

"Oh ye of little faith."

Iain smirks and walks away.

A few minutes later, I get stuffed into Rory's Mercedes with Lachlan, Erica, and their baby son. Thankfully, the bairn doesn't cry. He sleeps for the entire three-hour drive to Dùndubhan. Maybe it's three and a half hours. Feels like even more than that, though, since I have to listen to my brothers and Erica blethering about what they should do with me. Nobody needs to "do" anything. I'm fine. Aye, the woman I love essentially told me "away and chew a brush," but I'm not that easy to offend.

If my family decides to help me, though, I won't have much of a choice. Unlike my brothers, I don't mind if the MacTaggart clan butts into my love life. Let them have at it, I say. Whatever they do, it won't make a difference because they don't know Calli the way I do.

The garden party turns out to be a nighttime gala with white lights strung up around the garden and a metal fire pit. We roast sausages and marshmallows over the flames, and everyone blethers for hours. I want to go home and sleep, but I won't disappoint my family by leaving early. Since the MacTaggarts are never rude, they wrap up the celebration before ten o'clock.

Iain offers me a ride to my home on the outskirts of Ballachulish and says good night without getting out of the car. A ride in Iain's dilapidated Land Rover doesn't relax me since the vehicle seems to have no shocks. My erse hurts by the time I shamble into the house, and I don't even bother undressing. No, I just drop onto the bed and fall asleep within a minute, maybe less.

I dream of Calli, of course. Dirty dreams. So no, I don't mind the torment those fantasies inflict on me, not at all.

While I eat breakfast in the living room, I wonder what to do about my other problems. I'm skint, as everyone knows, and now I've got the Seona rubbish too. How much longer will I be able to afford the mortgage payments on this house? How long can I keep my office? The construction company had been dormant for too long after my accident, and I haven't had the money to get it going again.

I'm just finishing up my breakfast when someone knocks on the front door. I set my bowl of oatmeal on the coffee table and wander to the door, swinging it open without peeking out the window first to see who's there.

Rory skims his gaze over me and lifts one brow. "Going casual these days, eh?"

He's being sarcastic, of course. What's wrong with my clothes? Maybe I'm not wearing a shirt, and my pajama bottoms have leprechauns on them, but that doesn't make me any less manly. Jamie gave me the leprechaun pajamas because she didn't think I would wear them. Naturally, I do wear them, for the sole purpose of proving her wrong. But now Rory is studying me like he thinks I must've gone off my head. I might not have shaved this morning or yesterday, and it's possible I forgot to comb my hair, much less shower, so… Aye, he probably has good reason to think I'm barmy.

But I'm tired, that's all.

"Get dressed," he says in his stern-solicitor voice. "It's time to get off you erse and take legal action against Seona Ross."

"Donnae want to destroy her, Rory."

"You need to demand a paternity test, Aidan. Once you know for certain you are not the father of her child, she will have no legal grounds to demand anything from you."

"Aye, fine, let's get it over with." What if I am the father? I can't think about that until I know the truth.

But on this afternoon, on my first full day away from Calli, I make one very important decision. I decide I need to ring her every day to make sure she knows I haven't given up on us and I will never will. Words won't convince her, so daily phone calls feel like the best way to demonstrate my commitment to us. Our conversations have become awkward and uncomfortable, but I know things will get better. They have to. Calli says she's told her brother and her cousin about the marriage fraud the *cacan* Rade sweet-talked her into committing. At least he can't hold that over her head anymore, especially since he is as guilty as she is. More guilty, in my opinion.

The days drag by like I'm walking through wet cement. Seona refuses to have a paternity test, so Rory has filed the paperwork to get a court order. Naturally, Seona keeps demanding money. I take my solicitor's advice and cut off all contact with her, which includes blocking her number on my mobile. How long will it take to force her to have a paternity test? Even Rory can't say for sure.

Two weeks drag by like I'm trapped in purgatory for all time. But finally, I have news Calli needs to hear. Rory told me this afternoon, in his home office at Dùndubhan, but I've needed this long to drum up the courage to ring Calli. Rory suggested I spend the night here, and I agreed because I'm too knackered to drive. Well after midnight, I head into the sitting room. Then I dial her number.

It rings three times before I hear her lovely voice. "Hello?"

"Calli, it's me."

"How are you?" she asks, though I can't tell anything from her tone.

"Exhausted but fine." I pause for a heartbeat, then lower my voice to a husky whisper, "I've missed you."

"Oh Aidan, I've missed you too." She falls silent for a couple of seconds. "No wonder you're exhausted. Why are you awake? Isn't it two a.m. over there?"

"It is. Planned to get some rest and ring you in the morning, but I cannae sleep."

"Is there news?"

"Aye." Why do I feel anxious? This is good news I'm delivering. I haul in a deep breath and tell her. "The baby's not mine."

"Did she lie?"

"No, not quite. After the results came in, she admitted she'd slept with someone else while she and I were together. She couldn't know which of us was the father."

"You're always very careful to use condoms."

"I am, but no protection is perfect. Mostly, she wanted me to be the father because this other man was a one-night stand. She doesn't know his name, much less how to contact him."

"What about her demands for money?" Calli asks. "What excuse did she give for that?"

"Desperation. She's alone and running out of money. Her family moved to Australia last year, and she's been embarrassed to tell them about her troubles."

I'd hoped Calli would sound happier about this news. The last barrier to us being together has been shattered. Instead of being happy, though, she still sounds guarded.

"Seona doesn't want money anymore," I say. "My sister Fiona has a friend in social services who's helping Seona. Her mother's coming here to be with her until the baby's born, and after that, they're all going to Australia."

"I'm glad she's getting what she needs."

"This means it's over. We can be together, Calli."

Silence. It drags on and on while I listen to the faint static in the background of our call.

"Are you there?" I ask.

"Yeah, I'm here. I don't know if it's a good idea."

"What?"

"Us. We haven't known each other long. A couple weeks, really, and I'm not sure that's enough."

I blow out a sigh that probably sounds irritable. "How long would be long enough? A month? Six months? I love you, and you love me. More time won't change that."

"I thought I loved you. Maybe we've both been blinded by two weeks of incredible sex."

"What we have is more than sex, and you know it." I groan, unable to hide my frustration and weariness. "You've had too much time to think and come up with reasons we don't belong together. I know you worry you don't know me, but you do. What happened with Rade, the problems Tara and Gavin had, those have nothing to do with you and me."

"I thought I knew you. Then you announced we were moving to Scotland."

"Wasn't an announcement. I'm sorry I upset you, but I didn't mean it as an order. We can talk about the options."

"My home is here. Your home is there. What's to discuss?"

"Why won't you come visit me here?" I try for a reasonable tone, but I don't think I succeed. "At least see what it's like before making up your mind."

"If I don't want to move there, what then?"

"Told you before, I'll live in America if that's what you want."

"And you'll hate me for making you leave your beloved homeland."

"For Christ's sake, Calli. What do you want me to say?" I take several slow, deep breaths while I try to regain my composure. This call hasn't gone the way I'd imagined, not at all. "We can work it out. Please stop looking for excuses to end this."

"Bad things happen," she says. "Life has taught me to expect them. Good things are rare, and I can't risk it on the hope we might beat the odds."

"Please don't do this. I'll fly over there, and we can talk in person."

"I'm sorry. You'll never know how much being with you has meant to me, but I can't do this. Goodbye, Aidan."

She hangs up.

And I hurl my mobile onto the coffee table and sink into the sofa. A slew of Gaelic curses tumble out of me, then I realize what I need to do. The baby news hasn't made a difference. Neither has talking to her. I need to try something I have never done before, take the biggest risk of my life, and pray I can get through to Calli this time.

I run to Rory's office to grab the supplies I need, then I go back to the sitting room and settle onto one of the high-backed chairs near the big windows. Aye, it's the middle of the night. Maybe this is the right time to do what I have in mind. Maybe exhaustion has loosened me up enough that I won't hold back. I have a clipboard on my lap with sheets of writing paper clamped onto it. I lift the expensive pen I borrowed from Rory's desk and poise it over the paper.

Then I touch the pen's tip to the first sheet and just do it.

"In the name of transparency," I write, "I should tell you Lachlan sent Erica a note after their breakup. That's not why I'm writing to you. Lachie only managed two words, and I have much more to say."

Aye, I do have a lot to tell her, but I suffer a brief moment of paralysis before I can make myself go on.

"I've never loved anyone but you," I write. "Those weeks with you were the best of my life, and I believe with all my heart we will be together one day. You are the love of my life. I know you're afraid, but staying away from me won't make you feel any safer. Don't give up on us. Come see me, or I'll come to you, and we'll take as long as you want getting to know each other. Please give us another chance. We have as much time as you need to work out where to live, but we can't do that unless you let me see you. Please. You are *mo chridhe*—my heart—and you always will be. I'll love you for the rest of my life and the whole of eternity. All my love, Aidan. PS, let Tara and Gavin read this because you need their support."

Before I can lose my nerve and rip up the letter, I fold the page and slip it into the FedEx envelope I'd found in Rory's office. In the morning, I rush to the nearest place where I can drop off my envelope for overnight delivery.

All I can do now is wait and hope.

Chapter Thirty-Three

Three days go by with no word from Calli. I'd sent the letter overnight, and I know it was delivered. If she doesn't want me, she could at least say so. But I don't believe she feels that way, not for one second. Today, I can't take it anymore. I need to do something, anything, to take my mind off Callie, so I drive to Lachlan and Erica's farm in the hills surrounding Ballachulish.

Yesterday, my brothers cornered me in my office—which is just a trailer with desks, chairs, file cabinets, and other boring stuff—and insisted on giving me money.

"Call it an investment or a grant," Lachlan said. "Either way, you are taking the money. No more 'ahmno that skint' or 'I donnae need charity.' We've decided, and you will agree."

"Thank you, Lachie," I said, "for the generous 'investment' you're trying to ram down my throat. But you need to come up with a new line. The investment-slash-grant nonsense is getting old."

"Rory had rolled his eyes then. "We finally realized you won't accept anything from us unless we force you to do it."

"It's tough love," Lachlan announced. "Get used to it. Oh, and Iain wants to be your first new employee."

"But he's an archaeologist. I'm a general contractor."

"You know as well we do that Iain hasn't been an archaeologist for a long time. So haud her wheesht and hire him."

I saluted, in a way that wasn't entirely un-sarcastic.

But I politely declined my brothers' offer of an investment-slash-grant. I need to get my company on a stronger footing on my own, without relying on my family to prop up my business. Maybe that's foolish and stubborn, but it's how I feel. Besides, I believe with a conviction that has no factual basis that things will work out, and soon I'll be able to hire back any of my former employees who haven't found work somewhere else. Iain has already volunteered to be my first new hire.

Now, a day after that "tough love" rubbish from my brothers, I'm in the garden behind Lachlan and Erica's house planting seeds. It's a way to distract myself, nothing more. After marrying the bonnie Erica, Lachlan decided to become a farmer. They even have cows. Aye, my uptight oldest brother owns livestock and grows vegetables. Sometimes I think I've fallen through a black hole into another universe that looks just like the old one but has Farmer Lachie in it.

While I'm knee-deep in dirt and seeds, I swear I hear someone calling my name. It's so distant that I can't be sure. No, I must have imagined it. Lachlan bellows loud enough it echoes off the mountains, and Erica would've come over here instead of calling out to me.

I focus on the ground and the task I volunteered to do. It's not helping, though. I'm not distracted from thoughts of Calli. Instead, I keep wondering where Calli is and whether I should go back to my original plan and fly to America to kidnap her. While I consider the idea, I move to the left, still kneeling, and bend forward to place seeds in their wee holes. I think I'm planting spinach, but I'd dumped the seeds into my hand and tossed the packet away, so I'm not sure. This has to be the most boring job in the world. Well, except for being a solicitor. That sounds even more mind-numbing. Why am I torturing myself with farm work? I never want to become a farmer. This is Lachlan's dream, not mine, but I have nothing else to do to occupy myself, not until my company lands new clients.

"Aidan."

My entire body goes rigid. I know that voice. Christ, I'd recognize it even if Calli had laryngitis and could only croak words. Every hair on my body stiffens while an odd shiver tingles over my skin. *She's here.* I uncoil my spine until I crouch upright, my head still aimed away from her. I'm having trouble catching my breath. Did I hallucinate her voice? One way to find out. With a slow and deliberate motion, I set down the spade I'd been holding and place my palms on my knees. Though I can't speak yet, I take several deep breaths to calm my racing heart.

Seconds tick by, bleeding into minutes. Why am I frozen here in the dirt? It's barmy.

"Aidan, it's me."

Finally, I manage to speak, though my tone comes out gruff. "I know. Ye think I wouldn't recognize your voice?"

I rise to my full height, slowly, still half-convinced I'm hearing things. Rolling my shoulders back, I turn to face Calli. Cannae move anymore, though. Cannae speak either.

She walks up to me, halting an arm's length away. "Hi. Erica said you were out here. I was hoping we could talk. No, that's not right. I need to talk, and I hoped you would listen. Please."

I'm still incapable of forming words, so I just stare at her. Calli is here. With me.

"I know I screwed up," she says. "I know you have every right to tell me to go to hell. No one's ever been as good to me as you are, and I let my stupid fears come between us. I used the past as an excuse to keep you at a distance, to keep from falling for you. It didn't work."

I search her face, but I don't see any fear there. Has she really overcome the past?

Calli shuffles one step closer. "I made so many mistakes in my life. I thought I didn't deserve happiness, didn't deserve someone as good as you. God, you are so good. You make me feel like I'm not a criminal, like maybe I could have someone who loves me and treats me with respect. A man like you." Her voice broke on the last word. She moves a little closer, gazing into my eyes with unwavering focus. "For years, I've hidden from life because I felt guilty for breaking the law to help Rade, sure I'd be found out and locked up. I couldn't believe anything good could happen to me, but then you barreled into my life and turned everything upside-down in the most incredible way. The whole thing with Seona threw me for a loop, and you were right. I had too much time to think of lame reasons to stay away from you. The truth is, I love you so much it terrified me. But not anymore."

My lips twitch a wee bit. She flew all the way to Scotland to find me and tell me all of this. She must still love me, aye?

"What I'm trying to say," she says, "is I am so sorry. I'll do whatever it takes to make up for hurting you."

I should say something, shouldn't I? But my voice has abandoned me.

"You said you'd wait," she begins, spreading a palm on my chest, barely touching me. "Said you'd wait as long as it took. These two weeks felt like an eternity. But hey, at least I didn't make you wait two months. We've got one up on Erica and Lachlan, right?"

The corner of my mouth ticks up a hair. My heart is racing again, and I cannae figure out why I'm standing here like a tree instead of kissing her senseless. I guess I still cannae believe she's really here.

Fanning both her palms over my chest, she leans in and angles her head back to meet my gaze. Though I keep my chin raised, I roll my eyes down to look into her emerald eyes. My throat has tightened, and my eyes burn like I might cry. Only Calli has ever made me this emotional.

"I love you, Aidan."

My brows furrow, and my eyes widen a fraction.

"Please believe me, Aidan. I love you so much I can't imagine my life without you anymore." She skates her palm across my chest until it bumps over a small, hard shape beneath my shirt. She taps one fingertip on the circular object. "What is this?"

I duck my head, turning it to the side, my eyes closing. Aye, I'd bought the bloody thing for her, but now that she's here and I know she still loves me, I can't move a muscle to show her how happy I am to have her with me.

Diving her hand inside my shirt, she pulls out the object—a diamond engagement ring, dangling from a long silver chain. She runs her finger over the shiny gold band. The diamond glitters in the sunshine as bright and perfect as the love I feel for her.

Rubbing her thumb over the brilliant stone, she looks up at me, though I can only see her out of the corner of my eye. "I'm not giving up. I'll come back here every day, ten times a day, to beg you to forgive me if that's what it takes. I'll stalk you until you either take me back or have me arrested. Hell, I'll strip naked and run down the streets of Ballachulish screaming your name. Don't care about dignity or pride anymore, all I care about is you."

I rotate my face toward me. *Speak, ye eejit, before she leaves.*

She waits for my response as seconds elapse, and she bites down on her bottom lip.

I clear my throat. "Well, it took you bloody long enough. Thought you'd never come to your senses."

"You mean—" She gawps at me like she hasn't understood what I said. "Do you mean you forgive me?"

"Nothing to forgive. I knew you'd turn up eventually. You are hopelessly in love with me, after all." I smirk and wink. "Just like I predicted you would be."

A wee sob bursts out of her. She slumps into me, her forehead falling to my chest. I wrap my arms around her soft, warm body and tuck her snugly into my embrace. I don't care if she announces we have to move to America. I will go anywhere with her.

I crook a finger under her chin and raise her face to mine. "Did you think I'd give up so easily? A few weeks is nothing. Told you I'd wait as long as it took, because you're worth it."

"I know, but I told you—"

"Hush." I hold her face in my hands, brushing her tears away with my thumbs. "If I learned anything from Lachlan and Erica, it's that second chances come along if you're patient. And when you get a second chance with the one person you love more than anything, you jump on it."

"I spoke to Erica back in the house. She said I...broke your heart."

"You did." I keep my hands on her cheeks to stop her from flinching away. "Easy, *mo chridhe*, I'm not a weakling. I can handle a broken heart." I tilt her head back, slanting mine down to within an inch of her face. "Now it's your job to heal it."

She glances at the ring, which she'd been twisting around her fingertip, carving out a red line in her flesh.

"You spoiled the surprise," I say, snatching the ring away. I yank it, snapping the chain and letting the silver links plummet to the ground. I hold the ring between my thumb and forefinger. "This belongs to you."

"You still want to marry me?"

I shake my head, because she is adorably obtuse. "Havenae you been listening? Ahmno letting our second chance slip away."

"You're jumping on me?"

My lips curve into a smile. "That'll come next, you can count on it. First..." I drop to one knee before her, raising the ring, and gaze at her beautiful face that's filled with love. "Calli Douglas, will you marry me?"

"Yes." She holds up the appropriate finger, ready to accept the ring. "After my divorce is finalized, of course. That happens in less than seven weeks. Can you wait?"

"To marry you, yes." I slip the ring onto her finger. "To make love to you, no."

"Get up so I can kiss you senseless."

I surge to my feet and pull her into my arms. "I missed you."

"And I missed you so much. Can't believe I took so long to come here."

"Thought you were going to kiss me."

She throws her arms around my neck and crushes her mouth to mine. *Bod an Donais*, I've dreamed of this moment for two weeks, to have Calli in my arms, kissing me. I let myself relish the softness of her lips, the way she plunges her tongue between my lips the second I give in and open for her. She explores me with long, lazy strokes of her tongue like she wants to relish the taste of me after all this time apart. I lash my tongue around hers, molding my lips to her mouth.

Though we break the kiss, my lips graze hers when I speak. "I love you, Calli. Would've waited forever, but I had no doubt it wouldn't take that long."

Calli combs her fingers through my hair. "We are meant for each other. No other man on earth could understand me like you do."

"Stopped thinking we don't know each other well enough, eh?"

"The letter changed everything. You have a real way with words."

"I wasn't sure you'd like what I wrote. Never said flowery things like that before."

"What you wrote made me cry." She trails her fingertips down my cheek. "In a sad way at first, but later in a good way. I read the letter again on the plane. You amaze me, Mr. MacTaggart."

"You amaze me too, Mrs. MacTaggart."

She raises her brows. "Getting a little ahead of yourself, aren't you?"

"Always. Impulsive, remember?"

She laughs, then kisses me and touches me like she means to never let go. I hadn't written those words in the letter to impress her. It had all been true. I will love her for the rest of my life and whatever comes after that, until all the stars have died and there's nothing left except the two of us.

I glance around, lips compressed and eyes narrowed, while I search for the right spot.

"What is it?" she asks.

"Looking for the closest place where I can strip you naked."

"Outside?"

"Not making love to you in my brother's house, when he's home with his wife and bairn." I catch sight of the perfect spot and smile with satisfaction, then I sweep her up into my arms. "Found it."

I carry her toward a small grove of apple trees laden with ripe, red fruit and set her down on the grass beneath the largest tree, in the umbrella of its shadow.

Gazing up at the blue sky, I settle in beside her. "Growing apples in the Highlands is a difficult task. Almost takes a miracle to keep them growing and bearing fruit. Must be good luck to make love under the fertile bows of a Scottish apple tree."

"Are you implying this is a magic fertility tree?"

"Maybe it is." I dig a condom packet out of my pocket, holding it up. "I've been carrying this around so I'd be ready whenever you turned up. Should we use it?"

"What exactly are you asking me?"

I lay a hand over her lower belly. "Would ye like to start trying for a bairn today?"

A sexy smile curls her lips, and she snatches the condom packet from my fingers, tossing it aside. "Does that answer your question?"

I chuckle. "Well enough, aye."

Lying stretched out on the green grass, elevated on her elbows, she watches me shed my T-shirt.

"By the way," she says, "Rade insisted on giving me a financial settlement to compensate me for the years I gave him."

I pause with my jeans half unzipped. "Did he?"

"Yes. A hundred thousand dollars."

For several seconds, all I can do is stare at her, but then I grin. "I'm marrying a rich woman."

"Does it bother you?"

"Not in the slightest."

She clasps her hands over her belly, her feet shifting in restless movements.

"What is it?" I ask.

"Even though we're not married yet," she says, "I'd like to give you some of the money, to get your business going again. We'll be sharing everything soon enough, and I don't want to wait."

I stand here speechless, my hands lingering on the waistband of my jeans. Though I'd rejected Rory and Lachlan's offer of financial help, I don't want to say no to Calli. She's going to be my wife, and maybe sharing in her divorce settlement is the right way to begin our life together. Besides, I know she needs me to accept her generous, loving offer.

"I could be a manly man and say no," I tell her. "But I can tell you want to do this, and I can't deny my future wife anything."

"Thank you. I hope this doesn't wound your male pride."

"Donnae worry, love. Ahmno sensitive."

While I resume unzipping and push my jeans down, exposing my stiffening cock to her, she observes with growing lust that I can see in her expression. I've missed her passion, and I cannae wait to be inside her again.

"I do love watching you strip," she says. "Maybe I should stuff a few hundred-dollar bills in your waistband."

I kick my jeans away. "You get me for free. Donnae take my clothes off for money, remember?"

"Oh yes, you did mention that once upon a time."

Now I stand completely naked before my fiancée. The way she looks at me, I know I won't last long once we start shagging. I'm addicted to Calli's body. I'm addicted to everything about her, from her smile and her laugh to her incredible passion, and even her stubborn side.

I kneel over her, my knees straddling her thighs. "Time to unwrap my gift."

And she is a gift, the most precious one I've ever been given. I will spend the rest of my days proving to her that she means everything to me. No, I'm not a stripper. But just like in the club that night, I will follow her anywhere. She belongs with me, and I belong with her.

Our new life together begins now.

Chapter Thirty-Four

Eight Weeks Later

I am a married man. No one in my family thought I would settle down, but I proved them wrong. My family loves me, but I'd never had a serious girlfriend until I met Calli, so I can't blame them for assuming I'd stay "Don Juan" forever. Two hours and forty minutes ago, Calli and I said "I do." Now, here I am about to ravish my wife for the first time—the first as her husband. I shagged her plenty back in Michigan, and here in Scotland when she found me again, but now everything has changed.

Calli lies naked on a king-size bed inside our new home, a two-story farmhouse a five-minute walk from Lachlan and Erica's place, watching while I kick off my shoes. I'd watched her undress too, and I felt a wee bit disappointed when she removed her wedding dress. I might have gotten choked up when I first saw her in that frock. She looked like an angel with a halo of fiery red hair, and her emerald eyes shined like she might cry too.

My wife eyes my kilt while licking her lips and arching her back. My growing erection probably has something to do with that look on her face. I love the way her rosy nipples have gotten stiff and the skin around the peaks has pebbled. It might mean she's cold, but today, it means she cannae wait to have a poke. I know she likes my outfit—tuxedo on top, kilt in the middle, and more formal wear on the bottom. No underwear, but only Calli and I know that.

Lachlan had teased me about my clothes, but I think he's just jealous that Calli hunted me down to beg me to marry her, while Lachie had to plead and humiliate himself and virtually stalk Erica to get her back.

Aye, I've outdone my brother. And aye, I will mercilessly harass him about that.

While my wife follows my every movement, I take hold of the kilt, and with one flick of my wrist, send it plummeting to the floor. Since I'd already removed the rest of my clothes, I'm ready for action. My cock waves in the air, as anxious as I am to shag my wife, and a drop of moisture clings to the crown. I love it when Calli licks that off, but I have other plans right now.

I kneel at the foot of the bed. "Wish you'd let me take you to a posh hotel. It is our wedding night. Or afternoon."

Since she had insisted we not have sex yesterday or last night or this morning, my bride was anxious to get me alone and naked. I whisked her away from the reception early. She all but begged me to fuck her. That's not me being sarcastic. Calli said, "Please, please, please, Aidan. I need you now."

Satisfying my wife is my top priority.

"Rather start our life together in the home we'll share," she says, and tickles my knee with her toes. "You know I don't care about fancy stuff. I want you. That's all I need, today and every day."

"It's all I need too." I crawl up her body until I'm straddling her on my hands and knees. I stop with my head over her belly. "We are going on the honeymoon, even if Lachlan did pay for it."

"Lachlan *and* Rory. It was their wedding gift to us. Can't wait to see the French Riviera. Sure you don't mind bringing the puppies with us?"

"Wouldn't be the same without the furry lassies." I duck my head to swipe my tongue over one nipple. "Though I'm glad Jamie took them for tonight, so I can have you all for myself. Cannae wait to see you lying nude on a private beach, for no one but me to see."

"You have become rather possessive of my body."

I kiss her belly. "Let me show you how much I covet your body."

She bends one knee and grazes it against my cock. "I covet yours too."

I hiss in a breath when she hooks her leg around my hip. "*Thig mi air do mhuin.*"

"No clue what that means, but I'm game for anything."

"Means I'm coming to mount you." I lay a hand on her belly, gliding it lower and lower until my fingertips tease the hairs on her mound. "No need to *fannadh* anymore, unless you want me to watch."

"I want you inside me."

"*Dé an doimhneachd?*"

"You have got to teach me Gaelic. What's that one mean?"

"How deep."

Lifting her hips, she presses my palm into her mound until my fingers skim her clitoris. "Deep as your *slat* can go. I want you so deep inside me I can feel you come, like you're a part of me."

"We are a part of each other, *mo leannan*." I thrust my hand between her folds, caressing the skin and fondling her clit. When she arches her back and moans, I grin. "I'm impressed you learned a Gaelic word all on your own. *Slat*? Never taught you that one. Where'd you learn it?"

"Rory told me."

My hand stills, and my eyes go wide. "That bloody *bod ceann*—"

"I'm kidding," she says with a laugh. "Your brother's not a dickhead. But I learned *slat* from the internet."

"Did you now." I begin to stroke her again, slowly, intensifying her need until she's wriggling against my palm and clenching her fingers in the sheets. "I'm going to show you things the internet cannae teach ye."

"No better teacher than Aidan the Magnificent."

I pull my hand away, glide a palm down to the insides of her thighs, and spread her wide for me. "We come together this time."

She smiles, the expression infused with all the lust and love we feel for each other.

How did I ever get so lucky? But it wasn't really luck. Fate showed us the way. If I had never gone to that club... If Calli hadn't been searching for a stripper... Would we ever have crossed paths? I believe we would have because this was meant to be.

And I donnae care if that's romantic rubbish.

I plant my hands on either side of her, my arms straight and my face above hers. "I love you with everything I am."

"I love you, Aidan, so much."

No more words are needed. I show her what she means to me by sliding inside her slowly, tenderly, loving the look on her face—pain and pleasure, two sides of the same coin. Her body fits me snugly, like it was made for my cock. We were made for each other, for sure, in every way. I couldn't have found a more perfect lass for me if I'd scoured the globe in search of her. Calli is my other half, like the second face of that coin.

She clings to me while I begin to pump my hips, pulling out of her and then driving deep inside again, keeping the pace measured and rhythmic, wanting this to last as long as humanly possible. With her heels flat on the bed, she lifts her hips to meet my thrusts, her mouth open on a string of moans and gasps. The slickness of her body feels so bloody good, and I cannae look away from her face. I pump faster, harder, grunting every time I lunge inside her and blustering out a breath when I retreat. She locks her legs and arms around me, begging me to never stop, to make her come, to never stop.

Her body goes rigid. Her lips part, and she stops blinking, her gaze nailed to mine. I pound into her at a frantic pace, making her cry out.

At the instant the orgasm wrenches her body, my release jets out of me into her depths, and I throw my head back, shouting a long litany of Gaelic. She clutches me with her entire body and cries out several times. I pump into her twice more, then shove a hand down to massage her nub, determined to see her climax through to the very last spasm.

I collapse beside her and pull her into my arms, cradled against me. We're both breathing hard, nearly breathless. She rests her cheek on my chest.

"The wedding was beautiful," she says, "but this was more fun."

Aye, nothing compares to making love to Calli. But the wedding had been quite an experience too, with both of us reciting our vows on the same hillside where Lachlan and Erica had held their wedding. It lies just behind their house, and in the summer, it's blanketed with purple heather. Though I'd been determined never again to reenact any part of my brother's love life, Calli had disagreed.

"It's appropriate," she told me. "After all, we might never have met if you hadn't gone to Dance Ardor hoping to re-create Lachlan's journey to love."

Aye, she was right. My clever wife usually is.

"Weddings are for the guests," I say, back in the present with my naked, sated wife. "This was for us."

"I finally got to meet the infamous Rory, but I didn't see the caber."

"He was in a good mood today, because of the wedding." I shake my head. "The man needs a strong woman to shake some sense into him."

"I'm sure he'll find the right girl someday."

"Not unless she ties him up and drags him away from his office."

"Let's not talk about your family anymore tonight."

"Anything my wife wants." I roll onto my back, taking her with me, and she winds up sprawled over me. With my fingers, I trace small, delicate circles on her back. "Should I worry about your brother's intentions with my sister?"

Calli laughs.

And I know why. Maybe I can't read her mind, but I know my wife well enough to realize she's remembering a certain incident during the wedding reception, which had been an outdoor affair held at Lachlan and Erica's house. Gavin and Jamie had been engaged in a secret conversation some distance away from us. While Calli and I watched, the two of them slipped away from the crowd to a spot off to the side where they could have some privacy. I'd spotted the pair and poked my wife in the ribs, my lips twisting as I nodded toward Gavin and Jamie.

"What are they up to?" I had asked Calli.

She shrugged. "No idea. Maybe a quick tryst."

My mouth opened, but for several seconds, I couldn't speak. "Bad enough he had her in a hunting shack in the woods."

"Young love. What can you do?"

I've forgotten all about that now, what with my sensual wife ensconced in my arms. All right, maybe I haven't forgotten. But I've made a conscious decision not to think about it anymore. I'm in such a good mood today that I don't even care if Gavin Douglas has a poke with my sister.

Calli props her chin on my chest. "Gavin and Jamie may be the next couple to tie the knot. Do you have a problem with that?"

"Not so long as he treats her right."

She lightly rakes her nails down my chest. "You mean as long as he doesn't act like the two Scotsmen I know, who seduce us American girls at first sight."

"Exactly."

A mobile rings, muffled but nearby. She sits up, making an adorably pinched face like she's trying to decide whose mobile that is. "Sounds like mine."

Of course it's hers. Mine rings with bagpipes.

"Let it go," I say. "We're on holiday."

"Better check it, just to be sure."

I wriggle out from under her and march across the room to dig her mobile out from under her wedding dress, which had wound up piled on a chair. I glance at the phone's screen and curse in Gaelic.

"What's wrong?" Calli asks, sitting up.

"It's the surgery." I toss her the mobile.

She catches it in one hand. "My checkup? Probably calling to tell me the blood tests were fine. It was a standard physical, that's all."

"They called on our wedding day. Must be urgent."

"Don't turn into a worrywart. That's my job." She holds the phone to her ear. "This is Calli."

Since I can't hear the other side of the conversation, all I can do is wait and worry, though I don't develop any warts from doing that. Calli's eyes have widened a touch. Is it bad news after all?

"Surprise?" she says.

The word must mean it's good news. Right? Of course, there are bad surprises too.

I glance down at my naked body. Is that a wart forming on my cock? Need to stop fretting.

"What?" my wife virtually shouts. "That's incredible. I thought it would take longer to happen, but this is such perfect timing. Thank you for calling. I have no idea what to say."

Calli listens briefly, then says goodbye to the other person. She drops her mobile on the bed and looks at me.

I grasp her face in my hands, searching her eyes. "What is it? Are you ill?"

"No, not at all." She lays her hands over mine while tears trickle down her cheeks, and then she smiles. "We're having a baby, Aidan. I'm pregnant."

For a few seconds, I stare blankly at her. Did I hear that right? Did she say what I think she did? *Aye, of course she did, ye numpty.*

I let out an ear-splitting, uproarious whoop, throwing my head back while I fling my arms wide. The whoop segues into laughter, and I leap onto the bed, bowling Calli over with me. Tangled in each other's arms, we laugh and cry and kiss. Yes, I cry. A wee bit. Not enough to count as crying, really. Our kissing grows more heated while our hands grope each other's bodies and my *slat* starts to swell again.

I lick and nibble a path down her neck. "This requires another celebration."

"You mean sex."

"Would ye rather drink champagne?"

"Oh no. I want sex, right now."

Bod an Donais, is it any mystery why I love this woman?

I push up onto my knees. "I'd wager we made the bairn that day under the apple tree."

"The magic fertility tree? I think so too." Her lids flutter shut when I skim my hands up and down her body, exploring every curve and dip. "This might sound weird, but I'm looking forward to coming back after the honeymoon and getting to work. Cataloging your uncle's piles and piles of family papers and historical books is like catnip to a librarian."

"I'm looking forward to working with my new partner." I dip my tongue into her belly button, swirling it until she gasps. "The best partner a man could want. My bonnie, clever wife."

Settling onto the bed beside her, I rest my head on her belly and press my ear to her womb. My lips form another smile, a softer one this time. "I was right again. Said you could give me everything I wanted, and you have."

"Don't get arrogant about it. You might be wrong at some point."

"Maybe." I kiss her belly and smirk. "Donnae hold your breath, though."

She grabs a pillow and whaps me on the head with it.

I pepper kisses over her silky skin, up between her breasts, to the hollow of her throat. There, I breathe words against her flesh. "I want you again, but only if it willnae hurt the wee one."

She seems puzzled for a moment, then understanding irons out the wrinkles on her forehead. "If you mean the itty-bitty fetus growing inside me, nothing you do is going to hurt it."

"Good." I roll us both over, with my wife on top. "But to be safe, you should take the reins this time."

"Oh, I see. This is for safety." She spreads her hands on my chest and pushes up into a half-sitting position with those bonnie breasts dangling in front of me. "I thought you just liked watching my boobs bounce."

I wag my eyebrows. "That I do."

She raises onto her knees, closes her hand around my cock, and positions the head at her opening. "You ready for hot, married sex?"

"We've already done that, *mo leannan*."

"But this time it's hot, married, we're-having-a-baby sex."

"Ah, that is different."

With her hand still sealed around my *slat*, she says, "Aidan, you've given me everything I didn't know I wanted. Let me show you how grateful I am."

She slides onto my cock, inch by inch, while her cream coats my flesh and the heat of her drives me mad. My wife keeps tormenting me with that body until I'm seated snug inside her, then she exhales a satisfied breath.

I grasp her hips and give her a wicked grin. "I'm grateful I found a wife who's such a great fuck."

She slaps my chest. "Arrogant Scot."

"Cheeky American."

What do we do for the rest of the night? Shag each other mindless, of course. That's what honeymooners do, though our official honeymoon doesn't begin until tomorrow. I cannae wait to see the French Riviera for the first time, with my new wife, but that experience will pale beside the miracle I've been given. My perfect woman crashed into me in a nightclub and changed my life forever. If I had never tried to re-create Lachlan's happy ending, I might never have found mine.

But I did. Nothing else matters.

Well, nothing else except making sure my wife comes for me so many times she can't walk in the morning. She doesn't need to walk. I'll carry her to the car, and onto Lachlan's jet.

I gaze up at my wife while she rocks her hips and plants her palms on my chest. She gives me a saucy smile, then bends to whisper in my ear, "Ready to rock the house, Kilt Boy?"

"Aye, let's make noise."

The past means nothing anymore because I have the perfect future ahead of me—ahead of us.

And it's time to make this house rock like an earthquake.

Epilogue

Ten Months Later

Newlyweds are meant to be shagging relentlessly and ignoring their families because they're too wrapped up in each other to give a toss about anything else. Aye, that's what Calli and I should be doing. Maybe we've been married for almost a year, but that still puts us in the honeymoon phase, and if I have my way, we will never leave that phase. But instead of having a poke with my wife, we're babysitting my brother Rory. Aye, that means we got Jamie to babysit our wee daughter, Sarah, so we could chaperone my brother as part of a bloody insane plan to "help" Rory find his "happy ending."

I thought "happy ending" meant an orgasm, but then, I'm a man. I expect definitions of words and phrases to stay the same, but women come up with different ones every day.

So aye, babysitting Rory is exactly what I'm doing on this bonnie day, under a clear blue sky. My wife talked me into this, but Erica had suggested it. Naturally, Rory has no idea what Calli and Erica have cooked up for him. They claimed I had to be the one to talk Rory into this outing because I lie better than Lachlan does. Not sure if that's a compliment.

Why are we treating a thirty-nine-year-old man like a wee bairn? Because our wives told us to. Need I say more?

Lachlan and I should never have let our wives become friends. Now they believe Rory needs to find "true happiness" with "the right woman" who will show him how to "let go of the past." Neither of those lasses has ever seen my brother in his full-on Ogre of Loch Fairbairn persona, so they have no clue how he'll react to their meddling. Even I'm not sure. But Lachie and

I seem incapable of denying our wives anything—even if what they want is to interfere in Rory's life.

That explains why, on this beautiful Saturday afternoon, I've given up the chance to make love to my wife so I can "cheer up" my brother. Rory has pulled ahead of us by a few paces, which gives me a chance to talk to Calli.

"What are we doing?" I whisper.

"Helping Rory."

"The bloke seems fine to me."

Calli rolls her eyes. "Men are so blind. Your brother has gotten way more withdrawn and morose lately. He snaps at everyone."

"Aye, he needs a good shag. Let's send him on a business trip, since that seems to be the only time he'll touch a lass."

"You don't know for sure he has one-nighters when he's away from home." She takes hold of the collar of my T-shirt. "Come on. Don't you want to make Rory feel better?"

"Aye, but donnae get any barmy ideas. I won't be 'hugging it out' with Rory, or having a heart-to-heart with him, or—"

"No," Calli says like I'm a silly eejit. "Erica and I have a better idea, and your mom agreed with us."

"Do I want to know what you women have cooked up now?"

She pats my cheek, smiling with a mischievous gleam in her eyes. "We're stepping up the campaign to arrange for Rory to bump into single women whenever he's out and about."

I groan. "Bloody hell, Calli. Rory will break out his guillotine and behead us all for this."

"Don't be silly." Her brows lift. "Does he really own a guillotine?"

"No idea. But it wouldn't surprise me." Since I know I can't stop this meddling rubbish, I sigh and give in. "I assume there will be an accidental encounter while we're babysitting Rory this afternoon."

"Yep." She tickles my chin. "Might be more than one, just to make sure."

"More than one?" I toss my head back and groan at the sky. "You lot are determined to drive my brother insane, aren't you?"

"Relax. It'll be fine. And we're almost to the first stop—the café."

My brother stops dead on the pavement, then twists his head around to flash us an annoyed look. "Why are you two walking so slow?"

"It's called strolling, Rory," I say. "The rest of us donnae like going on a forced march at top speed."

He grunts and starts walking again.

Calli elbows me in the side. "Catch up before he speeds right past the café."

"All right, all right." I sprint to catch up to Rory and step in front of him, forcing my brother to stop. "Ah, let's go into the café. A wee piece would hit the spot, aye?"

"Not hungry."

"Have a glass of whisky, then." I nod past him, toward my wife. "Calli needs a break, and she loves the *cranachan* they make at the café."

Rory sharpens his gaze on me. "What is really going on here, Aidan? I've never seen you this determined to force me to have a piece."

"Or a drink. Your choice."

"My choice was to stay home, but you lot dragged me into the village for 'a day of relaxation and fun.' I'm not feeling relaxed or entertained."

I slap his arm. "Give it a try. For Calli."

That's a low blow, and I know it. But I'm desperate. My wife won't give up until we've dropped a lass into Rory's lap, literally, at the café. I want my brother to be happy, but this doesn't seem like the right way to make that happen. Cannae manufacture happiness.

Well, I suppose I sort of did. When I insisted Calli would fall in love with me.

Rory rolls his eyes and twists his mouth into an expression that I know well—part resignation, part annoyance, followed by acceptance of his fate. "Have it your way. Let's go into the ruddy café and have a piece. But I'm not eating *cranachan*."

No one knows why Rory hates that dessert, but he always has.

"Fine," I say. "No *cranachan*."

I wave to Calli, who trots over to us, then we all head into the café, though Rory insists we sit outside instead of taking a table in the interior of the restaurant. He stalks over to a table beside the wrought-iron railing that hems in the outdoor section and drops onto a chair. Calli and I sit across from him.

When the waitress arrives, Rory waves away a menu and growls, "Ben Nevis. Make it a double."

That would be Rory's favorite single-malt Scotch whisky. Some of our cousins like Ben Nevis too, but Lachlan sticks with Talisker. I'll drink any whisky, but Calli still despises it and only consumes alcohol in the form of Atholl Brose, though not since she got pregnant.

Calli and I order *cranachan*, with one glass and two spoons.

Our food and Rory's drink have just arrived when it happens.

A bonnie brunette walks past us, then whirls around as if she's only just noticed the three of us sitting here. Though I'm dead sure Calli has never met the woman, the brunette smiles and speaks to my wife. "Calli, how nice to see you and Aidan again."

Now I supposedly know her? *Bod an Donais*. Erica and Calli roped me into this nonsense without even telling me.

"Mary," my wife says as if she's greeting an old mate, "it's so nice to see you too. Why don't you sit down with us? There's an extra chair beside Rory."

My brother's eyes go wide, but only for a second. Then he clenches his jaw and aims his steely glare at me.

I shrug.

Calli waves toward the empty chair beside Rory. "Please sit down, Mary."

Rory's eyes narrow so much that they're almost closed, and a muscle ticks in his jaw.

As the brunette settles onto the chair beside him, Calli says, "Rory, this my friend Mary MacCallister. She's a paralegal. Mary works in Inverness, but she really wants to move home to Fort William." My wife puts on the least convincing look of innocence I've ever seen and flutters her eyelashes. "Gee, that's not far from Loch Fairbairn, where you work, Rory."

I wouldn't blame Rory if he let his head fall onto the tabletop. I feel like doing that too.

Do I see smoke curling up from Rory's ears?

Mary flutters her lashes the way Calli had done a moment ago, and she smiles at my brother. "You are a braw man, for sure. I've heard how powerful you are in court too."

The lass seems sincere in her desire to ensnare my brother, but Rory only grinds his teeth harder, making that muscle in his jaw pulse again.

And he's glaring at *me*. This barmy plan wasn't my idea.

Rory shoves his chair backward with so much force that it topples into the bloke sitting at the next table, behind my brother. But Rory isn't paying attention to that. He jabs a finger in my direction and snarls, "You lot need a new hobby. Do not ever set me up like this again."

He storms out of the café.

I hurry after him, but don't reach him until we're a block from the restaurant. Then I grab his arm to stop him. "That wasn't very nice, Rory. Mary seems like a sweet lass, and you behaved like a snarling beast."

He sighs, and his entire posture sags. "I'm sorry, Aidan. But I do not want to date anyone. Never again. Understand?"

"All right, aye. But honestly, I don't know if anyone can stop Erica and Calli from meddling in your life."

He swings his head toward me. "Don't worry about that. I'm away to New Orleans, to meet with an American mate so I can learn more about the legal system over there. I'll be gone…for a good while."

"Donnae need to run away."

"Not running. I need a holiday."

"But you said it's work."

He rolls his eyes, the way he loves to do. "A working holiday."

Aye, only Rory would try to combine the two and think it makes sense.

"I'm done with women," he says. "Please leave me be."

Then my brother walks away.

When I get back to the café, Calli is waiting for me on the pavement alongside the wrought-iron railing.

"Where's Rory?" she asks.

"Gone." I sling an arm around her waist as we head back toward where I parked our car. "You and Erica are rubbish at meddling. Please don't do it anymore, not to Rory."

"We'll get better at it. I promise." When I try to glower the way Rory does, she pats my chest. "Don't worry. We will leave your brother alone."

Thank heavens for that.

My wife smiles up at me with her green eyes glittering. "Rory's off the hook. That means Erica and I can focus on Jamie and Gavin. Their long-distance romance is causing them lots of stress."

I let my head fall forward, shut my eyes, and groan.

Want more of Rory MacTaggart? Experience his story in *Rory in a Kilt*, book three in The Ballachulish Trilogy.

Did you miss the original version of this story told from Calli's viewpoint? *Wicked in a Kilt* is available now everywhere.

Love the

Check out the

series too!

Visit
AnnaDurand.com

to subscribe to her newsletter
for updates on forthcoming books in these series
&
to receive free gifts for signing up!

Anna Durand is a bestselling, multi-award-winning author of contemporary and paranormal romance. Her books have earned bestseller status on every major retailer and wonderful reviews from readers around the world. But that's the boring spiel. Here are the really cool things you want to know about Anna!

Born on Lackland Air Force Base in Texas, Anna grew up moving here, there, and everywhere thanks to her dad's job as an instructor pilot. She's lived in Texas (twice), Mississippi, California (twice), Michigan (twice), and Alaska—and now Ohio.

As for her writing, Anna has always made up stories in her head, but she didn't write them down until her teen years. Those first awful books went into the trash can a few years later, though she learned a lot from those stories. Eventually, she would pen her first romance novel, the paranormal romance *Willpower*, and she's never looked back since.

Want even more details about Anna? Get access to her extended bio when you subscribe to her newsletter and download the free bonus ebook, *Hot Scots Confidential*. You'll also get hot deleted scenes, character interviews, fun facts, and more! Plus you'll receive the short story *Tempted by a Kiss* and mutliple bonus chapters in both ebook and audiobook formats.

Visit AnnaDurand.com to sign up.

www.ingramcontent.com/pod-product-compliance
Lightning Source LLC
Chambersburg PA
CBHW070941190726
48292CB00004B/1291